THE
PLASMA
CELL
REPORT

A NOVEL

JOEL GEIDERMAN

RIVER GROVE
BOOKS

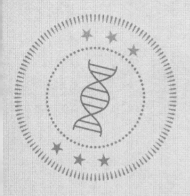

THE PLASMA CELL REPORT

Report of the Select Presidential
Commission on the Plasma Cell Project

Published by River Grove Books
Austin, TX
www.rivergrovebooks.com

Distributed by River Grove Books

Design and composition by Greenleaf Book Group
Cover design by Greenleaf Book Group
Cover images used under license from ©Adobestock.com

Publisher's Cataloging-in-Publication data is available.

Print ISBN: 978-1-63299-795-1

eBook ISBN: 978-1-63299-796-8

First Edition

***

For Mom

***

CONTENTS

PREFACE

We present the narrative of this report to the President of the United States, the United States Congress, and the American people for their consideration. The Plasma Cell Commission ("the Commission"), composed of ten commissioners, five Democrats, and five Republicans selected and approved by elected representatives of the United States, under the direction of the Chief Justice, has prepared and signed this report without dissent.

The President and the Congress created the National Commission on the Plasma Cell crisis to answer troubling questions. The mandate given to us was sweeping. We were asked to examine "all related facts and circumstances" and report back to the American public.

In early May 1987, a scientific discovery was made that became a dire crisis for the United States and threatened to destroy society and mankind as we know it. The events described herein undoubtedly altered the course of history in America and the world. This report was pieced together from interviews, diaries, government files, recordings, and other sources available to the Commission. Most quotes are *verbatim* to the extent transcription of the spoken word allows. In a few cases, in order to complete the narrative, possible thoughts have been interspersed, which all members have agreed to insert. All evidentiary materials have been ordered to be retained in the original and converted into a digital or a succeeding format and be stored in perpetuity in the National Archives. They are in a classified appendix to this report.

With this as a background, the Presidential Commission on the Plasma Cell Project respectfully presents its findings to the American people. To protect sources and methods, some names or sensitive information have been redacted on the advice of the Commission's legal counsel or other federal agencies. Unless otherwise authorized by Congress and the President, related materials will remain sealed for no less than forty years from this date. Earlier release of any details or documents will be punishable by a penalty of up to life in prison and a fine of up to $1,000,000.

Respectfully submitted in Washington, August 8, 1990.

PROLOGUE

T he government's Citation flew its star witness along with two federal agents in an easterly direction, landing at the general aviation airfield near Dulles Airport. The lights of the Virginia suburbs outside the nation's capital shimmered. The plane taxied and came to a halt on a quiet tarmac. Three black cars immediately encircled the aircraft, and federal agents took up positions surrounding it. The plane's door opened and its staircase deployed, after which the witness scurried down the stairs. He was handed off to two federal marshals and got in an armored black Cadillac.

As the car drove east on I-66, the occupant's mind drifted to memories of Katie and Atlanta until the Watergate complex came into view on his left side and startled him back to the present. As the car crossed the graceful Potomac, the majestic and well-lit Kennedy Center came into view. The witness leaned forward and peered between the front seats. Washington was magnificent at night. His heart pitter-pattered as he saw the stately white marble Lincoln Memorial to his right and, in the distance, the Washington Monument.

The car continued along Constitution Avenue and stopped at a red light. On the left was the National Academy of Sciences building with a statue of Albert Einstein in front of it. The car continued past the South Lawn of the White House and the Ellipse, stopped at 15th Street, and waited to make a left turn. A few blocks to the right, across the mall, were the US Mint and a site where ground had recently been broken for a United States Holocaust Museum. The passenger thought it ironic that his own parents escaped anonymously from Nazi hell in Tyrol, Austria, by a matter of days, and by tomorrow, the entire world would know his name.

The car pulled up in front of the Willard Hotel, where he was approached by three fresh agents who escorted him to the registration desk on the left side of the ornate lobby.

"Doctor?" the desk clerk asked.

"Yes."

"We have been expecting you. It is an honor to meet you. Your accommodations are on the eighth floor. It appears you will have the whole floor to yourself. Your room number is 818. I will write it down here for you."

"Thank you," the replied.

Two agents stayed in the lobby, and two went with him to the eighth floor. Still others sat outside of the hotel. The DC police and the FBI were determined not to have a Jack Ruby–style event occur on their watch. Once in his room, the guest ordered a cheese board, a Caesar salad, and a glass of white wine from room service. When he finished, he watched the news for a while but got tired of hearing his own name. He took a Restoril and went to sleep. The next few days would be grueling.

* * *

The next morning the doctor got into a black armored Suburban with his team of lawyers. Two federal agents were in the front seats. Along with several police cars, the vehicle was part of a small motorcade that would make the ten-minute ride to the Capitol Building.

He arrived at the east steps at the same time as FBI Director Turner. The two men shook hands as dozens of cameras recorded the moment. The doctor wore the same Armani suit he had worn to the funeral three years earlier, although it didn't drape quite as nicely over the body armor he was wearing. He marched up the long stairs, accompanied by his team of attorneys and flanked by bodyguards. The steps were lined with reporters and camera people on the east side of the magnificent seat of the US government.

"Doctor, have you ever worked for the CIA?" one reporter asked.

"Have you ever worked for the Mossad?" a reporter from *Le Monde*, the French news service, shouted.

"Can you confirm that Katie Shepard is dead?" another queried.

"Is any serum stored away?"

The doctor himself did not know the answer. Despite his silence, the questions kept coming.

"Did you ever sleep with Katie Shepard?" another inquired. Washington leaked like a sieve.

"Is the Medical Board investigating your license?"

The witness's blood boiled, but he had been prepped for this moment and took the questions in stride. He might have made a few mistakes along his uncharted path, but he hadn't asked for any of this. He deeply felt he had been looking out for the good of his country.

Finally, at the top of the steps, a seasoned reporter looked at him sympathetically and told him, "Thank you for your service."

He nodded and smiled at her before taking long strides, two steps at a time, into the Capitol Building, prepared to tell whatever he knew about the Plasma Cell matter, as he had done behind closed doors for the past two and a half years.

At the bottom of the steps, T-shirts were being hawked: *The Plasma Cell Hearings*, they read. Katie's image, leaked from Atlanta, appeared on the front of some of the shirts. The doctor appeared in a separate frame than her on others. Shirts, stocking caps, and baseball caps read *Katie Lives*, reflecting a conspiracy theory that had sprung up in the far right and far left media. Later in the day, hot dogs, knishes, pizza, ice-cold soda, shaved ice cones, and folding hand fans with Katie's image on them were sold at the entrances to the Capitol Building. Visitors hoping to get a seat at the hearings camped out. It was a circus-like atmosphere.

* * *

The Senate hearing room is smaller than it looks on television, the doctor thought. Standing television cameras and bright lights lined the rear of the room and made it feel even smaller. Several press pool photographers sat on the floor and clicked away with their still cameras as the witness was sworn in. The witness raised his right hand and when given the choice of affirming or swearing, he answered, "So help me God." He took his place at the witness table with his lawyer at his side and focused his attention on the chairman of the intelligence committee. Director Turner sat behind them.

The head of the intelligence committee, an octogenarian man with a shock of white hair and a generous portion of adipose tissue and skin hanging from his neck, spoke with a Southern accent. "Thank you for testifying before us today. I want to remind you that you are under oath. You have the right to refuse to answer any question in order to avoid incriminating yourself by invoking the Fifth Amendment. Doctor, let me say thank you for your service to the country. The senior senator from Delaware will have five minutes to begin the questioning."

"Thank you," the senator responded, staring coldly at the witness. "Can you please tell us how you first came to meet Katie Shepard?"

DAY ONE

May 3, 1987

I was so much older then
I'm younger than that now.

—BOB DYLAN, "MY BACK PAGES," 1964

A NEW ADMISSION

"Dr. Insbrook," JD Hartigan, the eager young intern, said as he caught up with the medical director of the medical center. "Are you busy? I would like to tell you about a fascinating patient I just saw."

Insbrook smiled, in the manner of the father of a teenager. "Sure. How are you doing, JD?"

"Good, Dr. Insbrook. I was out a little late last night and would still like to get out for a run, but I'm almost done."

"I have a few minutes, too, but let's keep it brief," Insbrook told him. "Tell me about him. Or her."

"Her: a new patient, Katie Shepard. I will present her formally tomorrow, but I wanted you to see her before I do," Hartigan said as they walked toward the woman's room. "Mrs. Shepard is a sixty-three-year-old woman who came in through the ER after she rear-ended another car at slow speed. She complains of palpitations, dyspnea on exertion, weakness, myalgias, and symptoms of a urinary tract infection." When they arrived at her door, Hartigan stopped and let the senior physician enter the room first.

"Mrs. Shepard," Hartigan said. The young woman in the bed sat up. "I would like you to meet Dr. Insbrook, our medical director."

"Hello, Mrs. Shepard," Insbrook said, somewhat startled by her appearance. She appeared to be quite young—in her late twenties perhaps.

"Thank you for coming to see me," Katie responded. "I'm hoping to get out of here soon. I'm feeling better."

"How old did you say you are?" Insbrook asked. He looked scornfully at Hartigan, thinking he must have been out *really* late last night. Perhaps all night.

"I'm sixty-three," she said without hesitation.

"Um-hum." Insbrook swallowed hard as he contemplated his next question.

Katie was stunning. The most striking of her features was her smooth, silky skin, completely free of wrinkles or blemishes. Her hair was shoulder-length, chestnut brown at the roots but otherwise blonde, her eyes wide and chocolate brown, her lips pink and well-shaped. She was simply beautiful. The rest of her body, as far as he could see under her hospital gown, was quite youthful.

He composed himself and approached her. "Could you open your mouth so I can examine you?" He looked around with a tongue depressor and flashlight and noted that her inside cheeks were pale. He inspected her hands. Her increased pulse rate automatically registered with him. He took note of her white fingernail beds and turned her palms over, comparing her pale ones to his own. She was sick.

"You seem to be anemic. Do you bleed heavily during your periods? Do you eat meat, or are you a vegetarian?"

"As I told the young doctor," Katie answered with a bit of irritation, "I went through the change fifteen years ago, so I don't have periods anymore. And yes, I like steak as well as cheeseburgers. I'm from Milwaukee, and that's what we eat there—steak and cheese. Have you not heard that? Watch a Packers game, doctor. It would be good for you."

"Hmm," Insbrook muttered. *One thing is for sure*, Insbrook thought to himself, *this woman is not sixty-three years old and has not been through menopause.* He was feeling a physical attraction to her, and he was only holding her hand.

"Exactly what brought you to the hospital?"

"I've been telling the same story all day," Katie said in frustration. "Look at the chart. It was a minor auto accident. My car tapped a guy's bumper. I think he stopped short, so it's probably his fault, but I don't care. I'm not suing him." She wiped her eyes with a tissue as tears began streaming down her cheeks. "Is anybody going to actually help me here? How about if you answer *my* questions?"

"I am sorry," Insbrook said. "Please don't cry. We're here to help you. First, let me finish a brief examination. I'm going to quickly check you over, and then we'll talk."

Katie nodded. He gently lifted the back of her nightgown and listened to the woman's lungs with his stethoscope. Then he walked to Katie's other side. She dropped the front of her gown slightly. *Hers is a body of perfection*, he thought as he looked at Hartigan. *Sixty-three?* The intern quickly buttoned his long white coat to cover what he could no longer conceal.

"Katie, can you tell me your birthday?" Insbrook asked, doing a mini mental status exam.

"September 14, 1924," Katie said without hesitation.

"And today's date?"

"Today is May 3, 1987. I am in a hospital in Cincinnati. George Washington was our first president. Franklin Roosevelt was the president when I was a child. OK? I know you think I am crazy, but I'm perfectly sane. Can you both get that through your heads? Leave, please. Allow me my privacy. I am *not* crazy."

Then Katie broke down. "This whole thing is crazy. I don't know anymore. I can only tell you what happened to me. I realize how young I look. Honestly, I have enjoyed being young for the second time, but I *am* sixty-three years old. I have a daughter almost twice your age," she said as she pointed to Hartigan.

"God help me," she begged. "Please, God."

Insbrook sat down next to Katie and stroked her back in an attempt soothe her. "I'm sorry. Please don't cry. We'll leave in a minute."

"No, no—actually, please don't leave." Katie had changed her mind. "It's time I told my story to someone. That's what I decided I would do while lying in your emergency room this afternoon."

"Dr. Hartigan and I are here to listen to you," Insbrook told her. "If you want to tell us your story, we'll listen."

"I know you will think I am insane which is why I haven't told anyone before, not even my daughter. I don't know where to begin, but I'll give it a try."

Hartigan opened a notebook he kept in his doctor's coat and began writing.

"I was born in Milwaukee in 1924. I was baptized as Katie Iverson. My father was John Timothy Iverson. He owned a liquor store, and my mother was Elizabeth, a housewife. I grew up Catholic, so there should be plenty of church records. I was an only child."

"Go on," Hartigan told her reassuringly.

"After I graduated high school, I got engaged to a young man whose father owned the Milwaukee State Bank. He was quite wealthy. This young man would have inherited everything one day, but he died storming Utah Beach on D-Day, June 6, 1944. At the time, I wished I had died with him. I mourned for six months. After a while, I got a job in a bakery, where in 1946 I met a man named Sherman Shepard. He was twenty-five, and I was twenty-two. Within a year, we got married and established our floral shop."

"Where was the wedding held?" Insbrook asked, testing Katie's ability to provide details.

"In the Church of the Blessed Sacrament on 41st Street, Milwaukee," Katie responded. "Look it up.

"A year later, Isabella was born. She was a wonderful daughter, and it has hurt me greatly not to see her these past few years. But what could I do? Look at me. I don't understand what has happened to me." Katie's voice began to crack; she sipped water from a cup by her bed.

"What do you think has happened to you?" Insbrook asked quizzically.

"I don't know. I may be insane, but this is the way I remember my life. I'll give you names and places. There must be some kind of records you could check." Tears once again began trickling down Katie's cheeks.

"And where did you and Sherman live?"

Katie reached for a tissue and continued. "We lived in Milwaukee at 7741 Phillips Avenue. I voted there multiple times. As Katie Shepard, of course, not Iverson. Is that something you could check?"

"I'm sure we could," the younger doctor answered.

"Isabella married a nice man named Ben Jacobson when she finished college in 1969. I never held it against her or him that he was Jewish, but of course, there was no church wedding, so there are no church records to check for that."

"Go on," Insbrook asked. "What became of them?"

"Ben wanted to become a professor, so they moved to Madison, where he would fit in better and could work at the university. At first, I saw them three or four times a year, then less and less. I have two grandchildren and miss them dearly. I send cards or call them on occasions. I promised the oldest one I would come to his Bar Mitzvah later this year, but how can I possibly do that with the way I look?"

The two doctors looked at each other skeptically. Hartigan looked guilty for even bringing his director into the room. This was one of those times when, in terms of practicing medicine or helping a patient, the two of them thought they were wasting this Sunday afternoon. Yet, it was such a refreshing break from their routine. Patients with mania often spoke the way Katie did, and it was amusing. Insbrook was convinced the woman suffered from some form of psychosis beyond his scope to deal with. Entranced by Katie, he patiently listened to her remarkably well-constructed tale as he promised he would.

"I was aging. Graying, wrinkling, gaining weight. Spreading out. Sherman was a sick man. He was overweight, had heart trouble and diabetes, and became impotent early on. I was depressed. I went through the change late, perhaps around 1972. Dr. Samuel Barrett was my gynecologist. He did pap smears on me, and once he did a uterine biopsy on me. You could probably get my records from him. Last I heard, he was still practicing in Milwaukee. Very nice man.

"By 1981, Sherman died. I was fifty-seven years old and all alone. I didn't want to burden my friends or my daughter, so I kept to myself and cried a lot. No one cared, and after a bit, even my friends stopped calling me. My sister-in-law, Violet, was alone; she was a widow like me and lived in Columbus, where I visited her. Columbus is a lovely town, so after a few months, I went back to Milwaukee, sold the business, settled my affairs, and moved there to make a new life. But I had no idea how different it would be. Soon after I moved, I began to feel different. I had more energy, although I hadn't noticed major body changes yet. Those began right after Violet died, about five years ago."

"Violet?" Hartigan asked. Katie was going too quickly.

"Yes, my sister-in-law. Sherman's sister. She had a stroke and died a few months after I moved. Then everything began happening to me. My old figure, my natural hair, my voice—it all started coming back. In all, it took about six months, and since no one in Columbus knew me, no one noticed, except for a cashier at Safeway who once said something, but then she left her job. At first, I thought I was losing my mind, but then I accepted it."

"Go on," Hartigan asked, fascinated. "Then what?"

"I had to buy new clothes so I wouldn't look ridiculous as a seemingly twenty-eight-year-old girl walking around Columbus in old ladies' clothes. I got a job as a hostess in a restaurant where I socialized after work and soon began to date men who were much younger than me. A few times, I even slept with them. I know it sounds a little ridiculous. I had to make up a whole life story to tell them. Put yourself in my place. Was I wrong for keeping my secret to myself?"

"You weren't wrong," Insbrook told her. "Then what happened?"

"How could I explain any of it to my daughter? She wouldn't have approved of what I was doing. Then I started getting terrible bone and back pains. I've been in intense pain of late."

"Did you ever use drugs for your pain or while you were socializing?" Insbrook asked.

"Not really. I smoked marijuana once or twice. And I tried cocaine once on a date. I didn't like it. They gave me a couple Tylenol number threes, but they don't work, so I just take a little plain Tylenol now."

"How about drinking?"

"I never was a big drinker," she said. "Maybe an occasional glass of wine or two."

"Go on," Insbrook said.

"I kept my secret to myself. I called my daughter from time to time, but I never mentioned what had happened to me. At first, she noticed that my voice had changed, but she got used to it. I presume my inflection and accent hadn't changed.

"I've already told you about the medical problems I'd been having—the pain in my spine and joints, the constant ache in my hips. As I told the young doctor in the ER, the pain started way before the accident today. I thought it was from the aerobics classes. Maybe it's just arthritis. I don't know—you are the doctors."

"Any other problems?" Hartigan asked.

"I've been a bit short of breath on occasion, but that has largely gone away. And now I have this bladder problem. I am a sick old-young woman. Or young-old. Honestly, I really don't know what I am."

Insbrook was mesmerized. Not knowing what to think, he looked at Hartigan. Something strange was happening. The color was gone from his face. He looked disquieted and confused. Insbrook rubbed his chin. "That was a fascinating story you told us, Katie. Do you think that you could repeat it if we were to ask you?"

"Of course I can repeat it. It's my life story."

"All right. Get some rest now, and we will see you tomorrow," the senior doctor told her. "We will do everything we can for you. Ask the nurses to page Dr. Hartigan if you need anything."

"OK. Thank you, doctors. I'm going to try to call my daughter now. It's Sunday."

The two physicians walked into the hallway, and Insbrook looked through the notes Hartigan had prepared. "Remarkable young woman. She is disoriented, but consistently so," Insbrook said. "You should add to this note a little bit, but I agree with your impressions. Excellent job, Hartigan."

"Thank you, sir," the intern replied. "But something happened in there. For a moment, you believed her, didn't you?"

"That's nonsense," Insbrook answered defensively. "I did not believe her," he said as if trying to convince himself. "Are you familiar with any of the organic brain syndromes, such as early onset dementia or Korsakoff's syndrome?"

"Yes, Korsakoff's psychosis is caused by thiamine deficiency, sometimes seen in alcoholics or in people on extreme weight-loss diets. They suffer false or fabricated accounts of recent events."

"Exactly," said Insbrook. "How do you diagnose it?"

"As I recall, the two salient features are retrograde amnesia—the inability to recall well-established events that are expected to be recalled—and an impaired ability to acquire new information," Hartigan answered. "As a result, the patient resorts to confabulations as a defense mechanism."

"Correct," Insbrook said. "A feature of these psychoses requires that the patient is alert and capable of making appropriate deductions from given premises and can solve problems logically going forward. So, in this case, Katie doesn't want to let on to what she can't remember, so she makes things up. It sounds as if Mrs. Shepard is confabulating, doesn't it?"

Hartigan nodded.

"Read about it so we can discuss it during tomorrow morning's rounds," Insbrook said. "Why don't you see which drugs or natural medicines can cause this? Check a lithium level on her, too, and a CT scan of her brain."

"Will do," the resident answered. "What do you make of her bone and joint pains?" Hartigan inquired.

"Maybe it's related to her aerobic classes. She's very fit, but maybe she overdoes it. It also goes along with what she's making up—the aging thing, part of her confabulations. Any other ideas?"

"I think we need to rule out a space-occupying lesion of the bones," Hartigan replied. "Myeloma, amyloidosis, or something like that, although she is quite young for those."

"Good thoughts. Let's get some X-rays. Let's also ask for an ortho consult. It sounds like she'll be with us for a while," Insbrook told Hartigan. "Have you tried to reach any family members yet? I suppose that would be difficult."

"I'm sure it will be. After all, Sherman is dead, and I don't suppose there is an Isabella or a Ben," Hartigan responded. "But if she gives me any phone numbers, I'll try them. Someone may know who she really is. Someone may be looking for her."

"Good thought. Did you say she would be my patient?" Insbrook asked.

"Yes. As of now, she's on the teaching service because she can't produce a valid insurance card. What she has is an out-of-state insurance card that is five years old. The finance folks are attempting to verify it."

"Let's try to clear up this woman's medical problems and then get her transferred to the psych service. Follow her there and let me know what they find. Quite an unusual case. We might want to write up a case report on her. Get some sleep tonight, JD."

"I will, and I will keep you informed, sir. See you tomorrow."

* * *

Inside room 641, Katie Shepard sat up in bed. She reached for the telephone on the nightstand next to it. "Operator. I would like to make a long-distance call to Madison, Wisconsin. The number is 608-555-7280. Please charge it to my account in Columbus, Ohio, 614-555-4218."

In Madison, a black wall phone rang. A slightly graying, attractive woman in her early forties got up from the dinner table to answer it. "Hello."

"Hi, Bella," the patient in 641 said. "It's me, Mother."

"Oh, hi, Mom. We were just talking about you. How is your trip to Cincinnati going?"

TARGET PRACTICE

On the night of May 3, 1987, in the United States, and early the next morning off the coast of Somalia in the northeast Horn of Africa, a clandestine operation was underway. Somalia was little known to most citizens of the United States and had been politically drifting for years, falling into the hands of vicious and corrupt warlords. It was a paradoxical cauldron of devout Islamists, avowed secularists, terrorists, traffickers of women and children, opium dealers, arms sellers, money launderers, and a shadowy group of government regulars in charge of mines that contained some of the most sought-after minerals in the world. It was considered the most failed state in Africa and had been called "the worst country in the world."

Somalia, situated in the Horn of Africa between Ethiopia, the Gulf of Aden, the Somalian Sea, and Kenya, has ancient roots as a trade center and, like much of its region, at one time or the other in the past had been controlled by Portugal, Germany, the Ottoman Empire, the British Empire, and finally Italy. In the late 1960s, UN geologists allegedly discovered huge deposits of uranium and other rare minerals in the Somali interior. It was at that point that Somalia's capital, Mogadishu, and its hapless citizens became of interest to the United States and the West, China, and the Soviet Bloc. The game was on, and not all players were playing by the same rules.

As a result of Somalia's mixed and rich pedigree, its inhabitants commonly inherited maritime skills, mercantile instincts, and knowledge and experience in piracy. By 1987, pirating comprised a sordid, deadly, and significant source of income for the warlords, many of whom spent their days intoxicated on the juices of the khat plant they commonly chewed, native to the equatorial region of Africa. High on its effects, the warlords, their gangs, and even their young sons regularly took pleasure in the women and girls in their midst as they were trafficked. It was a situation that alarmed and disgusted the US president, his vice president, and their generals and put Somalia on a short list of targets for future interventions the US population was likely to back. For Americans who knew history, the Barbary Wars during the times of Jefferson had been fought over piracy and the concept of freedom of international waters. The current president, with his vice president at his side, vowed in a Rose Garden speech, with the ceremonial Spanish king in attendance, "Piracy will not stand with my administration," a favorite phrase of his administration and a polite way of delivering a threat backed by the strength of the US military when it could be openly deployed.

In late April 1987, Somali pirates seized three Norwegian-flagged oil tankers and a Liberian-flagged ship that turned out to be transporting missiles, advanced radar installations, and other sophisticated arms from the United States to an allied country in the Middle East. According to intelligence sources, the seizure of the arms-laden vessel was probably inadvertent since the ship was disguised to look like a trawler. The vessel and its contents became a sticking point in negotiations to free the Norwegian tankers in exchange for a tidy ransom to be paid in unmarked US dollars. The pirates became emboldened once they realized they had seized American secrets along with valuable cargo and wanted to extract a higher price. In addition to US bills, they wanted the United States to include millions of dollars' worth of gold bullion. The United States understandably had no interest in acknowledging or revealing the existence of the fourth ship, including to Congress, making a rescue mission off limits to the Navy SEALs and other known Special Forces. Hence, a stalemate ensued. However, as one intelligence source testified to the Commission, "They had deuces, and we had aces. They never had a chance."

Between the hours of 21:00 and 22:00 in Washington and Maryland (the exact time remains classified), a team of sixteen National Security Agency (NSA) amphibious commandos launched a counterattack on the disguised ship in the middle of a moonless night. They parachuted into the ocean from thirty-five thousand feet, some with their fellow commando dogs in service to the United States, and swam several miles to acquire their targets. One dog drowned along the way, but not his master, who eventually shot the pirates' captain squarely between his eyes with a tumbling high-caliber bullet that ripped off his upper face and frontal skull and bizarrely exposed his frontal lobes, bleeding from a bridging vein that connected them to the skull and scalp. After another shot penetrated front to back through the left eye. Later, the commando calmly and proudly took pictures, his right foot resting on the corpse.

"Target practice," he testified to the committee, dressed in a black ski mask and fatigues, with his voice scrambled. "The fuckers killed my dog. Those fuckers killed my dog," he sobbed in the SCIF of the Capitol as he pounded the green cloth–covered table with his fist. Other NSA commandos were divers who operated out of NSA espionage vessels disguised as fishing trawlers. They quietly, surreptitiously attached explosives to the hull of the US vessel in case the primary mission failed—which, if detonated, would have sacrificed American lives but was the operational plan in the event the ship and its contents could not be liberated. Other NSA teams were deployed in groups of three to liberate the Norwegian tankers, easy targets while their crews slept. The teams had practiced for fourteen nights on full-scale replicas of the boats in the Caribbean.

Aboard the primary target, pirates had their throats slit or were garroted, manually strangled, shot, or thrown overboard. One terrorist who dreaded and feared dogs and could not swim jumped thirty feet to his death in the choppy waters below. Logs and records were quickly seized, placed in waterproof pouches, and removed. The synchronized operation was over in seven and a half minutes. No American lives were lost. Before midnight, a man identified in this report only as the Chairman received a call confirming the mission's success.

"Good night, honey," he said as he pulled up the duvet, switched off the table lamp, and turned on his right side. "I will be gone for a few days."

"Good night. The girls will miss you," the voice under the sheets next to him came back, referring to the two loyal dachshunds sleeping at the foot of their bed. "I will miss you too."

DAY TWO

May 4, 1987

In youth, the days are short,
and the years are long.

In old age, the years are short,
and the days are long.

—POPE PAUL VI

YOU DON'T WANT TO KNOW

Christopher Bouchikas awoke, eased himself out of his wife's arms, and quietly made his way into the bathroom of their Alexandria, Virginia, home. He looked back at Diana, his wife, sprawled across their bed. She kicked the remainder of the sheets off.

Quite the specimen I married, he thought to himself. Time for another baby, as they had recently discussed. He just needed to find the time.

Bouchikas's sleepy gaze was now back on the toilet bowl as he watched the water yellow. He ran warm water in the sink and scrubbed his chiseled face, lathered on shaving cream, and puckered his angular jaw to shave and get ready for his day.

"Christopher," Diana whispered faintly.

"I'm sorry. I should have closed the door."

"That's OK. Will you come and kiss me?"

"I know what you want," Chris answered quietly. "I'm running late. Go back to sleep."

"Just a little kiss. Then I'll go back to sleep," Diana promised.

Chris's hands were wet, and his face was full of Gillette's finest, as he made his way across the large bedroom, clad only in his boxers, and sat down on the edge of the bed whereupon he planted a foamy kiss on her strong Mediterranean nose. "I love you, honey," he said affectionately, before hurrying back to the bathroom to finish shaving.

"What time is it?" Diana inquired, half asleep, when he returned to start dressing. "I was hoping to talk to you about something this morning."

"It's six o'clock, honey."

"Six o'clock? Christopher, my Lord. It's six in the morning, and you're running late? When you took this job, eight was early. I used to be up with Nicky watching *Sesame Street*, and you were still sleeping. Now you tell me six is late. You can't do this, Chris."

"You caught me. I'm seeing a girlfriend before work. Hey, can we talk about this later? I have fifteen minutes before I have to leave."

"This is not a joke," Diana protested. "Don't you remember why you took this government job in the first place? To take it easy, to have time with your son and me. Now it's the same old thing. Can't you give that brain of yours a little time off and pay attention to us?"

Bouchikas sat silent as he pulled up his long black socks and continued to dress, not wanting to take time to respond or worse, to start the day with another argument, as had frequently been happening recently.

"Christopher," Diana pleaded, "I'm not saying this for me. It's about you and Nicky. I don't want to hurt you. I love you and hate seeing you working like a dog. Do you realize you see Nicky for all of an hour a day if he's lucky? Or are you kidding yourself? I hate to tell you this, but he doesn't even ask about you anymore when you're gone. I have to coax him to get on the phone with you, and he quickly loses interest. You are lucky I don't tell Mamá," she said, invoking Chris's mother, knowing she was his weak spot. "You are ruining all of our lives, Chris. Do you get that? This job will kill you and our marriage."

"I'm not doing this for myself," Bouchikas replied with conviction. "I believe our government needs me. Me—Christopher Bouchikas from Greektown on the south side of Chicago. Please give me some space for now. This job is bigger than I ever imagined it to be."

"Too big to tell your own wife about?"

"Too big to want to tell my wife about. It's punishable by life in prison, and you don't want to know," he said as he knotted his tie while staring into the mirror. "Do you want to know what I do? I told you before. Watch the nightly news. That's all I can tell you."

"I watch the news, but I don't know which parts you have anything to do with." Diana was brooding. She herself was a graduate of the Kennedy School of Government at Harvard. "Maybe I should sell *my* brain to the government too. And maybe they are also in the market for my body," she said as she slipped her gown off her shoulders, exposing her breasts and momentarily exciting her husband. "Mine isn't getting too much action here. Let me go back to sleep. I wanted to talk to you, but I don't feel well. I'm nauseated. Go do what you have to do."

"Kiss me," Chris replied. "I'll try to change things. I can't wait to see you tonight. We will have a special night. Wear your white teddy. It always drives me crazy."

Minutes later, Bouchikas walked down the stairs and quietly opened the front door. He took note of a man sporting a crewcut, dark suit, skinny tie, and sunglasses posted outside and another sitting in a black sedan across the street. Bouchikas picked up the *Post*, skimmed it, and dropped it onto the kitchen table for Diana to read later that morning.

Bouchikas felt tension in the pit of his stomach as he quickly poured cream into his coffee and mindlessly smeared cream cheese on his toasted bagel. He stood while he ate, watched two Golden Retriever puppies playing in the backyard, wishing he and Nicky could play that way. Diana was right; things would have to change. Bouchikas gulped down the rest of his coffee, put his dishes in the sink, and hustled out the front door. It was 6:20 a.m.

The black Town Car with diplomatic plates and blacked-out windows had pulled into the driveway, and Bouchikas climbed in. The car slowly drove through several neighborhood streets, rotated its license plates on a swivel, and ended up in front of a house that sat almost directly behind the Bouchikas residence, two blocks to the north. On command, the overhead garage door rolled open, and the sedan pulled forward. The door closed behind it once the engine was off. Later that day, Bouchikas, ironically, would be at work under the backyard, as Nicky played with his puppies above.

BEHIND THE GREEN DOOR

In Silver Spring, Maryland, Zvi Davis, a broadly built man with thick lips, wide-set, kind brown eyes, and swept-back brown hair entered a garage in the same strange manner as Christopher Bouchikas. He and his bodyguard and aide stepped from their car and walked to a box, where both men inserted a key they rotated clockwise. A metal plate in front of Davis glided sideways and exposed a keypad into which he entered a code. He received another code on the device he carried in his pocket and entered it on the panel. Like much technology being developed in public-private partnerships, it was hoped this dual verification device, which had been designed by government engineers and private industry, would find commercial security applications in the future. In response to the code, a steel floor panel yawned upward on hydraulic hinges and exposed a staircase that led to a basement. The two men removed and pocketed their keys and quickly trotted down the stairs. The heavy hatch shut behind them, the deadbolts securely locking into place.

Davis and his aide encountered a large metal door in the cave below painted with a fresh coat of celadon green paint. How this door and others like it at the National Security Agency (aka the

NSA) came to be painted green was a matter of curious history and lore within the Agency. In 1973, as the sexual revolution began, a pornographic "XXX" movie entitled *Behind the Green Door* went into wide release and became a mainstream sensation. The movie's star was formerly "the Ivory soap girl" described in a promotional campaign as "99 and 44/100% pure" named Marilyn Chambers. On a whim, the former occupant of Davis's location painted his door celadon and, in a playful triple *jeu de mots*, erected a sign above the prodigious green door that read: "Maryland's Chambers." When this play on words got around the Agency, the other Council members painted their doors similarly, and thereafter, the configuration and equipment enclosed in any secure NSA chamber were referred to as "Behind the Green Door." In fact, in communicating with one another, Council members would refer to themselves as either being behind the green door or not, referring to their presence in a secure NSA location.

After another sequence of codes, Davis opened the green door and entered the room under the famed "Maryland's Chambers" sign. The well-lit, technologically advanced facility he entered was referred to within the Agency as Little TEX, an acronym for TECCS (Tele-Electronic-Computer Communication System). The NSA liked acronyms. This whole structure, along with its sister complexes, were satellites for Big TEX, the massive Houston intelligence installation and bunker, the development to which Davis had devoted much of his adult life. All of the similar facilities were shrouded in secrecy, unbeknownst even to congressional oversight agencies. The particular structure Davis entered sat beneath four suburban homes and was encased in several feet of reinforced concrete at a depth twenty-five feet below grade.

Davis was an American success story. Born in Veliké Loucky, Czechoslovakia, in 1936, he moved to Budapest at the age of two. At six, his best friend was a boy named András István Gróf, later

Andy Grove, who would ascend to become one of the most prominent computer engineers in America in 1987. Gróf and Davis had
taken different paths out of Nazi hell. Gróf's family took on false
identities and were sheltered by righteous friends. Gróf married into
a Catholic family. Davis's family had no such friends in Hungary,
where the fabled blue Danube would, for months, flow red with
Jewish blood at the hands of the Arrow Cross. Fortunately, Zvi's
father had a box filled with gold bullion earned in the cattle trade,
along with two handguns buried under the giant walnut tree located
toward the rear of the family's large property. Having been tipped
off a few days prior to the liquidation of the ghetto and the subsequent transport of spring 1944, the elder Davis unearthed the
treasure chest and exchanged the bullion and the handguns with
the family's prayer books, candlesticks, prayers shawls, and *tefillin* in
the box. He buried them, pledging to retrieve them later when the
insanity of the Nazi era ended.

In those desperate times, the bullion bought transport for Zvi
Davis's immediate family, first through Slovenia and into the Alps
in the northeast corner of Italy. From there, additional gold, along
with forged papers, eventually took them to Ellis Island. Within
days of the Davis family's escape, Zvi's grandparents and most of the
rest of his family who were left behind were transported in boxcars
to the Auschwitz-Birkenau death camp and gassed and cremated
within hours of their arrival.

Once in America, Davis quickly learned English and attended
the esteemed Massachusetts Institute of Technology. He subsequently made a fortune in private industry. A few years later, he
made his way back to Budapest, this time paying off communists
for entrance into his homeland to dig under the walnut tree and
find the precious objects his father had left behind in the metal
box. For years afterward, Zvi Davis lived a devoted, pious Jewish-
American life. He donned his precious religious items every day,

worked long hours, raised a family, made a fortune, and contributed to numerous charitable causes.

Zvi's life changed when the offer came along to develop the most advanced computer system anywhere in the world, with no spending limits for an agency in the United States. In gratitude to his adopted country, he took a huge pay cut, accepted the job, and left Boston. The Chairman almost immediately recognized Davis's loyalty and brilliance and tapped him for the Council, where he became the Chairman's most trusted advisor.

Early this May morning, Zvi found himself behind the green door inside the ultimate man cave he had helped design, where before his workday, he entered the chapel, donned his tefillin and prayer shawl, and recited his morning prayers.

To the left, as one entered the workspace, on a wall twenty meters long, were five sets of Mem-Store information retrieval and storage terminals. Each Mem Store stood three meters high, was roughly the width of a deep freeze, and was stacked up and down with reel-to-reel tapes that slowly and continuously turned. Linked to supercomputers through a nascent worldwide network, these devices deciphered, sorted, analyzed (within the limits of their artificial intelligence abilities), and stored signal intelligence as it was being received from giant antenna farms and other listening posts and assets throughout the world. Newer digital storage capabilities were being developed to replace reel-to-reel magnetic tapes, which were subject to deterioration. The NSA's archival materials were being converted to digital copies twenty-four hours a day because it was feared that magnetic material was decaying rapidly—even when kept in cold dark storage. The material was voluminous and otherwise would have required warehouses full of tapes, papers, and microfilm. Collected information had increased exponentially since 1948.

Computer terminals arrayed on counters included terminals marked SIRPINET, GWAN, JWICS, TS/SI/TK/B Ops Net,

Multi-net, and NSANET. The NSANET was believed to be completely isolated from the network being developed worldwide to link information held in universities, defense agencies, military installations, embassies, and different countries. In academic circles, there was even talk of a commercial World Wide Web that would be open to the public, but no one knew how it could be easily searched by the average person who was unfamiliar with computer code. The NSA looked forward to such a network because it would open up whole new avenues for surveillance and data acquisition from individuals and other countries, with the ability to change or destroy someone else's code, data, or entire enterprises. Within the NSA's own network, the ability to operate secretly was of paramount importance in order to keep intruders out and prevent leaks. On NSANET, which ran on an exclusive backbone, every keystroke was logged, activities were audited or monitored, and evidence of downloading and printing of searched documents was flagged. Built for spies, by spies.

To the left of the stairs were living quarters that included a kitchen, bedroom, chapel, bathroom, exercise room, paneled library, and pantry, well stocked with a twelve-month supply of food, potable water, and other beverages, some stored in a state-of-the-art wine cellar. A power plant within a few hundred meters of the house was capable of supplying power to a cluster of government-owned houses, including the one Davis occupied. All were cooled by a complicated, redundant system that released steam into the atmosphere or heat into the Delaware basin dozens of miles away. In all, it was a technological marvel, kept out of sight and known to only a few people.

Zvi sat at the controls of his Little TEX node and directed his assistant to make phone calls and retrieve his boss's assignments for the day. Davis learned that Dalia Abrahamyan, Renee LeSayer, and he were on rotation in the NSA's administrative offices in Fort Meade, Maryland, outside of Washington. Bouchikas would be at work beneath his residence. George Christianson, Preston Knox, and Alan Atlas would be in Houston at Big TEX. Harvey Kraft would be working from his location in West Virginia. Davis rose and stuffed a stack of papers into his briefcase as his assistant punched in a code. Another giant door above the complex opened. The two men scurried up the stairs, entered the car, and left for work, hoping to avoid DC's rush hour. It was 7:30 a.m.

MORNING ROUNDS

Katie Shepard's day began early as the phlebotomy team drew her blood before 7:00 a.m., followed by breakfast at 8:00, after which she was sent for a chest X-ray. Katie felt visually assaulted by the environmental service workers staring at her as she was wheeled through the hall in her nightgown. She was parked in her wheelchair outside the radiology suite for an hour while waiting to have her chest X-rayed, a procedure that took a minute and a half. Back in her room, she climbed out of the wheelchair and scooted into her bed under the gaze of the transporter. Katie hoped she would find a bit of privacy and peace and quiet for a while. She was in a miserable mood.

Insbrook suddenly appeared at the entrance to Katie's room. She found him to be attractive.

"Oh, hello, doctor," she said. "Would you mind coming back a little later? I'd like to take a nap. I hardly slept last night, and it's been a long morning. I'd also like to shower and put on some makeup before I see you."

"Sure," Insbrook told her. "I'll come back later."

A SHADOW GOVERNMENT

By 11:00 a.m., Davis had attended two meetings focusing on NSA-designated Category III items. Afterward, Davis returned to his office and reviewed the most urgent items on his report.

Working with the Department of Defense (DoD), the NSA had recently developed a classification scheme for threats to national security. The DoD intended to share the classification schemes with relevant government agencies, including the Centers for Disease Control (CDC), in an attempt to standardize nomenclature among them.

There were 1,008 items classified by the NSA as Category V, defined as "situations being monitored" (SBMs) by a federal agency. Category V items reached the Agency via thousands of channels. Most items originated from open news sources, while others came from intelligence sources and were transmitted for analysis to the NSA. Somewhere in between, from Guam to Puerto Rico, data was intercepted around the clock by electronic and human screeners who matched the messages against established criteria to determine whether an item qualified as a conceivable danger to national security. Messages were received and processed by multiple screeners working independently to ensure that no problem could be overlooked or unsuppressed. One special team of screeners consisted of blind people whose keen sense of hearing was exploited to detect signals on intercepts that sighted screeners might miss. Category V items were processed by NSA lower echelon officers (LEOs) whose task was to assess a problem, follow it, and submit a brief report on its status within twenty-four hours of detection. Most of these items fell by the wayside without NSA intervention.

Category IV items were "situations of interest" (SOIs). There were 217 such items listed on Davis's report. These were still handled by lower- and middle-echelon officers, with reports spot-checked by higher-level officials. After twenty-four hours, SOIs received a secondary review by another agent. This system ensured threats of significance would not be either bungled or intentionally suppressed.

Category III were "items of concern" (IOCs) with respect to national security. They mandated review by an upper-echelon officer or one or more members of the Council. On May 4, 1987, there were a total of forty-five IOCs, easily managed by an agency with nearly one hundred thousand known employees.

Category II items were "items of very high consequence" (IVHCs) to national security. Under NSA bylaws, a Category II designation required a meeting of no fewer than five Council members, including the Chairman. There were no Category II items on the morning of May 4.

An example of a Category II item declassified for this report concerned the events surrounding Iranian attacks on shipping lanes in the Straits of Hormuz that were meant to disrupt Western commerce. While the administration contemplated a covert reflagging of Kuwaiti tankers, five NSA councilors approved a more aggressive operation. The plan was a simultaneous attack on all Iranian vessels in the area by a school of never-before-used stealth nuclear submarines operated by Navy Special Forces that bore no ultrasonic signature, were untraceable to any sovereign country, and carried an arsenal of Soviet-style torpedoes stamped with Cyrillic lettering, painted with slogans in Arabic, and with enough firepower to destroy the entire fledgling Iranian navy. The goal was to keep international shipping lanes in the Persian Gulf open to unimpeded traffic for years. The Iranians heard leaks about the Western operation, got cold feet, and backed off their attack. Whereas they had succeeded in their provocation of the United States nine years earlier, they weren't yet prepared for a full-scale war with the world's greatest superpower.

If three out of five NSA Council members and/or the Chairman deemed an item to be an "item of clear and present danger" (ICPD) to national security it was labeled Category I. Such a designation necessitated a full NSA Council session be convened. All members would remain together until the issue reverted back to a less serious level or was resolved. According to Davis's report, there were no Category I items on May 4, 1987; there had not been one since the time of the Libyan air strike twelve and a half months earlier.

The NSA with its far-reaching network of operators was a major focus of the Plasma Cell Commission's report. By 1987, for more than thirty years, the NSA had used military intelligence, foreign intelligence, the CIA, the FBI, global communication companies, and worldwide media services to monitor events in the world that could threaten national security. The NSA collected an enormous horde of its own intelligence through an elaborate system of listening posts on land, at sea, in the air, and in space. By 1987, NSA hardware and software were the finest money could buy. The bulk of the NSA's intelligence web was Zvi Davis's conception.

The NSA's network of listening posts was a technological marvel to behold. Its ground-based components were in the main composed of huge antenna farms situated in quiet locations such as Vint Hill Farms, Virginia; Cheltenham, England; Edgell, Scotland; and

Hokkaido, Japan. By 1956, the network expanded to include posts in Turkey, Iran, Morocco, and Afghanistan. Known sites numbered ninety and stretched from the Arctic to the South Pacific. Other ground-based hardware that helped information pour into the NSA included microwave receivers seated atop US-owned buildings around the world and those located in microphones and transmitters hidden in building walls, typewriter keys, and high-tech items. Embedded transmitters also made their way to countries in the Soviet Union, Central Europe, Cuba, parts of South and Central America, the Middle East and Asia with Agency help as part of high-tech transfers.

There were also Sturgeon 637–class submarines with advanced NSA capabilities that replaced less sophisticated ones previously located aboard more vulnerable vessels such as frigates and destroyers that operated on the open seas.

By the 1980s, it was America's domination of space that proved decisive in US superiority over the Soviet Union. Space-based components included four signal intelligence satellites in geosynchronous orbit whose purpose was to intercept electronic information from around the globe. "Keyhole" satellites could photograph objects four inches wide and send pictures to TV monitors on Earth at the speed of light. A fleet of SR-71 reconnaissance planes could fly at speeds in excess of 3,000 miles an hour at heights of 85,000 feet, during which they could film 60,000 square miles and spot a mailbox on a country road and simultaneously determine its address via a global positioning satellite. In 1985, the space shuttle Discovery launched the MAGNUM SIGINT satellite at the enormous cost of over $300 million. Other systems enabled the efficient management of the United States' multitude of satellites and enabled the secure downlinking and distribution of data to dispersed NSA facilities. Much of this capability was the brainchild of Davis and his team at Oxford, MIT, Cal Tech, Stanford, and in private industry.

How did the NSA keep track of all of this data? On a real-time basis, it didn't. Much of the data, referred to as "chatter" in the intel community, was stored and could be searched afterward if necessary by recognition technologies applied to digitally stored data.

Two recent examples gave the American public and the rest of the world insight into the astonishing listening capabilities of the NSA. In 1983, the Soviets were revealed as liars to the rest of the world when the United States released transcripts of three hours of cockpit conversations that revealed the premeditated nature of the downing of a Korean Air Lines jet that had veered into Russian territory. If the United States was monitoring the activities, why did they not warn the jet to get back on course? The Secretary of Defense later explained it was only after the aircraft was downed that appropriate tapes were located and analyzed, but he assured a House committee that intelligence agencies were developing methods to monitor chatter in real time. Sure enough, by 1985, NSA-supplied information pinpointed the precise location of the Achille Lauro hijackers aboard an EgyptAir craft after it left Egyptian airspace, leading to the aircraft being forced down in Sigonella, Italy, after a harrowing encounter with four US F-14 Tomcats who threatened to shoot the plane out of the sky.

In addition to its own raw data, the NSA had access to classified congressional reports and White House briefings, including the daily national security briefing presented to the President first thing every morning. It was the Nixon White House, whose beliefs often paralleled the NSA's, that first championed the idea that any matter that even remotely threatened American stability, be it political, military, biological, or economic, should be covered by the label of a national security threat and eliminated by whatever means necessary. Such activities were meant to be curtailed by post-Watergate intelligence reforms but were largely restored after the Iranian hostage crisis and the 1980 election.

Sources told the Plasma Cell Commission that when the NSA could exert its influence through other agencies of the US or other governments, it did so. Occasionally, however, in the interest of preserving national security at whatever cost necessary, it acted as a maverick agency to effect its policy decisions. As demonstrated in this report, by 1987, the NSA had effectively morphed into a shadow government of the United States.

Davis reviewed the day's voluminous reports and then headed to another meeting that attempted to control world events. Davis was already tired; age-related fatigue was beginning to set in.

THE BOMBINGS OF SEPTEMBER

I t wasn't until 9:00 a.m. that bachelor Harvey Kraft got out of bed, ate his room service breakfast consisting of a croissant and a pot of coffee, and read the *Wall Street Journal.* When he finished, he showered, dressed, and strode down a long corridor, peering through ten-foot-tall picture windows, and admired the manicured landscape of the Greenbrier Resort grounds on this spring morning. As he arrived at the end of the hallway, he was met by a broad man attired in a bellman's outfit, a listening device in his ear and a concealed service weapon under his jacket, who took out a set of keys and opened a door marked *Service.* They rode the elevator down for what seemed like an eternity and arrived in the basement where they saw an anteroom and, of course, the green door. As Davis had done in Maryland, Kraft opened the door and was greeted with bright lights and a bevy of technological equipment. He sat down at his console to review the reports that were prioritized for his perusal and to continue working on his ongoing assignments. He expected a ten-hour workday ahead of him.

As he had eaten his croissant that morning, Kraft was reminded of the last major NSA operation he had directed. The information the NSA scooped out of the ether with its vast system of listening posts was normally supplied not only to Kraft and the other councilors but to a variety of "customers," including allied governments in most cases. The year before, it was the NSA that supplied the Joint Chiefs with the vital intelligence that pinpointed the exact tent in which Libyan leader Muammar Gaddafi would be sleeping on the night of April 14, 1986. This would surely have resulted in his death had the initial military plans, which called for six 1,000-pound bombs to be dropped on the Bab al Azzizia barracks in three separate bombing raids spanning three hours, been followed. Instead, two such bombs were dropped by only two F-111s during an eleven-and-a-half-minute raid. The original plan would have required the French government's approval for American bombers to fly over its sovereign territory. France had initially signaled its willingness to go along with the plan but then cowered and declined, fearing terrorist retaliation within its borders. Islamist cells with operational plans were known to be hiding in the Paris suburbs.

The uproar over the French turnabout shook the halls of power within the White House, NATO, the Pentagon, the CIA, and the NSA. The CIA particularly fumed because they had expended assets and risked US lives and the lives of foreign sources in order to pinpoint the arrangement of tents in Gaddafi's nomadic compound and his exact sleep location on the night of the raid; it was known to have changed nightly. The French government did a poor job of trying to close the diplomatic gap between it and its allies. While ambassadors and generals exchanged dirty looks and angry notes and heads of state exchanged heated and occasionally foul words via supposedly secure phone lines, the NSA did nothing, and it accomplished its goal. Kraft had been the one to deliver a plan to the Council that would punish France so they would change their ways.

Without warning, beginning on the morning of April 15, the flow of vital Communications Intelligence information (COMINT) to friendly foreign governments, aside from Thatcher's in London (who could be trusted not to share it), slowed to a trickle. Daily briefings on Soviet troop positions in Eastern Europe became limited, and information on Libyan troop movements in Chad, where French troops were engaged, was cut off because of "malfunction of satellite resources," according to the Pentagon, per the information given to them by the NSA.

French President Mitterrand not only had to contend with an angry United States. He also had to deal with an angry French public who had, in public opinion polls conducted the day after the raids, expressed overwhelming dissatisfaction with the decision to deny air space to the United States; embarrassed diplomats who were made to look duplicitous and self-serving; generals who felt responsible for letting down their brethren on the other side of the Atlantic; and with an enraged intelligence service that had been exposed as being inept and under-funded without American help. Several high-level officials resigned. Others begged their American counterparts for restoration of COMINT communications. The American President, however, and his advisors could honestly deny they knew of no orders coming from the White House, State Department, Department of Defense, Joint Chiefs, or the CIA that halted signals intelligence flow to France.

The well-orchestrated effort by the NSA sought no permission or prior approval because none was needed. In fact, few knew of the decision to not share signals intelligence, a key to ensuring the deniability of the plan. To be sure, the policy shift was not shared with any foreign entities. In its own subtle way, the NSA got its message out to the so-called friends of the United States around the world. Only one short message would ever be sent by the NSA regarding this matter, and it went directly to Alain Dupontier, head of Direction Générale de la Sécurité Extérieure (DGSE), the French equivalent of the NSA. "You should not have interfered with

Mother Nature. Instructions will follow." Mother Nature had been the code name for the raid in Libya.

The pressure began building in France the first week of September 1986, less than five months after the truncated American assault in Libya failed to kill its target. The French had been soft on terrorists for more than a decade and had caved or even been sympathetic to their demands. Now, they would pay the price.

As background, during the 1970s, secret agreements between the governments of Italy and France, the PLO, and related terrorist groups were concluded that assured free passage, diplomatic recognition, and room to operate for these groups in both countries. The French were badly scarred by their Algerian experience, and the Italians were starved for cash, so both were eager to accommodate these players. In addition, and perhaps more importantly, both needed Middle East oil. Non-state actors established safe staging bases in Western Europe, from which, in 1982, pro-Palestinian Marxist extremists carried out the assassination of Lieutenant Colonel Jack R. Ray, a US military attaché, and Yaakov Ben-Simantov, an Israeli diplomat. In a turnaround in 1986, the law-and-order government of Premier Jacques Chirac proceeded to place George Ibrahim Abdullah, a Lebanese citizen, on trial for those crimes. Still not understanding the dangers of appeasement, in the summer of 1986, French intelligence officers met with representatives of the Lebanese Armed Revolutionary Factions (FARI) to work out a deal in exchange for leniency in the Abdullah case. Those dealings encouraged more kidnapping, including that of French journalists who were held as hostages in Beirut.

The Bombings of September—*Les Attentats de Septembre* as they were known by the French public—began on September 4 and continued for nearly two weeks, growing increasingly deadly as time passed. The first bomb, at the Gare de Lyon, produced no fatalities but caused fear throughout the public who relied on this transit hub. It was followed by a message to the government from a murky group closely linked to, if not one and the same as, FARI. Their message: Free Abdullah, or else.

The first fatal attack came on September 8, after authorities refused to bow to a deadline for the release of Abdullah and two other accused assassins. A bomb exploded at the post office of the Hotel de Ville, the city hall of Paris, killing one person and wounding eighteen, including a *mère supérieur* out for a stroll, who resided in a convent near Notre Dame Cathedral. Four days later, the bombers struck again at a crowded cafeteria restaurant in Plaza La Défense, killing two people and wounding thirty-four. Several witnesses reported seeing a young man in the toilet room. He never returned to claim the backpack he left behind, a bag loaded with explosives and shrapnel packed inside a pressure cooker that subsequently detonated. The man leaving the backpack fit descriptions of Abdullah's brother Rahi.

Paris authorities reasoned whoever was responsible for the attacks—be it Abdullah's family members or other extremists—were most likely taking their orders from handlers in the Middle East. Even if their masters were in France, some communications must have left France to parts of the Middle East, and authorities reasoned that with the ability to monitor these, they could find the bombers. Only the NSA had the means to do this.

Jacques Chirac, who was both the prime minister of France and mayor of Paris, had verbally challenged the terrorists prior to the stepped-up bombings. This time he responded with more draconian measures. He ordered one thousand crack soldiers to beef up patrols along French borders, and police were given broad powers to detain, interrogate, and transport suspects. Police raids on suspected terrorist safe houses intensified, and numerous suspects were rendered to a third country for interrogation. Chirac imposed restrictions on all foreigners entering France, with the exception of Common Market nationals and Americans.

On September 14, a few minutes before Chirac went on air to announce his new measures, a package was discovered under a table at the Pub Renault, a popular cafe on the Champs-Élysées. The policeman trying to remove the parcel was killed as it exploded, and twenty others were wounded. The next day, a bomb exploded outside of police headquarters near the Palais de Justice, killing two people and injuring forty-one others. A third bomb in the bustling Montparnasse area ripped through several bistros, sending hundreds to overloaded hospitals. For good measure, a small kosher restaurant in the Marais district was bombed simultaneously, killing two non-Jewish employees and wounding a pair of newlyweds celebrating their honeymoon.

Paris was in a state of panic. Parisians stayed in their homes. Theaters, restaurants, and department stores were deserted. People avoided the Metro, putting more cars on the streets, where they were routinely stopped and searched, creating massive traffic jams. The large stone *jardinières* that usually lined the Champs-Élysées were carted away during an all-night operation in order to remove them as depositories for bombs. The famous boulevard itself was now patrolled by elite troops openly carrying assault weapons and was nearly devoid of civilian traffic. Meanwhile, the airport and train stations were jammed with foreigners trying to leave and French citizens trying to reenter. Hotels that relied on tourists sat empty.

French intelligence services were rendered impotent as a result of the loss of NSA eyes and ears. Alain Dupontier, the head of the French DGSE, and the current chairman of the NSA were friends of sorts, belonging to the same "fraternity" as were the heads of GCHQ in London, the Mukhabarat in Cairo, the Mossad in Jerusalem, and others. Under extreme pressure from his government,

Dupontier dispatched an urgent message to the Chairman: "COMINT urgently needed. It has been cut off. *Expliquez, s'il vous plaît.*" Employing an infrequently used channel of communications, one that left no trace of itself, the Chairman's reply was simple: "Our ally, the French Republic, should not have interfered with Mother Nature."

In fact, there had been a warning issued earlier, prior to the Libyan operation to kill Gaddafi. In the hours before the E-111s and EF-111s took off from their bases in Britain for their 2,400-nautical-mile flights around the coast of France, Spain, and Portugal, last-ditch efforts were made to change the minds of the French leadership. A course involving an overfly of French territory would have cut the trip by 1,200 nautical miles in each direction and allowed much heavier runs at lower risk to personnel. A diplomatic effort by the US ambassador to the United Nations had failed, as did those by other high-level contacts.

It was during that window of opportunity in April 1986 that the Chairman of the NSA, at the advice of Kraft, dispatched a trusted courier to Paris to deliver a sensitive message to Dupontier. Meeting midway across the Pont Neuf bridge, the elegant and formidable seventeenth-century structure spanning the Seine at the tip of Île de La Cité, the courier delivered a note that began with the admonition: *Ultra Secret: Detruisez apres Avoir Lu* ("Top Secret: Destroy after Reading"). It went on to say, in French and English: "If France does not cooperate, she will be on her own. Mother Nature is vital to the interests of the United States." The French unity government was indignant over American interference with their internal affairs and ignored the message. "A great-sized monster of ingratitude," the Chairman wrote in his journal, quoting Shakespeare's words in *Troilus and Cressida.*

On September 17, 1986, at 6:30 p.m. in Paris (thirty minutes past noon in Washington), two men in a black BMW slowly drove past the Luxembourg Gardens, turned down the Rue de Rennes, and cruised lazily down the busy Left Bank thoroughfare lined with cafes, shops, and flower stands. Nearby, in front of a discount clothing store called Tati, one of the men briefly donned a face mask and placed several parcels into two large trash receptacles before speeding away. The packages were loaded with an estimated three kilos of high-grade explosives and an assortment of nuts, bolts, razor blades, and carpenter's nails. When they detonated fifteen minutes apart, they killed seven people, including first responders and children, and injured or maimed 120 in the bloodiest single massacre yet of civilians in Paris. Heads, limbs, and other body parts were found a block away. It was subsequently learned the license plate on the BMW had been captured by NSA satellite cameras and was traced to members of the Palestinian Liberation Front.

Within thirty minutes of the Tati blast, a government Concorde left Charles de Gaulle Airport on its way to Andrews Air Force Base in Maryland. When the supersonic jet came to a stop, a helicopter carried a high-ranking French general to the roof of the State Department building—eight stories above grade. By 7:30 p.m., Washington time, a top-secret *Ordre Irrévocable an Exécuter* was in the hands of the President of the United States and soon in the hands of the Joint Chiefs and intelligence agencies. The order was an ironclad, nonrevocable authorization for American aircraft to overfly French air space during any future attack on terrorist targets in Libya, Syria, Iran, Sudan, Iraq, Lebanon, or other unspecified countries for as long as Francois Mitterrand remained president of France. It bore the full weight of authority of the French government, at least until the government changed. It was signed by the hand of Mitterrand and bore his seal.

The Bombings of September ended with the discount store bombing. The terror cells in Saint-Denis were located and eliminated, along with the two men in the car who bombed Tati. Paris slowly returned to normal.

As Kraft prepared for his long day, he took solace in how his plan had succeeded so brilliantly eight months earlier.

A VISIT WITH KATIE

Shortly after noon in Cincinnati, Insbrook paid a visit to Katie Shepard. Katie looked up from the newspaper she was reading and glanced skeptically at the ruggedly handsome physician.

"Hello. What?" she said. She had grown hostile to strangers entering her room.

"I just wanted stop in and see you on my rounds."

"That's nice. What kind of doctor are you, anyway?" Katie asked, feigning indifference to him and looking down at the newspaper.

"An internist. An endocrinologist, to be specific," he answered. "Don't worry about words. I just wanted to ask you a few more questions."

"OK," she said, standing up and moving to the window. "I don't have much to do anyway. What is it you want to ask, doctor? I told you everything yesterday. But I'm not sure you really know what goes on in this hospital. I haven't been in a hospital since I had my daughter forty years ago, but this is not the one I would recommend to anyone now. Back then, people were polite, and it was quiet. If you are the director of this place, why don't you direct your people to treat patients with a little more respect? Why don't you direct your workers not to stare and make comments as patients are wheeled through the halls? Why don't you direct your doctors to let a patient know what is going on with them instead of running in and out of a room every five minutes? And why don't you direct the nurse down the hall to stop calling me 'honey' and treating me like a child? Apparently, I am sick with some kind of medical illness."

Insbrook tried to reply, but Katie continued speaking over him.

"So, Mr. Medical Director, you came to ask me questions? I have a question. How can a sixty-three-year-old woman look like me? You tell me. That's what I'm here to find out. I'm sure you have a couple of fancy East Coast degrees on the walls of your office."

Insbrook didn't answer this time. He sat quietly and listened.

"I know it can't happen. This doesn't happen," Katie Shepard repeated. "I am a rational person, but I cannot explain it. I have lived through it, though," she said emphatically.

As Katie stood in front of the hospital window, the morning light silhouetted her shapely form through her nightgown. "I have to get out of here; that's what I have to do," she said. "I have to prove it to myself. I'm going back to Columbus." She turned and faced Insbrook. "You can come with me if you want to see where I live, but I'm going home. I drove to Cincinnati to see a friend, and the next thing I knew, I was admitted after a car accident. I wish to sign out, please. You can't keep me here."

"Mrs. Shepard," Insbrook began, "you can't leave. You are a sick young woman, and we are trying to help you. Why don't you sit down again so we can have a conversation? So far, you have done all of the talking. I've considered everything you have said, including your criticisms of the hospital, and I will do what is within my power to solve the problems. On another day, we can talk more about those issues. Right now, I'm here to talk about yours. Is it OK if I ask you a few questions? And then you can ask me some."

Katie sat down. "Can I go first?" she asked.

"Sure," Insbrook replied.

"Can you tell me what you're doing for me?"

"What do you mean?"

"Well, I'm here in your hospital. What are you doing for me? I am sitting here while I presume you collect money from my insurance company."

"Therapeutically, we're doing nothing," Insbrook told her. "This is the diagnostic phase. After we make a diagnosis, we will see what we can do to treat you. Let me see if I can list the problems we have discovered so far. It appears you are anemic. Once we determine the cause of that, we can treat it.

"Do you think you ever drink and forget to eat?"

"How would I forget to eat?" Katie replied. "I like food. Not yours particularly, but in general, I do. Pardon me, but your food tastes like cardboard."

Insbrook liked Katie's sassiness. He was tired of the "yes, sirs" he heard all day. He continued. "You complain of painful urination, and you have a UTI. We are culturing it so we know how to treat it. We will also do tests for STDs since you admit to being sexually active."

"You make it sound like I've admitted to a crime," Katie protested. "You know what? Leave. Get out of my room, please. I didn't ask you to come into my room in the first place. My private life is none of your business. What do you admit to?"

"I didn't mean it that way. That's just the way we speak in medicine."

"Then try speaking like a human being," Katie said. "Go on."

"We also plan to examine your blood and look for a reason for your arthritic complaints. And we will screen your blood for coincidental abnormalities. It's probably all normal, but we'll see if anything turns up."

"Maybe I could leave some blood and urine with you and get out of here. Frankly, sir, you seem like a nice man, but I want to go home."

"No, we need you here. We are also going to have a psychiatrist see you. I'm sure you understand."

"I expected it, but I don't *understand* anything."

"Katie, in terms of your anemia, what can you tell me about your menstrual periods?"

"I don't bleed at all," she said. "My last period was about eighteen years ago."

"And when you . . ." Insbrook cleared his throat, then continued, "got younger, your periods did not return? Why would that be?"

"I read up on it. My theory is that I ovulated all of my eggs, and then, no matter what happened, it was finished. That's what I have been thinking. My libido came back, but not my periods."

"Interesting theory. You're a bright young woman. Can you tell me once again who your primary care doctor is?" Insbrook asked.

"I haven't seen a doctor for five years. I've avoided them. But as I told you, when I lived in Milwaukee, my gynecologist was Dr. Barrett. He should have my records. Why don't you talk to him, assuming he is still alive?"

"At this point, I won't assume anything," Insbrook said. "I'm going to have you sign a release form, and if Dr. Barrett has any of your records, he can send them to us. What about your daughter?" Insbrook asked, testing her recall. "You haven't seen her at all?"

"Isabella?"

"Isabella."

"I haven't seen anyone after the physical changes except people I've met in Columbus. Oh my gosh," Katie said. "I just remembered something. There's something in my purse I want to show you." She reached for her leather purse and shuffled through loose tissues and makeup. "I have a card here. Oh, here it is." She handed the doctor a postcard, postmarked from Anaheim, California, the previous December 23 and addressed to Mrs. Katie Shepard in Columbus, Ohio.

Dear Mom,

*Things are beautiful here. It's so warm! We took the boys to
Disneyland today, and they loved it. Next stop, San Diego. Then
maybe Tijuana. Merry Christmas.*

Love,

Bella, Ben, and the kids

The doctor was perplexed. "Can you give me a phone number
where Isabella can be reached?"

"Yes. It's 608-555-7280. Oh shit, I just remembered that they
were going to a medical convention this morning. They'll be home
Wednesday night. I'll try to convince Isabella to come here once she
is back. I want to tell her everything, if you will help me."

"Of course I will, Katie," Insbrook said as he held her hand.
But then, he ran his hands through his hair. *Help me? Dr. Barrett?
Isabella? Growing younger?* Here was a gorgeous, sensuous young
woman—who frankly was arousing him as she was silhouetted in
front of the window—telling him about her middle-aged daughter
and two grandchildren. Did he believe this? Why did she suddenly
realize Isabella was at a convention? This wasn't the game he had
come to play. He became edgy and abruptly stood up to leave.

"Where are you going?" Katie asked, now disappointed. "Can't
you stay a little bit longer?"

"I would love to, but I need to run now. I have a lot of patients
to see," Insbrook said nervously. "I'll come back later and tell you
what we have found."

Tears began to well up in Katie's eyes as she sat with her hands
on her temples. "Kill me, kill me, please kill me," she whimpered
pathetically. She flung her handbag off the bed, its contents scattering across the floor. She threw her newspaper on the floor and
curled up in the bed, sobbing.

"Get this out of me," she muttered. "Please, get this devil out of me!" she screamed as she wrestled with her gown.

Feeling increasingly uncomfortable, Insbrook quietly said, "Katie, please don't cry," as he backed out of the room. "I promise I will help you."

NUPTIALS MADE IN HEAVEN

C hristopher Bouchikas sipped a glass of orange juice as he read the reports that had accumulated overnight. He was seated behind the cockpit in a captain's chair; in front him were spread notes and papers on a wooden table. He was aboard *Perseus*, one of a fleet of unmarked jets that shuttled NSA Council members between cities. The plane was making its way toward NSA headquarters in Houston. *Perseus* was a Gulfstream IV, smaller than its sibling *Sylph*, a 727-23 that was capable of carrying larger groups. Several other small jets, other fixed-wing aircraft, and helicopters located around the globe completed the NSA's fleet. Airline tickets for these trips did not exist. No Such Airlines.

Bouchikas was the son and grandson of Greek immigrants—his father a Greek-born professor of history, and his mother a chemist who moved from Athens to the United States in 1950. His beloved grandfather opened his restaurant in Chicago's Greektown the same year. Christopher was born six years later while both of his parents were teaching at the University of Chicago. He became a local sensation as a five-year-old when the *Hyde Park Herald* carried accounts of how he could read and comprehend adult novels and solve junior high school math problems. By age eight, he could sight-read Rachmaninoff's *Concerto #3* and play it on the piano. Christopher entered college at the University of Chicago at the age of twelve, where he achieved a bachelor's degree in electrical engineering in three years. He went on to receive his doctorate in the field from the University of Michigan while at the same time studying political science.

In 1976, at age twenty, Bouchikas was studying for a third degree in economics at Harvard when he met Diana. Diana and Christopher were practicing members of the same Orthodox Church and were aware of each other through friends and family but had never met before their chance meeting in Boston. They fell in love on their first date and married in Chicago later that summer. It was a marriage made in heaven.

By 1978, as the Iranian revolution simmered, the couple had moved back east and Bouchikas served in the State Department in Washington. He was fluent in French, Arabic, English, and Greek and proficient in Farsi, skills that were found useful. The scholar advised on matters of Indo-Asian and Middle East politics, economics, and energy. His advice to the CIA was to assassinate Ayatollah Khomeini in Paris. His counsel was ignored, but the outcome he predicted if they didn't do so proved prescient. He subsequently received high marks from the Departments of State, Defense, and Energy. Despite this, Bouchikas was relieved of his duties in early 1981 when the new administration cleaned house and installed their own people.

Bouchikas was bitter at first and felt he had prostituted himself while working for the government. A professor of economics once told him, "When you work for the government, it's like being a two-bit whore. When you're needed, you're needed, but when it's over, nobody remembers your name." The professor was wrong, though. The government would remember his name.

In 1981, Bouchikas moved to the private sector to try his hand at making money, beginning with firms that were part of the military-industrial complex. He started at a think tank based in Virginia, before being recruited to the more lucrative jobs in California. There he worked on various assignments, including, for a short period of time, the much-maligned Strategic Defense Initiative. At the same time, he was contracted to network and lobby with congressmen to help establish a private equity firm with influential connections that was launched in May 1984. All the while, Bouchikas's moves were being tracked by the Department of Defense, the FBI, and the CIA, all of whom were interested in his service.

As a result of large salaries, shrewd investments, and his contacts both on Wall Street and in Washington, by 1986 Bouchikas had accumulated assets worth many millions of dollars, more than enough to satisfy his lifestyle for years to come. It was at that time that out of a sense of patriotism sprinkled with a bit of intrigue he went to work for the CIA. Soon after, he was approached with an offer from a closely tied agency, which further piqued his interest. Thus, by late that year, at the age twenty-nine, he was taken into the ranks of the NSA and became the youngest member of its elite governing council. He and his family then moved to their home in Alexandria, from where, it was promised, he would help control world affairs for the foreseeable future. He was also guaranteed a generous salary and pension as well as an extremely large life insurance policy. To Bouchikas, it seemed to be another marriage made in heaven.

DIRECTIVE #9

A black SUV waited at Hobby Airport to drive Bouchikas on the twelve-minute ride to the Federal Building, below which was housed Big TEX. The building stood on what thirty-five years earlier was ranch land owned by early settlers of Houston. In 1955, the property was purchased by private investors with laundered funds provided by the CIA. The CIA was not legally allowed to buy land inside the United States without congressional approval and allocation of funds by the GSA, but an exception quietly published in the Federal Register allowed the NSA to do so. Over the next few years, under great secrecy, an underground vault that reached 120 feet below grade and spanned 282 acres was constructed; it would house a completely self-sufficient intelligence facility supposedly capable of withstanding a nuclear assault. When the facility was complete, two modest buildings that served as entrances were constructed at the perimeters while the rest of the ranch was restored to its original appearance, and the canvas-covered fences that surrounded the property were removed. With the expected growth of the metropolis rapidly approaching the area, and with the help of Rep. Sam Rayburn, plans for a federal office building were approved for the site. That building, completed in 1964 along with several support buildings—commercial office buildings, a retail section, and an adjoining park, fountains, promenade, and parking structures—now stood atop the one-thousand-acre site. The Federal Building built above the NSA headquarters also served as a good cover for those who made daily trips to the complex. As a bonus, the NSA made a windfall on its land holdings, helping to establish a large slush fund that grew with the go-go years of the 1960s and beyond.

The history of how the National Security Agency, the nation's most secret intelligence agency, came into existence requires a little background to explain. The need for a centralized Communications Intelligence (COMINT) gathering agency that could intercept and decipher foreign messages became highly apparent at the start of American involvement in World War II, following the surprise attack on Pearl Harbor. Thus, the Special Branch of the War Department's Military Intelligence Service was born. Soon after, the Special Branch took over for the Signal Security Agency that had been under the control of the Signal Corps that was housed at Vint Hill Farms, Virginia, from 1929 to 1942.

In May 1949, the Special Branch gave way to the Armed Forces Security Agency (AFSA), placed under the direction of the military's Joint Chiefs. The mission of AFSA, whose very existence was top secret, was to place the conduct of communications intelligence and security of that information under one authority within the military establishment. The activities of this newly formed agency were beyond the reach of even the President, as set forth in the infamous National Security Council Intelligence Directive #9 of 1948, which for unexplained reasons excluded such authority. Rather, AFSA was under the direction of the Armed Forces Security Agency Council, comprised mainly of representatives of each of the armed services branches plus an outside chairman. In 1949, AFSA operated exclusively out of Washington, with all signals intelligence concentrated at Arlington Hall and all communications operations housed at the Naval Security Station on Nebraska Avenue.

A change in AFSA's mission occurred in the late 1940s when, in addition to it being the intelligence gathering unit for the armed forces, it began to receive and process requests for intelligence from other agencies of government, including the FBI, the CIA, and the State Department. Ultimately, the competition for AFSA's services by so many government agencies overburdened and weakened it. AFSA came under political attack during the Korean War because of the poor quality of its communications intelligence and for not knowing the People's Republic of China would enter the conflict on the side of the North. When information on this immense intelligence failure reached President Truman, he set about to correct the problem. He initially appointed a committee to study it and subsequently adopted nearly all of the committee's recommendations. Chief among them was the establishment of a new, super-secret agency that would replace AFSA. Of nonpareil significance was that this new organization would continue to operate with the full protection of Directive #9, i.e., beyond the reach of the president. It followed that on October 24, 1952, President Truman signed an executive order, a vague, seven-page presidential memorandum, that established the clandestine National Security Agency, unaccompanied by any legislation that set limits on it. The Commission concluded that it should, therefore, not be surprising that the NSA eventually evolved into an operational unit that operated at times as a shadow government of the United States.

Truman was a man who knew firsthand the power of the atomic bomb to wipe out an entire city. He feared that an attack on Washington could lead to a crippling of America's ability to respond, especially if the entire intelligence gathering and cryptologic apparatus were located there. He therefore ordered that communications intelligence operations be well removed from probable targets. The original location chosen for the NSA's headquarters was Fort Knox, set in the backwoods of Kentucky. That choice, however, was met with resistance from young civilians who made up the bulk of the NSA's brilliant mathematicians and scientists. As an alternative, it was proposed that two facilities would be built, linked together electronically as best they could at the time. One would remain in or around Washington, and the second would be built at a distant site. This fit in with the NSA's philosophies that redundancy was the key to survival and almost no cost was too much to bear.

The Washington area site for NSA headquarters was a relatively easy choice. Fort Meade, Maryland, located roughly midway between the District of Columbia and Baltimore, sat on a huge parcel of government-owned land that was perfect, out of range of known nuclear weapons at the time, with easy access to metropolitan Washington via the highway. The compound of buildings eventually built there occupied 350 out of Fort Meade's 1,000 acres and would be the official headquarters of the NSA. The Houston location was decided upon later. Its southwestern location was desirable to a young generation of scientists who could not afford adequate housing near Washington and were attracted to the Sun Belt. In the days of larger throw-weight bombs and precision-guided intercontinental ballistic missiles, a location twenty-two miles from Washington no longer afforded adequate protection from a nuclear attack. Eventually, the complex in Houston surpassed the massive Maryland installation in both size and strategic importance. The up-and-coming high-tech hubs of Austin and Dallas were in close proximity.

* * *

Once inside the main building of the massive Houston complex, Bouchikas pressed the elevator button for Level 2. The levels were

numbered from the bottom up, i.e., the deepest level carried the low-
est number. What he believed to be (and, indeed, what was) Level 1
housed the NSA's massive state-of-the-art computer system, a computer's computer if you will, along with its elaborate cooling system.
This enormous one of a kind computer was the literal and figura-
tive foundation of Big TEX and was the brainchild of Zvi Davis.
Operating the system required an army of full-time programmers
and was believed to be at least thirty years ahead of any computer
in the world. All told, the behemoth could perform one quadrillion
calculations per second. Level 1 stretched for several city blocks and
was divided like the human brain into left and right hemispheres.
The western end of the building was code-named Carillon and was
made up of ten IBM 360/65s strung together in parallel, while the
eastern end consisted of a twelve specially configured Cray-2 systems.
Other components that connected the two, a virtual brainstem, were
developed by the Department of Defense and are classified. The
whole structure was encased in thick concrete, impervious to both
water seepage and temperature changes. Redundant cooling systems
shunted the tremendous heat generated by these computers to locations in the Galveston Bay. A failure of the cooling system would be
catastrophic, causing the destruction of the computers, their data,
and all human life that could not escape to the surface in a short
time, a difficult task without elevators or lights. The energy source
for all this came from several small nuclear power plants located
inconspicuously nearby.

Several features of the NSA's computer network were of vital importance. First, no one other than the NSA shared the network. Eighty
percent of its terminals were in the building that housed it; the rest
were in redundant NSA locations or were housed "behind the green
door" in installations in and around Washington, all owned by the
NSA. Communications were encrypted by the NSA's cryptographic
team, the world's best. Terminals outside of the Houston headquarters

used NSA technology to unencrypt messages and deployed what is known as the RSA algorithm, a synchronized code that changed several times per second. A tiny delay in synchronization would render the system inoperable. In 1987, it was estimated that it would take 10^{1024} years for the next fastest computer to crack the NSA's code. Nevertheless, fearing the system might eventually be subject to a brute force attack or another unknown method for accessing it, Davis and his team concentrated on a concept called quantum computing based on the mathematical work of Paul Benioff. Quantum computing would expand its complexity in a thousand dimensions. The Commission found that no such computer currently existed and concluded it probably never would.

There were six elevator banks and twenty-four elevators in the lobby of the building. Elevators going to different levels and sections of the building had separate guarded entrances, key to ensuring the separation and anonymity of people who functioned in various capacities within the NSA complex. It was ingenious how so many people in the same building were isolated from one another. People working a short distance from one another horizontally or vertically would, by design, never see each other's faces or even know of their existence. The inaugural director of the NSA, Lieutenant General Ralph Canine (pronounced Ka-neen), was so preoccupied with operational covertness that he reportedly never physically occupied his Fort Meade office. In fact, during his five years on his job, few who worked at the NSA's headquarters building knew what he looked like.

Most of Levels 2 and 3 of the Houston building were restricted to Council members and a handful of other high NSA officials. Level 2 housed offices, conference rooms, classrooms, breakout rooms, and living quarters, while Level 3 contained auditoriums, a library, a lounge, a theater, leisure facilities, and, strangely, ethnic-themed restaurants that rotated on a daily basis. Level 4 consisted of other sundry administrative spaces, while Levels 5 and 6 contained parking spaces and maintenance facilities.

As Bouchikas descended, he wondered if levels unknown to him existed. The scholar thought it possible that what was Level 2 to him might be someone else's Level 3. Bouchikas was not alone in such suspicions, which was inherent in the espionage business. To look over one's shoulder was a way of life. Anyone who asked questions was looked upon with suspicion themselves. The culture of the Agency was such that orders were carried out without knowing who ultimately was giving the order. Better not to know, an arrangement akin to that of the Mafia.

Who ultimately *was* giving the orders? Even as a councilor, Bouchikas was not entirely sure. He thought he was close to the top of the organization, but he was uncertain of that as well. The man he took orders from was called the Chairman, but who, if anybody, gave orders to the Chairman? Was the NSA really running parallel and sometimes counter to the administration of the President, as Bouchikas was led to believe, or was the NSA, in fact, taking orders *from* the President? Or were the generals giving the orders? Bouchikas didn't really know the answers to these questions with certainty.

* * *

Bouchikas was in the office of George Christianson, a former State Department and CIA official.

"Is anything new happening in that stack worth knowing about?" Bouchikas asked, gesturing to a pile of files on Christianson's desk.

"South America is wrapped up," Christianson told him.

"I read the file on that. The President is a clever man on foreign policy," Bouchikas said, "which is a good thing because he's handcuffed on most matters at home these days. Did he have to pay a price down there?" Bouchikas asked.

"You know the answer to that, Chris. Pallets of cash flown on CIA airplanes, right into the hands of the dictators. It makes me sick."

"I worry about the man's judgment lately," Bouchikas commented. "Any new word on his health?"

"They say he's stable, meaning not great. He seems to have good days and bad days," Christianson told him. "Look, you know how I feel about him personally, but we do all right by him. With somebody else, the Agency might not get away with all this."

"Get away with all this." What did the NSA get away with? Historians will likely say the NSA was an agency that got away from its original mission. Surely, they will say it was an agency that believed it could get away with murder.

Bouchikas looked at his watch. "Sorry to cut this off, George, but I must get to my next meeting. I just stopped in to say hello."

DAY THREE

May 5, 1987

*To know how to grow old is the
masterwork of wisdom
and one of the most difficult
chapters in the Art of Living.*

—HENRI-FRÉDÉRIC AMIEL

THE DREAM IS OVER

P hilip Insbrook began his day at 6:30 a.m. in order to get some of his administrative work out of the way, including completing mandated forms, answering mail, and returning phone calls. Among the items he was completing was a census report that included the number of patients admitted to the hospital in the last twenty-four hours, the total number of inpatients, lengths of stay, numbers of ER visits, and statistics on births, deaths, communicable diseases, and public health problems including those related to the raging epidemic of HIV/AIDS. Payment sources were also compiled, including Commercial, Medicare, Medicaid, HMO, self-pay, county funds, and the like. The task was laborious and boring. Once compiled, the data was to be shared with government agencies, businesses, insurance companies, and researchers.

Insbrook thought computerizing medical reports was a good idea and would make his tasks easier. The health progress or regress of an individual could be followed over time. By analyzing matched groups, based on age, sex, race, genetic background, environmental conditions, food and alcohol consumption, exercise, and other etiologic factors, the "value" of interventions could be measured.

Appropriate interventions might theoretically add years to people's lives, whereas withholding them might be economically justified.

Such thoughts were disturbing to Insbrook, a frequently quoted medical ethicist. He was troubled that the entirety of medical research was aimed at the prolongation of life without regard for the quality of that life, especially the later years. To him, there was a point beyond which medical therapy exceeded its usefulness. He had recently published an editorial on the subject in the *Archives of Internal Medicine.*

> "The argument that no one has the right to play God falls apart when we look around at what we physicians do each day of our lives in medicine. This is not to deify the physician. Rather, the point is that those of us who live in a society with any semblance of order seek to change the natural course of things routinely. This is the charge of civilization; to positively influence our surroundings rather than accept the string of chance occurrences out of which life itself emerged and evolved out of the primordial sea."

Insbrook filled out a few other required forms, but his thoughts were consumed by Katie Shepard, about whom he had barely been able to stop thinking since their first encounter. He stood up behind his desk, picked up the phone, and dialed a five-digit extension.

"Six South? This is Dr. Insbrook," he said, staring out his window. "Do you have any new results on Mrs. Shepard?"

"Shepard? Hold on, and I'll check," a voice at the other end responded. Insbrook sat down on the edge of his desk and waited as the nurse looked through Katie's chart.

"Dr. Insbrook," the nurse said, "what would you like to know?"

"Give me whatever you have."

"OK, doctor. The urinalysis shows an elevated specific gravity, a low pH, high white cells, and many bacteria. The rest is normal."

"Please get a cathed specimen and repeat the urinalysis along with a culture? Also, dipstick it for protein. Do you have results for the BUN and creatinine?"

"Not yet. They lost the serum sample yesterday, and they are here now, drawing another one. I do have the CBC back. Do you want those results?" the nurse asked.

"Yes, please."

The nurse relayed Katie's blood results, as Insbrook listened attentively.

"A normochromic, normocytic anemia. It sounds like something may be going on in the kidneys," Insbrook said. "Ask the phlebotomist to draw an extra red top tube and run it, along with a serum iron and iron-binding capacity. I'll check on it later. See if you can get Mrs. Shepard on the schedule for an IVP too."

"Yes, doctor. I will take those as verbal orders," the nurse said.

"One other thing. How is she?" Insbrook asked.

"Who?"

"The girl. I mean the woman. Mrs. Shepard."

"She cried a lot last night, and the resident ordered something for sleep," the nurse told him. "Otherwise, she has been good. She really liked you, sir. She thought you were very handsome, doctor. She said she was sorry she got upset. She asked me if you were coming to see her again today."

"Yes, I will. I'll be there in an hour or two, right after I make my rounds. Will you let her know?"

"Yes, sir. I will."

Insbrook hung up the phone and paused before getting to the unpleasant task of filling out an incident report on a medical student who had died by suicide. He stood and walked to the window of his seventh-floor office where he stared at the pavement below. He conjured the image of Nancy Berman's shattered body lying there the night before. Nancy had been a medical student who wanted more than anything to become a skilled surgeon in order to emulate and honor her late father. She had been a patient of Insbrook's since she was age seven when it was discovered she had juvenile-onset diabetes.

Why was so little research time and money allocated to finding a cure for this disease? Insbrook wondered. Maybe not enough people shuddered at the word diabetes. Nancy did. It drove her out of her mind, especially when a retinal hemorrhage left her virtually sightless in one eye the week before. Her disease would likely have prevented her from getting a spot in the highly competitive surgical program she coveted.

Nancy knew too much about her disease to go on living with it. The end came a few hours after she scrubbed in on a below-knee amputation of a thirty-five-year-old diabetic woman. It was noted in operative records that during the surgery, Nancy's "good" eye became glassy, and her damaged eye drifted. Later, feeling weary and depressed, she took a plunge from a call room window to the Cincinnati pavement below. Her note to her family and boyfriend, cruel as it was, was simple: "My dream is over. I am out of here."

Insbrook stared at the spot on the hospital driveway where she landed. Her face had become unrecognizable and countless bones had been broken. Insbrook had watched Nancy being taken away in the coroner's van as firefighters unsentimentally hosed down the messy scene and crews sterilized the property around the medical center, restoring its serenity. *Medicine*, he thought, *can be a cruel and ugly business.*

WHATEVER CAN GO FORWARD
CAN GO BACKWARD

D r. Karl Gruber lifted his eye up and away from his Bausch + Lomb microscope and pushed his laboratory stool away from his bench. The scientist stood up and began nervously pacing around the room, concentrating deeply, deciding how he would phrase the next paragraph of his upcoming publication, "The Effect of Ambient Temperature on the Aging of Mouse Myocardium as Measured by Lipofuscin Deposits." Gruber was sure it would be published because he was the editor of the *Journal of Gerontology*. The researcher envisioned his article would appear in the same issue as an editorial he had been laboring over entitled "Toward a Multifactorial Theory of Aging." He had worked so long and so arduously on the *Journal*, as well as on his numerous research projects, that a friend jokingly warned Gruber that his research into aging would ironically drive the scientist himself to an early grave.

Karl Oscar Gruber was the director of the Institute for Gerontologic Studies at the University of Illinois College of Medicine in Chicago. Gruber's lab and his research group were widely considered to be the best in their field in the United States. They studied aging in all its aspects—clinical, biologic, sociologic, and economic.

His group had recently published a paper in *Nature* about the potential for exploiting pluripotential stem cells within fifteen years as a means of turning back the aging clock. Gruber's most recent discovery was telomeres, for which he was nominated for a Nobel Prize. Gruber had recently advised an NIH grants committee and counseled them that they should provide maximum funding for aging research because he was convinced that science would, within his own lifetime, discover a way to extend human life far beyond its current limits, especially with American wealth and ingenuity.

Born near Salzburg in 1939, Gruber was the only child born to poor, uneducated parents. When Karl was four, his father died of a massive heart attack at the age of fifty-two. Two years later, his mother died of ovarian cancer at age forty-four, leaving him an orphan. Karl was then placed in a Catholic home for boys where he behaved, studied incessantly, resisted the urge to enter the priesthood, and instead took up studies at the University of Vienna on a full scholarship as a result of his exceptional *Klausurarbeit* scores. There he received his doctorate in biology. Some speculated the age-related deaths of both of his parents motivated him to devote his life to study the mechanisms of aging. His doctoral thesis, which showed that nearly all species studied live to approximately the same age when measured in terms of total lifetime energy expended, catapulted both Gruber and his department to prominence in the field of gerontology. With the advent of better microscopes and newer analytic techniques, great strides were made over the ensuing decades that began to unravel the secrets of why all living things age and die. Gruber was responsible for many of those discoveries.

Gruber had been in Chicago for two years. Prior to Chicago, he had been in Cincinnati for two years, and before that, in Kyiv, in the far western part of the Soviet Union. Kyiv had been a hub of research into aging, generously funded by the Soviet government. Gruber, who never married, accepted a position at the Kyiv Institute of Gerontology in 1975, where for the next four years he worked and studied with American and other Western counterparts under an agreement on joint scientific and space exploration hammered out during the Nixon and Brezhnev days. There, he collaborated with the greatest minds in his field. It was during this period that Gruber became enamored with the United States.

In addition to collaboration, the United States was trying to drive a wedge between the Soviet Union and its satellite countries in its efforts to win the Cold War. Defections to the West by intellectuals, elite athletes, and artists were useful in this endeavor. Every defection was a blow to the feeble, tottering leadership in Moscow. While in Kyiv, with the aid of an American diplomat and the State Department, Gruber surreptitiously obtained immigration papers and a temporary work card for work in the United States. Shortly afterward, he came to the United States to present a paper at a World Health Organization plenary session and never returned home.

After Kyiv, it would be Cincinnati for Gruber, where he crossed paths with Philip Insbrook several times. They were the same age, with Austrian parentage, one Catholic and the other Jewish, and that difference spoke volumes for what they did and didn't have in common. Publicly, each had a healthy respect for the other as a preeminent scientist. Privately, Insbrook had quipped about Gruber in a memo to his dean, "His ideas are a bit crazy, if not dangerous. Perhaps he should go back to Russia." Nevertheless, the two men kept in touch with each other from time to time.

Parenthetically, Gruber's labs and offices on the southwest side of Chicago were close to the neighborhood where Christopher Bouchikas grew up. The Plasma Cell Commission's investigators discovered Gruber frequently ate at Christopher Bouchikas's family's restaurant; however, they found no other links between the two men. Like both mutations and evolution, many aspects of life are a result of pure chance.

* * *

While in Chicago, Gruber made an appearance on a segment of CBS's *60 Minutes*, followed by numerous appearances on late-night talk shows where he intrigued audiences with predictions of extreme longevity. His thick Viennese accent and shock of unkempt gray hair appealed to audiences as if he were a cross between Dr. Ruth Westheimer and Albert Einstein. In November 1986, he sat for an interview with *Rolling Stone* magazine in an article discussing aging rock stars, an excerpt of which follows:

> **Interviewer:** "What do you mean by a Multifactorial Theory of Aging?"
>
> **Gruber:** "We mean that up to this point, there have been several theories advanced as to why we age. Many identified factors are involved. If we control some of these, we can slow aging."
>
> **Interviewer:** "But not stop it?"
>
> **Gruber:** "For now, no, but one day, yes. If we could eliminate all of the known factors associated with aging successfully in one model, we would still only extend human lifespan by perhaps ten or fifteen years. While the Multifactorial Theory acknowledges the contributions of many known factors, there is still believed to be an as-yet-undiscovered final common pathway to aging. That is what we are searching for."
>
> **Interviewer:** "You have mentioned a hormone or enzyme. Could it be as simple as that? Could there be a single enzyme that is responsible for aging?"
>
> **Gruber:** "Most probably there is. Or the lack of it. Let me illustrate. Your readers who are gardeners may be aware that

in some species, senescence can be postponed if they are maintained in a juvenile state by pinching away new flower clusters before they blossom. From these observations, we hypothesize that at maturity, organisms begin to decline by producing a substance that initiates and advances aging. If that substance were to be removed or its production or mechanism of action blocked, the organism would likely be maintained in its healthy mature state indefinitely, barring trauma or infection, or the like."

Interviewer: "How close are we to discovering this common mechanism?"

Gruber: "It's difficult to say. It could be this week, this month, or this year. This much I am sure of: With concerted effort, we could have the answer by the end of this millennium. It is inevitable."

Interviewer: "You are dead sure we will solve this riddle. Why, Dr. Gruber?"

Gruber: "Because of the state of scientific research and technology. Today, we are one hundred times as scientifically advanced as we were ten years ago. In another ten years, it will be ten thousand times more. It is only a matter of time until we find the secrets for which we search. Remember this: We are not talking about magic. Underlying aging is a biological process. We will master it. Please do not doubt me. *Whatever can go forward can go backward.*" This was Gruber's favorite tagline.

Gruber set aside his manuscript when the morning mail arrived. It included a thick envelope from Kyiv, stamped in red in English with the same phrase repeated in Cyrillic script beneath it: "Photographs, Do Not Bend." The scientist removed a series of images taken through the electron microscope. He examined them, noting the subtle changes that indicated death at the cellular level after lab rats were injected with a concentrate taken from the serum of animals that had died at an early age with no cause found at necropsy.

It's the aging protein, he thought to himself. *It's all right there.*

GETTING PERSONAL

Insbrook gently knocked on the door of room 641 in the mid-morning, wanting to pay a brief visit to the intriguing patient inside before continuing his regular rounds.

"Come in," was the hurried reply from behind the door.

As Insbrook entered the room, Katie did not look away from the television. "*It Happened One Night*, 1934!" she shouted with excitement.

"What are we talking about now, my dear?" Insbrook questioned gently, worried about this latest outburst concerning events and dates from long ago. *Psychosis?* he wondered.

Katie turned away from the game show she was watching and smiled at Insbrook.

"It was a category on *Jeopardy!*. Best Picture of the Year," she explained. "I would have won one thousand dollars."

"Whew. I was getting a little worried you might be psychotic," Insbrook told her. "But that is the correct answer."

They both laughed as Katie turned off the television. "So, what's the latest? Do you have any news for me, or can I get back to spending time with Alex Trebek?" Katie asked. "He's a handsome man. Middle-aged—like you."

"Not too many labs are back," he answered, trying to keep it professional. "As we suspected, you are anemic and have a UTI, but nothing else is back yet. I only dropped in to make sure people are treating you better. I spoke with the staff."

"Almost everything is better. A guy in a suit who said he was a VP came and apologized to me. I guess you really *are* important. This place is not the Ritz-Carlton, but it will do—for a hospital. The food still tastes like cardboard, though," she said, looking over at an uneaten, unappetizing plate of cold scrambled eggs, a dry slice of toast, and a dish of cubed red Jell-O resting on a tray.

"Hmm. I will see if Wolfgang Puck is available," he retorted.

"And you, good doctor. How are you?"

"I'm fine. Busy," Insbrook told her.

"May I ask if you are married?" Katie asked.

"Divorced," was the quick reply.

"Do you live alone?"

"I have a houseman and a dog," Insbrook answered.

"A butler. You would, wouldn't you?"

"Mostly a driver, but Francisco also takes care of my house, gets my groceries, lets the dog out, those kinds of things. He lives in my house. He answers the phone when he is home and I can't. A little of everything, really. The man is so loyal he would take a bullet for me. I could hardly live without him."

"You do like women, don't you?" Katie asked coyly.

"Of course. Yes, I do. My wife was a woman, actually. I mean, yes," he said nervously, his hands in the pockets of his lab coat beginning to perspire.

"Lots of girlfriends, I bet," Katie said as she looked him up and down.

"I'm too busy for that," Insbrook explained. "But we shouldn't be discussing this."

"Too busy to enjoy life?" Katie queried.

"I know how to enjoy life. I could tell you about some of the finest hotels and restaurants in a lot of the major cities in the world," the doctor smugly assured her.

"Good. When I get out of here, you can take me to one of them. Or perhaps I will have you over for a homemade dinner. After all, you have been so kind to me. I'm a very good cook."

"Dinner sounds wonderful," Insbrook allowed, although he was hesitant. "I don't normally see patients outside of the hospital, but I might make an exception once you are no longer my patient, assuming you can actually cook."

"I've been doing it for nearly forty years, doctor."

"I like you, Katie." Now seated, Insbrook began to come to his senses. *I wish I hadn't said that*, he thought to himself. He leaned back and couldn't help but admire her. "Katie," he began, clearing his throat, "you are delightful, and I admit I would probably enjoy spending time with you in a different life. But it's probably not a good idea in this one."

Katie sat in silence, dead serious for a moment. She looked at the doctor with affection. "I like you too. Maybe sixty-three is too old for you," she finally said with a small, wry smile.

"I don't know if that will be possible in any case," Insbrook continued. "Katie, do you really believe you are sixty-three years old?"

"As opposed to what?" she asked coldly. "Twenty-seven, twenty-eight? How young do you like them, doctor?"

"I mean, you're not putting us on? Do you genuinely believe that?"

"Yes, I do. You think I'm insane. Is that it?" she exclaimed emphatically. "Get out of my room, then," she protested as she threw a napkin at him, playfully.

"I never said that," Insbrook said defensively. "Jeez, I don't know what to think. I think you are terrific. But listen, right now I need to continue my rounds."

"You seem to exit whenever it gets a little uncomfortable," Katie told him. "I asked you to dinner, and you gave me an excuse. Doctors. You are all brains and no emotions. Same thing for the last thirty-five years."

"Maybe so, but I do have to leave," Insbrook said.

"OK. But come back later," she said as she grabbed his arm. "I remembered I have something I put in the side zipper of my purse after the accident, when the police came to the ER, that may be of interest to you. They locked up my purse, but the nurse said security would bring it back later after it is checked for contraband."

"All right, I'll stop back after rounds," Insbrook said, reaching for the door.

Katie rushed over to the doctor and kissed him on his left cheek. "Thank you for stopping by, doctor. I'm sorry I was sassy to you. Please come back."

"I will," Insbrook responded. As he walked away, Insbrook sensed that his interest in Katie might be becoming a little more than just professional.

THE CARRYING CAPACITY

In a Level 2 conference room, on a larger-than-life screen, the Kodachrome slide in a circular rack changed to one of fading browns and browning greens. It was a picture of three deer, possibly a family, in a sparse, overgrazed clearing. The two larger animals lay dead, scrawny and malnourished, as evidenced by their patchy hides and protruding ribs. Standing next to them, looking directly into the camera as if seeking relief, was a wobbly-legged fawn, thin and barely alive. Far in the background, out of focus, were other animal carcasses lying in small groups.

The slide advanced. This time it was scrawny, malnourished, or dead people. A woman with a white head wrap lay sprawled in the road with her eyes open even after death as if she had collapsed in her tracks. Flies crawled on her lifeless face. Other human beings lay on blankets or sat on makeshift seats created from burlap sacks, emptied of NGO-delivered rice and filled with arid dirt, waiting for their turns to die. A potbellied child with prominent ribs and thin wobbly legs also seemingly gazed pathetically into the lens, as if appealing to the assembled group in Houston.

The slide flashed back to a scene of dead and dying deer. "Gentlemen," Dalia Abrahamyan explained from the podium, "this is the balance of nature. This is the way populations limit themselves in nature when they outgrow their resources." Dr. Abrahamyan advanced the carousel to a slide showing healthy deer playing and grazing in a lush, sunlit meadow.

"There is an ecological concept called the carrying capacity that refers to the number of a particular species an ecological system can sustain or 'carry' in good health. As a population increases to the point where it approaches or surpasses this capacity, factors are brought into play that limit it. These include predation, parasitism, hormonal and behavioral mechanisms, and competition for essential resources such as water, food, and shelter."

The slide changed to a scene of two fornicating deer.

"The reproductive capacity of individuals is meant to assure the continuation of the species, at least in some small numbers, should they fall on hard times, but when a population exceeds its carrying capacity," Abrahamyan explained as the slide changed to a rotting animal carcass, "some animals die. Only humans have the intellectual capacity to determine how abundant their supplies of food and other essential resources are and attempt to control their populations in some instances, generally in the West."

The picture changed to a photograph of a pack of brawny wolves ripping at the bloody flesh of an animal amid pure white snow. Abrahamyan continued, "The wolf and the mountain lion are the deer's natural enemies. Their populations vary with each other. As too many deer are killed off, the carrying capacity for the predator species is concomitantly decreased. Soon they, too, fall victim to competition and starvation. Once that happens, the deer population will again increase, followed after a lag period by an increase in the wolf and puma populations. This linked fluctuation between predator and prey has been observed in nature many times."

The slide changed. "Such a correlation establishes a population range that can be sustained by the ecological niche of the species, a range that is autoregulated," the population scientist explained. "Simplified, this is the balance of nature.

"The balance can be destroyed," she continued, "when predation is unnaturally removed from the ecologic environment. An inadvertent demonstration of this began in the year 1907. Prior to that time, a steady population of about four thousand deer existed and thrived on the Kaibab Plateau of Arizona," she said, displaying a picture of a healthy flock grazing. "This population level, well below the carrying capacity of the area, was stable in large part due to equally stable populations of pumas and wolves indigenous to the region. Then a so-called humanitarian endeavor was launched to free the supposedly vulnerable deer from their predators by exterminating the pumas and wolves. Without them, by 1925, the deer population of the Kaibab swelled to one hundred thousand, causing the area to be stripped of grass, shrubs, seedlings, and other vegetation needed to feed the deer. Within two years, over half the deer population starved to death, ultimately forcing the intervention to be halted. When the misguided adventure was over, the carrying capacity of the plateau fell below what it was in 1907 and took years to recover with the careful reintroduction of the predators.

"The underlying concept is simple. Birth and death rates must be roughly matched if there is to be ecologic and population stability. If one input to the equation drastically changes, the population will swell for a while but ultimately decline due to famine, pestilence, or disease." The slide changed to a picture of a mushroom cloud. "And in the case of humans, by war. Colleagues, we are not here to discuss deer and pumas."

Starving people appeared once again on the screen. "These are the tribespeople of Sudan. Their population has now exceeded the carrying capacity of their land, and millions face starvation. Our satellite images and intelligence inform us that this situation will not correct itself."

"So, Dalia, are you suggesting that there is a finite carrying capacity in Sudan, and we are approaching it?" Davis asked.

"We have reached it," Abrahamyan answered. "It pains me to turn my back on starving people, but I fear that in the end, we will see more malnourished children and dead women with flies on their lifeless faces than we have seen today. The problem is acute. Other parts of the world are not far behind.

"We could send food now," she continued, "but we are likely to see famine, food riots, and even water wars unless we can control the size of the population, and if not, our only choice is to let nature take its course. Sooner or later, it will be troops the United States will need to send."

The Chairman looked at his watch and spoke. "The hour is almost over. It is obvious, if our birth rate was suddenly increased, or conversely, *our death rate was suddenly and severely reduced,* that our national security could be threatened. We must be on guard against those possibilities. That is the lesson of the day.

"In ten days, Dalia will be presenting part two of this presentation, and we will have further conversation on the topic. Unless I hear objection, for now, we will not interfere in Sudan. We will also encourage other parts of our government not to interfere either, unless, of course, our strategic interests such as oil in Southern Sudan or access to one of our vital ports were threatened."

A VISIT TO THE LAB

By late morning, Insbrook stopped to see what surprise Katie Shepard had for him. He wondered again if his interest in this patient was becoming more than professional. He was also beginning to wonder why he kept considering evidence that she really was sixty-three years old.

Katie was in the shower when Insbrook arrived. When he checked her chart, it revealed no additional laboratory results were back, so he decided to pay a visit to the pathology department to try to expedite them. A visit from the hospital's medical director usually got their attention.

"Have you run the chemistries on Katie Shepard yet?" Insbrook asked.

"Katie Shepard. Shepard . . . let me see . . ." The technician thumbed through a stack of papers. "No, not yet. I'll run them right now."

Two minutes later, the results printed, and five were marked as abnormal. Most significantly, the serum calcium was critically high.

"Are you sure these are Mrs. Shepard's results?" Insbrook asked the technician.

"Yes—unless the phlebotomist accidentally mislabeled the tube," the lab tech replied.

"Do me a favor," Insbrook asked. "Have the nurse draw fresh tubes of blood. I'll sign an order when I get to her floor. See if you can get me the results to me as soon as possible. These results are consistent with a possible malignancy, so I would like to make sure these are Mrs. Shepard's before I say anything to her."

"I understand," the technician told the doctor. "It's a good idea."

Insbrook walked to another area in the sophisticated lab. "When you receive a sample for urinalysis on a woman named Katie Shepard can you run it for Bence-Jones proteins as well and page me with both results right away?"

"Yes, I will," the lab tech responded.

Insbrook then walked across the hall to the hematology lab. "Excuse me," he said to the lab technician, "will you see if you can find the blood smear on Katie Shepard, a patient of mine on 6 South, for me to look at?"

The tech dutifully searched a rack and handed the doctor the slide he requested. Insbrook hunched over and peered through the lens of a microscope at the slide, carefully counting cells and moving the stage of the instrument until the edge of the smear came into view. There he saw something highly abnormal: rouleaux formation, consistent with the disease he had in mind.

He looked alarmed and dialed the hematology consultant he had called in to see the patient. "This is Dr. Insbrook," he told Jack Shaw's assistant. "I need to speak to Dr. Shaw right away."

"Hold on," she said as she buzzed his office.

"Jack, it's Phil. I'm calling about the Shepard woman I asked you to see. She appears to be pretty sick on paper. She has a urinary tract infection and kidney pathology—and apparently a critically high calcium level. Her BUN and creatinine are both somewhat elevated. Not terrible numbers if she is sixty-three, but not good if she is in her late twenties. Aside from the calcium, her alkaline phosphate is 240, and her uric acid is 8.2. And the clincher: rouleaux formation on her peripheral blood smear. Put it together—to me, it's multiple myeloma. It's exceedingly rare under age thirty, I know, so maybe she really *is* older."

"Do you really think she is sixty-three?" Shaw asked. "I just finished seeing her. She's a young woman, Phil. Settle down."

"I don't know how old she is. I don't think she is sixty-three, but I don't know about being in her twenties either. If she has multiple myeloma, she has bone involvement. Textbooks say bone lesions usually appear after ten or twenty years. I don't think she's had this since she was three. Children with chronic illnesses just don't develop like her. Something doesn't add up, but I have a theory."

"I think your imagination is getting away from you," Shaw said.

"I'll order an immunoelectrophoresis and a skeletal survey, and I'll cancel the IVP. It's not safe with that creatinine level. Maybe you should do a bone marrow tap? Can you think of anything I'm missing?"

"No."

"I'll speak to the residents. I'm going to keep the psychiatrists away from her until we're finished. She's sick one way or the other, and I don't want them to upset her. I'll make sure she is comfortable. Call me if you think of anything else."

IN SEARCH OF A WINNER

T he President spent the morning in Washington, briefing cabinet members and a handful of Republican members of Congress on his South American trip. He had returned home with much-needed foreign policy and economic successes, including a commitment from Colombia and its neighbors to rein in the drug cartels, an agreement for exclusive exportation of oil to the United States from Venezuela, and an agreement by the Argentine government to stop flooding world markets with subsidized soybeans, poultry, and beef. In return, he pledged goodwill, rescheduling or relief of South American debt owed to the United States and the World Bank, and the mending of fences with the civilian government of Argentina after the split caused by America backing the United Kingdom during the 1982 Falklands War. The trip was being hailed as a great foreign policy achievement. This is what the bipartisan group of senators and congressmen were smiling about as they ate breakfast in the State Dining Room.

Afterward, the President and his two closest advisors retreated to the Oval Office. "Do you think this will take the focus off some of my problems?" the Chief Executive asked.

"Only to a degree," Steve Hazelton, the White House chief of staff, told him. "The Democrats don't average foreign and domestic issues and don't give you credit for anything good you might come up with at home. If you cured cancer, the headline in the *Post* would read, "President seeks to cut healthcare expenditures." They like to say you only do well at foreign policy because you have good people around you. The liberals want a big domestic issue, which probably translates to mean big spending."

"What about you, Dan?" the President asked Dan Dixon, his domestic affairs advisor. "What do you think?"

"I agree that our side cares about foreign policy while our opponents and their media allies focus on domestic issues," Dixon continued. "Their constituents couldn't find Argentina or Venezuela on a map, aren't farmers or ranchers, and don't give a rat's ass about unfair competition. I think you need a domestic achievement that plays well with the majority of Americans. Something big—perhaps in the healthcare realm. Betsy says they are planning to attack you on the Sunday shows this week for not caring about healthcare or childcare and ignoring the elderly. Those are the talking points, according to her mole at CBS. They want to distract from your achievements." Betsy was Betsy Friar, the combative forty-one-year-old presidential press secretary.

"Assholes," the President said. "What about the two hundredth anniversary of the Constitution that's coming up? Why don't we celebrate that? Fireworks on the mall and all. That's a good domestic issue."

"It's a sure thing," said Dixon. "But you will be out of office by '89, so the benefit will go to your successor."

"Oh, that's right, isn't it," the President conceded. "Then let's do it big this Fourth of July. What about that solidarity bunch in Poland?" the President asked. "Let's get them to fly an American flag off one of those ships at the Gdansk shipyard. Americans love the flag."

"That's foreign," Dixon answered. "And besides, people might get killed if they tried that. Here's an issue I wish we could tackle: The CIA and the FBI are at each other's throats. They're accusing each other of spying and stepping on each other's toes. Did you read my memo on this?"

"I skimmed it," the President replied. "Aren't we talking about scaling back some of that surveillance? I recall we were."

"Yes, we are talking about it," Dixon told him, "but the lawyers haven't agreed on a solution we could get through Congress. The CIA, the FBI, the military, and that gang in Maryland are each essentially operating autonomously. It's crazy and dysfunctional and it will bite us in the ass one day."

"What liberal moron at the ACLU dreamt up that scheme?" the President asked, as he anxiously tapped his manicured fingernails on his desk.

"In marriage, that's called an arrangement," Hazelton said. "It's also the law."

"Well then," the President said, "we still don't have an issue."

Just then, Stan Dillard, the attorney general, entered the room. Dillard was a physically large man, highly unpopular with the public, a longtime friend of the President who had also served as his campaign manager.

"Good to see you, Stan," the President told him. "Sit down. We were brainstorming on coming up with a popular domestic issue for me. Something to secure my legacy."

The President turned to his team. "Boys," he said, "please find me a winner. Make sure to include Betsy in your brainstorming too. She's one smart cookie, that one."

A JOURNEY TO MILWAUKEE

"**F**light 202 to Chicago with continuing service to Milwaukee will board in ten minutes," a voice announced in the small airport terminal. Insbrook thought it would be good to check in with Jack Shaw before he departed. In addition to being a practicing hematologist, Shaw was the hospital's current chief of staff.

"Jack, this is Phil," Insbrook began. "I need to be out of town tomorrow. Can you cover for me? My assistant has a list of the patients I am following. She will also give you some paperwork that needs to be filled out. Can you do it for me in the morning?"

"Sure, Phil. Is something wrong? Is everything all right with you and the family?"

"Yes, all fine, but something came up that needs my attention," Insbrook told Shaw. "When you make out the CDC report in the morning, can you please put a 'one' in the column for suspected or confirmed public health problems?"

"Yes, sure. I haven't heard about that yet," Shaw said.

"No one has. I'll probably cancel it. But it takes those bureaucrats at CDC two or three days before they pay attention to us, and if this is confirmed, I may want their help sooner," Insbrook explained.

Shaw didn't understand what Insbrook was talking about but went along with him anyway. "On another note, the oncologists agree that the Shepard woman probably has a plasma cell disorder. You were right, Phil. She's sick," Shaw told his boss.

"Yes. She's seriously ill. Under no circumstance should she leave the hospital. Get her committed, if necessary, but don't let her leave the hospital."

"This is all strange, Phil. Are you OK?"

"I'm OK. Trust me. I think I know what I'm doing. Look, Jack, my flight is boarding now. I have to go."

"Have an easy trip," Shaw told his colleague. "Call me at this time tomorrow, and I'll let you know what is happening."

"Will do. Bye."

Insbrook hung up the phone and looked down at what he was holding in his hand, glad that he hadn't told Shaw about what had happened when he went back to visit Katie Shepard that afternoon. For now, he thought, it was wise that only he knew about the tattered Wisconsin driver's license Katie had given him, a document attesting that, at least at one time, there was a woman named Katie Shepard who lived in Milwaukee and who would now be sixty-three years old, who looked exactly like the woman in the Cincinnati hospital room.

Of course, there were other explanations as to why the woman who called herself Katie Shepard was in possession of the old driver's license. But then, there was the recently dated postcard from California, and Insbrook's initial impression that her remarkably detailed account of her life sounded true. And there was the point that he himself often made to his students: If the odds of something occurring are one in a million, consider you might be dealing with the one. Academically speaking, each and every possibility must be ruled out or in. So, Insbrook was on his way to do just that.

Fortunately, it was not unusual for Insbrook to have Shaw cover his duties at the hospital so he could get away for a few days. With his wife and children living seven hundred miles away, there were few to whom he was responsible other than his patients and his dog. But he had Shaw for the former and Francisco for the latter.

Philip Insbrook, forty-eight years old, had attended the University of Virginia as an undergraduate, followed by Johns Hopkins for medical school, his residency and fellowship. He had a storybook American life. His mother, Anna, was pregnant with him in 1938 when she and her husband, Otto Itskowitz, fled Tyrol, Austria, outside the picturesque city of Innsbruck situated in the Swiss Alps. Anna and Otto, both Jewish, foresaw the Anschluss and were already under the cruel boot of Nazism by that time. Both had been excluded from their professions. Otto had had a close relationship with Sigmund Freud, who had already immigrated to America. Fortunately, because of Otto's training as a psychiatrist and Anna's as a pharmacist and proprietor of a successful *apotheke*, with the aid of a tidy sum of money paid by Anna's parents, the couple managed to obtain visas out of Austria directly to the United States.

Otto and Anna changed their surname to the Americanized Insbrook at Ellis Island in order for them to fit in before they settled in Virginia. Philip was born near the end of that year, in time to be born an American. His parents always marveled at this! In turn, Philip Insbrook loved his country.

After a stint at Johns Hopkins Hospital, Insbrook started at Albert Einstein College of Medicine in New York. He was subsequently recruited to Stony Brook University with the lure of a full professorship. At the age of forty-two, he again changed jobs to become the medical director of a university-affiliated suburban hospital in Manhasset. By the time the offer came from the University of Cincinnati Medical Center, Insbrook's wife, Doris, had had enough. Enough of the moving, the packing, making new friends, and adjustments for the kids. She had grown to resent Philip for always being told what to do and never consulted as to what *they* would do. "Ordered around like another intern," as she put it. Doris took a stand, refused to leave Long Island, and she told her husband if he wanted to take the job, he would have to leave her. He did. His teenage son and daughter chose to remain with their mother and their friends. Doris, feeling lonely and unsatisfied and perhaps a bit vindictive, took up with the children's former swim teacher, which infuriated Insbrook. They now rarely spoke without arguing.

Philip Insbrook was more than a professor of medicine and the director of an academic medical center. He was a philosopher, author, dreamer, and detective. His favorite literary character was Arthur Conan Doyle's Sherlock Holmes, inspired by the real-life Joseph Bell of Edinburgh, a nineteenth-century forensic pathologist. Both Doyle and Insbrook observed that it was always pathologists who examined specimens under a microscope or dissected mysteries in the autopsy room that had the final answer. A close friend of Insbrook's from medical school who had gone into the specialty was now a famous coroner who frequently appeared on television. She had been known to solve cold case murders, for instance, by matching a 0.5 mm x 0.5 mm piece of skin from under a dead woman's fingernail to a tiny avulsion at the base of an accused rapist's penis. It was this same spirit of questing to know the answers to all life's riddles and not to overlook the tiniest detail that compelled Insbrook to journey to Milwaukee.

Insbrook made his way to his airplane seat and quickly fell asleep for a short, much-needed nap.

THE GREENBRIER

Harvey Kraft finished work late into the evening and ate in a quiet corner of the lobby lounge, as he did most evenings, at a table reserved for him, set with white linen including two napkins, as if he were entertaining a guest. As a resident of the hotel, anything he wanted to order from the hotel's standard menu would be accommodated as long as it was ordered before midnight. On this night, he settled for beer-battered fried fish and chips and a cold draft Molson. The North Atlantic cod shipped in daily was particularly succulent and sweet this time of year.

The Greenbrier Hotel and Resort was a marvel to behold. Set on eleven thousand acres of wooded grounds and home to a world-acclaimed eighteen-hole golf course in Greenbrier County, West Virginia, its origins go back to 1778. Early visitors were encouraged to come to "take the waters" of Sulphur Springs and get away from the Potomac basin, lowlands, and swamps. Before air conditioning and air travel, its elevation of two thousand feet above sea level in the Allegheny Mountains near a shaded forest offered relief from the heat and humidity of the capital, two hours away.

By 1858, a resort and hotel were built on the original site at Sulphur Springs. During the Civil War, due to its strategic location, the hotel took turns being occupied by both sides and was used as a hospital and military headquarters. Following the Civil War, it became a vacation spot for both Northerners and Southerners, a fixture of early postbellum society, where political healing among the well-to-do on both sides took place. The completion of the Chesapeake and Ohio (C&O) Railway in 1873 significantly advanced the Greenbrier's fortunes and brought an influx of visitors from farther away. In 1910, C&O bought the property outright and embarked on the construction of a massive year-round hotel. C&O was trying to compete with Canadian Pacific to the north, which had already completed luxury properties in Banff Springs, Lake Louise, and Quebec City. The 250-room structure C&O erected opened in 1913 and formed the central wing of what today is a seven-hundred-room, thirty-three-suite, five-star resort with ten lobbies. To date, twenty-six US presidents, the Duke of Windsor along with Wallis Simpson, and numerous other heads of state and luminaries have vacationed there.

As if this rich history were not enough, in the late 1950s, the US government approached the owners of the Greenbrier to help establish an underground bunker to house remnants of the government in the event a nuclear attack destroyed or incapacitated the District of Columbia. It was part of a continuity of operations plan ordered by Eisenhower's Policy Directive 40, which also included continuity sites in Mount Weather, Virginia; Cheyenne Mountain, Colorado; and Raven Rock Mountain near the Blue Ridge summit in Pennsylvania, where a redundant underground Pentagon is also housed.

The bunker at the Greenbrier was constructed in plain view of the public between 1959 and 1962, while the Greenbrier Hotel was being expanded. Eisenhower and Kennedy each signed off on funding for the bunker project. Without public explanation, a seven-thousand-foot landing strip was built nearby. The entrenchment below Greenbrier—termed a fallout shelter when it was built—was

dug far below ground, encased in three feet of concrete, a half inch
of lead, a moat, a three-foot perimeter wall, and another layer of lead
shielding. Other details are classified. The massive blast doors leading
into the facility are specially designed to flex in response to the pressure of a nuclear blast wave and return to their normal shape after the
wave passes. The bunker is the size of two Walmart stores and con-
tains 1,100 beds, each eerily assigned to individuals by name, even as
would-be occupants came and went from their jobs, unaware of the
facility's existence. It is stocked with thirty years of food, with fresh
food and medicines rotated and restocked every six months by a shill
service outfit operated by a branch of the Army. An intricate air-con-
ditioning system not only cools the bunker but was designed to filter
out radiation. The effect is a constant flow of man-made wind that
blows through the facility. The existence of the Greenbrier bunker
was known to key members of Congress and the President but never
revealed to the general public before this report.

What was not known by anyone, including the executive or
legislative branches, was that at the time of the construction of
the Greenbrier bunker, a massive adjacent underground facility
was built to the northwest of the main complex by the NSA. It
is twice as large as the government's approved bunker, designed to
accommodate massive computers and provide data storage far into
the future. The West Virginia location was originally planned as
the backup site for the Fort Meade headquarters, but the advent
of higher throw-weight weapons, arsenals numbering in the thousands, and the doctrine of mutually assured destruction (MAD)
made Dr. Strangelove planners think twice. What if the entire DC
area were destroyed or became unlivable or unpassable? Perhaps
Houston was a safer place for a redundant site. It might also be
better to be located far away from Washington's eyes and ears. But
having already built the shell of the site in West Virginia, the NSA
made the decision to build it out as another backup, at least in

part because of its proximity to whatever remnant of government might survive as it contemplated a post-doomsday world. Also, it was NSA policy for at least one Council member to be in residence at each location and, to the extent possible, not be together in one location unless absolutely necessary so as to have one survivor run a shadow government if it became necessary. Dr. Strangelove planning, indeed.

Shortly after 11:00 p.m., after reviewing accumulated reports and briefing papers, Kraft finished his second beer, gathered his items, paid his bill, and left a generous tip, all in cash, the same way he covered his monthly tab at the front desk. No credit cards. No Such Account. He rode the resort's main central elevator and walked the long corridor to his luxury residential suite, where he headed to bed. He suspected he would have another long day ahead of him once the sun peeked its head above the Alleghenies in seven hours.

DAY FOUR

May 6, 1987

In youth, we learn; in age, we understand.

—MARIE EBNER ESCHENBACH

A PUBLIC HEALTH ITEM

Stuart Atherton was randomly assigned to investigate the Category V threat that came in from Cincinnati at 10:10 a.m. A young woman with an illness that carries a 60 percent five-year mortality was sick in a hospital bed in Ohio, but nothing was said about why she might present a threat. The last public health hazard to which Atherton had been assigned was in 1985 when it was reported there was an outbreak of bubonic plague in Nogales, New Mexico. The isolated case of plague was contained after the single reported death.

As for the present problem, the only information Atherton had was the channel by which the NSA was notified. It had originated at a state reporting center in Cincinnati. After seeing the report, Atherton spoke to his assistant. "We received an item I'd like you to start a file on. See if you can find out who is in charge at the University of Cincinnati hospital and get him or her on the phone for me. I'm sure it's nothing, but I want to get the matter off my desk."

All afternoon, there was no other information available. Atherton repeatedly tried to call Dr. Philip Insbrook, who had registered the item, but he was unavailable. Jack Shaw, the second in command at the institution, claimed to have no personal knowledge of a public health hazard at his hospital or elsewhere in the state. Atherton was suspicious that information was being withheld from him. He had no idea his assignment would ever be seen by anyone else at the Agency, but like his mentor, Atherton was a tenacious, thorough, and ambitious man. He worked late attempting to close out this low-level file as he had on hundreds of others before. The sooner he could put it to rest, the sooner he could get on to something more interesting than a possible public health problem no one seemed to know anything about. When he checked in with Alan Atlas, his mentor and handler, later that night he briefly mentioned the matter to him.

MONUMENT TO THE IDEAL DOCTOR

T here were four people in the waiting room, two of whom were pregnant. The one closest to term was with a man who held her hand in one of his and gently stroked it with his other hand. In front of the couple was a small green leatherette overnight bag and two pillows. Next to them, another pregnant woman sat alone, patiently knitting a baby's blanket. A middle-aged African American woman waited for her yearly pap smear and nervously fiddled with her hair as she read an old copy of *Reader's Digest* she had found on a side table. The doctor's office was tastefully decorated with a water feature meant to evoke life in the placenta and other art, including a large surrealistic Salvador Dali lithograph entitled *Monument to the Ideal Doctor*. Seated under the *Monument to the Ideal Doctor*, by himself, looking uncomfortable and awkward, was Philip Insbrook.

A man in scrubs stepped out of a long hallway off of which were six examination rooms. He was tall, broad, and handsome for a man in his early seventies. Looking over the edge of the half-height glasses resting on the bridge of his nose, the doctor spotted who he suspected was his distinguished visitor. He walked over and extended his hand.

"I don't think I have had the pleasure before," he began. "I'm Samuel Barrett. Dr. Insbrook, I presume?"

"Yes, Philip Insbrook. Call me Phil."

"Good to meet you," Barrett replied. "Call me Sam." The two men shook hands vigorously.

"It appears you have a thriving practice. An impressive office. Very nice."

"Yes, it's nice, I suppose. I still work twelve hours a day, though, plus the deliveries that can come at any time. These young doctors are smart; they won't work like me. But yes, it is a beautiful space, and I am proud of it. Come now, let's go sit in my office." The two left the waiting room and continued their conversation. "My nurse told me you needed to speak with me urgently. She said you just flew in from Ohio. Is that right?" Barrett asked.

"That's right," Insbrook affirmed.

"You are *the* Philip Insbrook, right? The one who wrote the editorial in the *New England Journal of Medicine* a couple of months ago about the non-publication of negative trials? Is that you?"

"Yes, that's me."

"Excellent piece. I agree wholeheartedly. A federal registry is an excellent idea. Tell me, what can I do for you?" Barrett was now seated authoritatively behind his large desk while Insbrook the detective sat anxiously in front of it, his legs tucked under his chair as he leaned forward.

"Sam," Insbrook said, "I'm not asking you to violate confidentiality, but I am seeking information on a possible former patient of yours. This could be helpful to a girl who came to us who is ill. She claims to have been your patient."

"You came all the way here from Cincinnati to ask about a patient?" Barrett asked incredulously.

"Yes."

"What's her name?" Barrett inquired.

"Katie Shepard," Insbrook told him.

"Katie Shepard?" the gynecologist said in surprise. "She's not exactly what I had in mind when you said 'girl.' Her husband was a friend of mine."

"Husband?"

"Sherman. We played poker together. He died, I'd say, maybe five years ago. Katie left town maybe a year later, and I haven't seen her since. I thought she might have sent for her records, but she never did. I thought she must have died. So she's still alive?"

"Yes. How did she look the last time you saw her?"

"Katie was always a beautiful woman. When she was young, my God, she was a total knockout. But, you know, age caught up with her like the rest of us. The last time I saw her, she had put on a little weight and was graying, but she was still attractive. As far as I know, she was healthy. What kind of problem does she have now? 'Girl'— you had me going," he said, laughing.

"We're suspecting multiple myeloma."

"Multiple myeloma? That's awful. Sorry to hear it. I'm still not sure why you are here, though. Is this some kind of research?"

"You might say that, but I can't go into it now," Insbrook said. "Let's just say she may be a reportable case. Is it possible your patient Katie Shepard has a daughter or a niece by the same name in her late twenties?"

"No nieces that I know of. And the only daughter she has is the one I delivered over forty years ago. She was a patient of mine too. Isabella . . ."

"Jacobson," Insbrook said, finishing his sentence in disbelief.

"Right, in Madison, I believe," Barrett told him. "Katie must be pushing sixty-five by now."

"Sixty-three," Insbrook corrected.

"That's right," Barrett agreed. "I did an endometrial biopsy on her the last time I took care of her. I hope you aren't here to tell me I missed something."

"No, no, you didn't. It's not that." Insbrook was afraid of what he would do next. But he felt procrastinating with small talk was like ordering needless lab tests after a diagnosis had already been mostly clinched. There was no use in asking more questions when he could easily get his definitive answer. From the pocket of his jacket, Insbrook pulled a folded piece of paper. "Katie Shepard signed this form for me for the release of her medical records. Could I take a look at them, please?"

Barrett leaned forward, took the form, and examined it, not wanting to appear lax in front of his distinguished guest. He asked his nurse to bring Katie Shepard's file into his office. In the meantime, Insbrook took back the release, placed it in front of him, and focused on its right-hand bottom corner. A minute later, the nurse handed Barrett the file, who in turn handed it to Insbrook and watched him leaf through it. Insbrook was visibly shaken as he saw the one thing he was looking for: the bottom line of a surgical consent form signed by a middle-aged woman a few years earlier. The signature was a near-perfect match to the one rendered the day before by the seemingly young woman in the Cincinnati hospital. Insbrook's heart raced, his nose flared, his skin flushed, he became clammy, and his visceral organs reflexively tightened. He struggled to regain his composure. "Could you have someone make a copy of this for me, please?" he asked softly.

"Certainly," Barrett replied.

"One more thing. I have this driver's license," Insbrook said, producing the license Katie had given him the day before. "Is this the same woman you treated?"

"Well, it was forty years ago," Barrett replied. "My God, she was something else. But can you tell me what you found? You look pale, Phil."

"Believe me," Insbrook replied, "I can't even begin to tell you."

* * *

Even as Insbrook spent the rest of his day taxiing around Milwaukee gathering other pieces of evidence, including tissue samples from the earlier biopsy, Katie's church records, some pictures he took of her high school yearbook, and Isabella's birth certificate, the fact that Katie Shepard had become some thirty-five years younger in appearance was already to him a foregone conclusion. Now, he was plotting what to do with his earthshaking discovery. He realized the importance of not letting this information fall into the wrong hands and desperately wanted to control the fate of the situation for as long as possible. He briefly considered not telling anyone what he had learned, allowing Katie to die of her disease, and taking her secret with her to her grave. But he knew the clinical course of multiple myeloma was variable, and the young woman he had come to like so much might live long enough for someone else to put her puzzle together. She seemed hell-bent on proving her story, which might not be too difficult once Isabella and Barrett were brought into the picture, and he was sure she would bring them into the picture before submitting to being committed to a mental facility, another idea that crossed Insbrook's mind. Except she didn't belong there and doing so would require a hearing after seventy-two hours, where she would surely tell her story. Insbrook felt that once somebody else discovered Katie's secret, what might become of the information could be disastrous. Unless he could bring himself to end her life, something that would violate his morals and values, Insbrook was faced with the task of deciding whom and in what manner he should inform that he believed Katie Shepard had within her body the key to unlocking the secrets of aging.

* * *

Late in the afternoon, while waiting for his flight, Insbrook called Shaw. "Jack, I'm sorry I couldn't phone all day. How is everything there?"

"Not great. I've had ten calls asking what our public health problem is. You wouldn't believe the harassment I've taken from these bureaucrats," Shaw said in an angry tone. "One guy called Atherton keeps calling me. He sounds like a goon. He claims he is with HHS in Washington. I don't know anyone at HHS. Do you know him?"

"I don't know the guy. What did you tell him?" Insbrook asked nervously.

"I told him I don't know anything about it, which was easy because I *don't* know anything about it. Frankly, Phil, I'm a little pissed off I had to do your dirty work. Next time, you do it."

"I'm sorry. There won't be a next time. This was a one-off," Insbrook assured.

"You're damn right there won't be a next time," Shaw said with a raised voice. "I haven't been able to get any of my own work done. We should discuss this when you are back tomorrow."

"I won't be back tomorrow, Jack. I have to go to Washington. Something came up. I hope to be back by Friday. Please forget about a public health problem. If the guy calls again, tell him it was an error."

"OK. I am sorry I blew up at you. To tell you the truth, I've been a bit on edge and depressed since my wife passed away."

"Sorry to hear that. Hang in there. It will get better. What about the young woman, Katie Shepard?" Insbrook asked. "Do you know anything new about her?"

"Yes, I do. The immunoelectrophoresis showed a monoclonal peak in the gamma region and Bence-Jones proteins in her urine."

"And the skeletal survey?" Insbrook asked.

"Abnormal. Big punched-out lesions in her bones, right where she's complaining of pain. You were right. It's pretty sad. To look at her, the girl could be Miss America, while in reality, she's dying of multiple myeloma."

"Yes, she appears to be. Now, here's what I want you to do. Get the interns and residents off the case. As soon as her medical workup is complete, transfer her to the psych team but continue to list me as her attending physician. Keep her in a locked ward, and please don't let them start chemotherapy until I'm back. It's probably a good idea to keep her a bit sedated too."

"That's one of the craziest things I've ever heard. I am not sure I can do that. What's this all about?" Shaw asked.

"I can't go into it now. Trust me; we're not hurting anybody. If you aren't comfortable doing it, I'll make the arrangements myself when I land in DC. Please, please don't discuss her case with anybody. I will be grateful to you, and you will understand one day. There are things I still need to work out."

When Insbrook got off the phone, he reflected on what Shaw had said about Katie Shepard: "She could be Miss America." Very possibly, she would soon be known as such.

MR. ATHERTON

L ate in the afternoon, Stuart Atherton made his final call to the Cincinnati Medical Center and caught Jack Shaw as he was leaving for the day.

"I just spoke with Dr. Insbrook," Shaw said. "We're sorry for the inconvenience, but there is no public health hazard to report. There's been an error. There is no reason for you to be involved."

"I need to know a little more about the nature of this error," an equally irritated Atherton said. "Your institution is supposed to be a screening center. Once a report leaves your location, a lot of time and effort is spent in investigating it. Whose error was this? Do you have a name?"

"Look, if you would like to discuss this further with Dr. Insbrook . . ."

"Yes, I would like that," Atherton interrupted.

"You'll have to wait until he gets back. He's out of town."

"How long will he be gone?" Atherton asked.

"I'm not sure," said Shaw. "If it's that important, why don't you leave your information with my assistant, and she will have Dr. Insbrook call you when he gets back from Washington."

"Washington?" Atherton questioned.

"Yes."

"All right. I'll call your assistant in the morning," Atherton said. The NSA officer was now suspicious of Insbrook, a man who filed an unexplained health report and left mysteriously for Washington. It was this shred of suspicion that led to Insbrook's every move and word being monitored.

Atherton began with the task of obtaining telephone records of calls placed from either Insbrook's personal or university account. What the well-trained NSA officer discovered raised concerns for him. Among the calls placed were those on May 5 from Cincinnati to Dr. Samuel Barrett in Milwaukee and to the National Institute of Health (NIH) in Bethesda. The next day, Insbrook again called the NIH from Milwaukee and subsequently called the home of Dr. Carly Steiner in Chevy Chase, Maryland. Later he called Dr. Karl Gruber in Chicago, Dr. Lena Gunderson in Sweden, Dr. Leonid Gregori in Kyiv, and finally Steiner once again. Why would an endocrinologist in Ohio, away from his regular job, be placing these calls? Atherton smelled that he was on to something.

Atherton thought he recognized the name Carly Steiner from his previous encounter with a health problem. He searched the name in Chevy Chase on his desktop terminal, and a profile instantly appeared. She was the director of the NIH, a position she had held for eleven months. Decades earlier, she had served her medical internship under Insbrook. Prior to being recruited to the NIH, she was a geriatrician practicing in Palo Alto, California.

Gruber was found to be a famed gerontologist who had spent time in the Soviet Union. A search on each of the individuals whom Insbrook had called revealed their connections to one another. The common link was gerontology. The list of people being scrutinized by Atherton and a small team now assembled under him grew quickly as they taped their sticky notes to a white grease board and connected them with one another. Atherton obtained a log of patients in Barrett's practice from insurance claims information and compared it to a list of patients currently admitted to the University of Cincinnati hospital. Katie Shepard was a match. She was added to Atherton's team's board.

By early evening, Atherton was in touch with a contact at the FBI headquarters in Washington. "There's a Dr. Philip Insbrook arriving from Milwaukee on United flight 818 in half an hour. He'll be meeting Dr. Carly Steiner of the NIH. Have one of your vans follow them. Find out where they go, what they do, who they call, what they say. Find out everything. Record everything and report back to me. I will owe you."

Atherton later called Alan Atlas, his friend and mentor at the NSA, to inform him. On a hunch, Atlas decided he himself would also listen in on Insbrook's conversations when he could. Insbrook had friends from Kyiv and other hostile locales. Many on the list of Insbrook's calls were foreign nationals. Atherton asked the FISA court for permission to surveil these people and their contacts in the United States, and the request was approved during a late-night session. At that moment, the private lives of Philip Insbrook and his associates, like those of thousands of other American citizens, became the subject of intense investigation and intrusion by a clandestine agency of the United States that was accountable to no one.

DAY FIVE

May 7, 1987

*Severities should be dealt out all at once so that
their suddenness might give less offense.*

—NICCOLÒ MACHIAVELLI

NO ROOM AT THE TOP

I t was 9:00 p.m. on Thursday night. JD Hartigan and his fellow intern Sheila Blackwell were seated next to each other, writing orders for the following morning.

"Nineteen more hours, and I'll get out of this place," Sheila lamented. "If I'm lucky."

"Then you can go home and crash and be back in the next morning," Hartigan told her. It was the time of the training year when interns became cynical and bitter, barely able to tolerate the dehumanizing rite of passage demanded by their chosen profession.

"Why don't you go home?" Sheila suggested to Hartigan. "I'll finish your work and cover for you. I have to be here all night anyway."

"Thanks, but I'm about finished. Before I go, I need to try the number Katie Shepard gave me one more time. She said it was her daughter's," he said, making air quotes with his hands. "Maybe it belongs to someone who knows her."

"She's pretty cute, isn't she?" Sheila teased. "You like her, don't you?"

"It's not that," JD protested. "I'm just being diligent. She is stunning, though. I don't think I've ever seen a more beautiful girl in my life."

"It figures, doesn't it? You meet someone like her, and she turns out to be totally crazy. Like the guy I met at the going away party last weekend."

"What guy?"

"I thought I told you. I met this gorgeous guy."

"And he was gay?"

"No, but that has happened too. Either that or a Republican. Anyway, you probably saw him. Maybe six feet tall, dark, beard, Armani jacket. Jeans. Stylish glasses."

"Oh, yes, I remember him. Cool guy."

"He was. Anyway, he drove me home, and we started . . . well, you know, and then when I asked him what turned him on, he said he wanted me to pee on him."

"No!" Hartigan exclaimed. "What did you do?"

"I told him I had just bought new bedding, so no way."

"You didn't tell me," Hartigan said.

"I wasn't about to advertise. I have my principles, after all," Sheila told him. They shared a laugh.

"Actually," JD said, "Katie isn't so off the wall. I spent a half hour in her room, and she's very cogent. We watched the news together, and everything she said sounded perfectly normal. She's quite aware and intelligent. She has a sense of humor. An old soul, if you will. She's normal as long as you don't bring up her age. She is convinced she is sixty-three."

"So, one minute, she's clear, and the next, she's psychotic?"

"Well, not really psychotic."

"Come on," Sheila laughed. "At least I admitted the guy who wanted me to give him a golden shower was crazy. This Katie babe has lost touch with reality. Nutso. Cuckoo. Get over her. I would fly over that cuckoo's nest if I were you. It's bound to hurt you sooner or later."

"A little cuckoo," Hartigan admitted, "but only when it comes to her age, and even then, it doesn't seem like she's lying. She's very convincing."

"I've heard that. I haven't talked to her myself. For some reason, it seems like mostly men go into her room."

"It kind of reminds me of that movie, the one about Kris Kringle with Maureen O'Hara and Natalie Wood when she was a little girl," Hartigan interjected. "The one they play on television every Christmas."

"*Miracle on Thirty-Fourth Street*," they said in unison.

"Yes, that one," Hartigan said. "Remember how the main character kept insisting he was Santa Claus, and he was so consistent about it and so convincing that after a while, people believed that he *was* Santa Claus? Katie is kind of like that."

"Right," Sheila said. "Only one thing. If you remember, the guy in the movie really *was* Santa Claus, if you believe in that. Do you think any of this is real, JD?"

There was silence for a few moments as both interns digested that thought. Hartigan interrupted the silence. "Hey, you remember what Chico Marx said, don't you?"

"No, what?" Sheila replied.

"*Asta* what Katie needs right now," Hartigan said in his best Chico imitation, "a sanity clause!"

The two exhausted interns shared another laugh.

"She sure does," Sheila answered. "I understand she's being transferred to the psych ward tonight. That seems precipitous. Weren't you and Dr. Insbrook in the middle of her workup?"

"Yes. I don't understand transferring her at this time of night either," Hartigan told her. "The nurse just said someone called in an order; I didn't get details. At this point, I just do as I am told."

A few minutes later, a man with a wheelchair appeared at the nurses' station. The transporter, dressed in hospital greens, was tall, lean, dark, and with a heavy beard shadow. He peered at Hartigan's face and name tag as the intern tried unsuccessfully to call the number he had been given, hoping to find a link to the outside for the young woman who had caught his fancy.

"I am here for Mrs. Shepard," the transporter told the charge nurse in an accent that sounded French, perhaps Farsi.

"We didn't expect you quite yet," the nurse told him. "She's showering. Can you come back?"

"I'll wait," the man said.

"It's up to you," the nurse told him.

The man seated himself in the darkened hallway, in a small alcove usually occupied by visiting relatives. In the shadows, he scouted the doorway of Katie's room, alternately looking at his watch and at the nurse. He studied Hartigan as he walked down the hall to leave the hospital. The transporter flexed the muscles of his toned biceps and ran the fingers of his opposite hand over the bulging muscles of his forearm. His eyes were dark and intense as he watched for Katie Shepard, pondering something deeply. Watching. Waiting.

"Mrs. Shepard is ready for you," the nurse informed the transporter. He jumped to his feet, stood up behind the wheelchair, and approached room 641. Fresh from a shower, Katie was arrestingly beautiful as she came to the door, momentarily startling the man who had come for her.

"I'm sorry to keep you waiting," Katie said.

"It's OK," he said. Katie sat down in the wheelchair with a plastic bag containing her personal belongings placed on her lap. She had been told she was being moved to a different floor more suited to her condition.

"Bye, Katie," the nurse said affectionately. "We'll come up and see you."

"Thank you," Katie replied.

The man who fetched Katie pushed her wheelchair to the elevator to take her to the locked psychiatric unit on the ninth and top floor of the hospital. The halls were quiet as visiting hours had just ended. The empty elevator arrived, and the transporter remained silent as he turned the wheelchair around, backed it into the elevator, and pressed the call button for the ninth floor.

Katie stared forward and silently contemplated her situation. Insbrook had phoned a couple of hours before, telling her he finally believed her and that he would be moving her to the psychiatric unit for her protection until he could figure out what to do with her. *Protection from whom?* she asked herself. Katie trusted Insbrook and agreed with his plan, but now she wondered whether Insbrook had told her the truth about why he was precipitously moving her and, in fact, thought she was insane. She herself had thought at times that she really might be losing her mind, and this could not be happening. She instinctively felt something was wrong.

As the elevator rose above the sixth floor, past the seventh, and on its way to the ninth-floor psychiatric ward, the transporter pressed the red stop button, which triggered a loud bell. He pulled a screwdriver from his pocket and jammed it between the stop button and the metal panel that housed it, forcefully poking the tool with the palm of his hand to disable the alarm. Security video showed the would-be assassin once again reaching into his pocket for a thin piece of rope that he pulled taut and slipped around Katie's neck as a ligature, intending to swiftly extinguish her life.

Katie's eyes widened as she struggled to preserve the life that had already been extended so bizarrely. She flailed wildly and with a burst of energy. Her momentum tipped the wheelchair forward on its front wheels, reversed its energy, and sent the chair backward at a high velocity, slamming the man behind it into the rear wall of the elevator cab. His head struck a protruding railing, and the would-be executioner was stunned, concussed, and sprawled out prone like a rag doll on the elevator's floor.

Katie scrambled to her feet, pulled the screwdriver out, and pushed the stop button, whereby the elevator proceeded up the one-and-a-half floors to the ninth floor. As the doors slowly opened, Katie ran, leaving the tumbled chair and the dazed transporter behind her. Once outside the elevator, she frantically pushed every elevator button, top to bottom, to send it away and slow its descent as she searched for a way out. The embattled woman ran toward the locked glass-enclosed entrance of the psychiatric unit as the elevator doors closed behind her. She rang a buzzer and pounded on the entrance, screaming desperately for help. A frightened nurse's aide approached the door and saw the bawling Katie Shepard as she peered through a small glass window. She impulsively turned and ran for help, not knowing exactly what to do.

Katie continued to pound and shriek, nervously looking back over her shoulder. She slapped her palm on the door, sweating, trembling, and shouting for what seemed to her to be an eternity. Then, slowly, ominously, the doors of the elevator behind her opened. Katie reflexively ran toward the stairwell door under an exit sign a few feet away, trying to avoid being trapped between the elevator doors and the entrance to the locked psychiatric unit.

As the elevator doors separated, the outline of her attacker again was visible; Katie spotted him. She desperately raced into the stairwell and scampered up the stairs, scattering her belongings, knocking over trashcans, pulling fire alarms, and sobbing as she ran for her life. As she arrived at the next level, Katie opened the door and ran through it, finding herself ten stories above the Cincinnati streets on the rooftop of the hospital. In the center of the roof was the hospital's heliport. After she raced as far as she possibly could to the edge of the building, she stopped and gazed down as she shouted at the top of her voice into the night air for someone to help her.

The rooftop door opened, and the shadowy silhouette of the persistent assailant passed under the glow of a single incandescent lightbulb suspended from a curved pole. Katie looked back, looked down, and inched closer to the edge of the building. In a flash, there was a blinding barrage of light. The heliport's floodlights illuminated the roof of the building and outlined the youthful form of Katie. A team of uniformed security guards, a doctor in scrubs, and a nurse arrived.

"Stop. Don't do it. Don't jump!" the nurse pleaded.

Katie froze as the team rushed to subdue her. In almost unintelligible speech mixed with hysterical sobs, Katie seemed to mutter, "Don't kill me. Please don't kill me." No one there was trying to kill her, the nurse thought. As the guards held Katie down, the nurse pulled a syringe loaded with 100 milligrams of Thorazine from her pocket and sedated the obviously delusional and suicidal young woman.

DAY SIX

May 8, 1987

*Our hope of immortality does not come
from any religion, but nearly all
religions come from that hope.*

—INGERSOLL

THE SMELL OF BLOOD
IN THE MORNING

The sun had been up for a half hour, and the orange-pink tones behind the low clouds in the distance began to give way to a clear blue morning sky. JD Hartigan, shimmering in a layer of perspiration, was doing laps around the quarter-mile track that encircled what was known on the campus as Frat Park. The park was wooded on three sides, with the fourth side backing up to a row of stately Greek-named fraternity houses, mostly built in the early part of the century. The perimeter of the park was comprised of a cinder running track. The grassy center was meant to serve as an intramural baseball, football, soccer, and gymnastics field. On this spring day, it would later be filled with young lovers, blankets, picnic baskets, dogs, and Frisbees.

Hartigan had already circled the track twenty-seven times and intended to do five more laps to complete his usual eight-mile run. At the far turn, a huge athletic man appeared at the edge of the track, having come through the woods on a bicycle path that led to the park. He was clad in blue shorts and a gray sweatshirt with its sleeves cut off and displayed powerful, toned thighs and proportionately larger Paul Bunyan biceps as he stretched beside his bicycle behind the track. The stranger's eyes watched intensely as the runners passed him.

Hartigan moved with long, easy strides at a steady, even pace. This was the comfortable part of his run, his muscles warm and loose but not yet tired. His body had released much of its overnight deposit of endorphins, the morphine-like substance responsible for the euphoria conditioned runners experience during long runs.

Hartigan steamed into the near turn, approached the fraternity houses, and entered his twenty-ninth lap as two students entered the infield to do sets of push-ups, while a little further along, another was intensely doing sit-ups. Hartigan's mind drifted to thoughts of his own college days, the fraternity hazing when he was forced to do push-ups and sit-ups when he was racked out of bed in the middle of the night. He thought it ironic that now, eight years later, he voluntarily woke up two hours earlier than he had to each morning to run eight miles to begin his day.

Meanwhile, the man at the edge of the track leaned over his bicycle and pulled a baseball bat from one of the wire baskets that straddled its rear wheel. In the opposite basket were several baseballs and plastic whiffle balls. He took the bat and examined it, cleaning the barrel with his thumbs. As Hartigan passed, the next two runners followed almost a half lap behind. The man with the Goliath hands holding a Louisville Slugger ran them up and down the shaft of the bat, caressing it before taking practice swings, cutting the air violently with his hips and shoulders in a synchronized swivel as he let loose the whiffle balls that traveled hundreds of feet effortlessly through the still morning air.

Hartigan was almost finished with his run and was beginning to feel tired. The young doctor, with a thirty-six-hour workday ahead of him, tried to focus on other things. On his mental list of things to do was to visit Katie again and attempt to call the phone number she had given him. He focused on the image of Katie. *Oh, she is magnificent*, he thought, closing his eyes. Making his way around the track in his final lap, her image pulled him along.

Hartigan was isolated on the ellipse now, about a quarter lap behind the other runners, as he again approached the man who had been hitting whiffle balls and baseballs at its edge. His heart racing, pouring sweat, Hartigan ran briskly toward the man who stood poised with the bat in his hands and who stepped toward the edge of the track and swung the bat.

For Hartigan, the scene was slow and surreal, with the end of the bat ever widening as it approached, seeming to take forever though there was not enough time for him to alter his course. His thoughts were jumbled up in a split second. His brain concentrated solely on the fact that his life would soon end. There was no other external stimulation, no other reality. An explosion of neuronal discharges raced around memory circuits for the last time, like one last firework display at the end of a baseball game.

A sickening *CRACK* rang out through the morning air devoid of ambient noise. All heads at the park turned toward the far corner of the track to see what had happened. Hartigan lay breathless and dead, his skull split open and his neck hopelessly broken in the first and second vertebrae, his spinal cord ruined. Blood covered his face and made an ugly red puddle on the track, glistening in the morning sunlight as it slowly seeped into the cinder. The smell of death permeated the warm air, as in a matador's ring at the final moment of victory over a hopelessly vulnerable bull. The man who had been swinging the baseball bat rode away through the woods on his bicycle.

ON THE ROAD IN MARYLAND

Dalia Abrahamyan, an accomplished scientist of world renown, was the Council member scheduled for a day off. The beautiful biologist and sociologist planned to spend her precious day off from the NSA in the countryside. Early that sunny morning, she and Steven, her current romantic interest, embarked on a daylong excursion to explore the pastoral coast south of Annapolis in the white Porsche she recently purchased with a portion of her Nobel Prize money. Dalia unwound as she left the NSA behind for the day, driving with the cabriolet's top down amidst the yellow birches, white pines, and poplars in early bloom. Later in the day, they would search for a bed-and-breakfast where they could share the bottle of white wine, brie, and fig spread she had packed, along with a freshly baked baguette they would pick up at one of Dalia's favorite spots along the way. This was ultimate bliss for her. She wondered to herself why she had ever taken her current job when she could spend more of life's finite days like this. Or have a baby and a husband, as her immigrant parents constantly begged her to do.

In fact, the NSA chose her, not the other way around. Abrahamyan was selected as a candidate for the position with the aid of a computer, by a formula, to fill a seat left vacant in early 1985 following the death of its former female occupant. Computer as headhunter, if you will. Her fluencies in Farsi, Arabic, Armenian, Russian, and English were valuable to the NSA, along with her academic credentials and overall brilliance. The thirty-seven-year-old scholar had had a successful career that demonstrated her legerity. She had graduated from Harvard at age twenty. Later, along with two British colleagues at Oxford, one a Black woman and one a White man, she won the Nobel Prize in economic sciences for their collective work on the economic effects of climate change caused by the destruction of the rainforests in South America. Subsequently, along with colleagues at Stanford, she engaged in studies into the biological and sociological aspects of human sexuality. Why, for instance, was male-on-male sodomy so common in some cultures and time periods while forbidden and punished by death in other places and times, including currently in her native country? Her research on this comprised the basis for her second doctoral thesis.

When she began with the NSA, Dalia was more than fulfilled by her position. She had grown up a poor immigrant and now had enormous resources with which to study and pursue her eclectic interests. Preparing and presenting seminars like the one she had delivered two days earlier on population control gave her great satisfaction; she also enjoyed the broad education she received through the rich resources available to her through the NSA's unique network and from her eclectic band of colleagues. She was well paid. Unfortunately, as time went on, Dalia felt more and more that too much of her life was spent in areas of little interest to her, including politics, money, and power. She was considering moving on.

For today, Dalia's cares were left behind. Sporting gold-rimmed Ray-Bans, she looked and felt beautiful and sexy this glorious morning as she sat braless in her flowery silk sundress, the breeze blowing through her flowing black hair. She hoped her most recent beau, a handsome professor of Italian literature at Georgetown, would prove more satisfying to her than deciding the fates of millions of people. Trying to escape the pressures of Washington and the NSA, she nimbly shifted gears and made her way southward along the scenic Chesapeake byway.

CHESS MASTERS

Alan Atlas, a fifty-five-year-old with quite the opposite personality of Dalia Abrahamyan, reported for duty at NSA's Maryland headquarters that Friday morning. Atlas was cold and calculating, with little interest in romanticism. A decorated West Point–trained military strategist, he had made his mark as an ace mathematician, statistician, and chess champion, an alpha male through-and-through. When Atlas was in active competition, he was one of the top chess players in the world. He liked to brag about the time when, during a weeklong competition, a Russian opponent dropped out due to a nervous breakdown—or, as the newspaper reported, mental exhaustion that caused his heart to race uncontrollably. Atlas had nerves of steel. With an IQ of 155, he was a certified genius, but like many in that range, he showed few outward emotions.

Atlas had few, if any, known friends or relationships. Other NSA Council members feared, disliked, and avoided him. His regard for individual human life was small, and he let his feelings be well known. Atlas was brilliant, but as if brains were not enough, he had also trained as a commando and still, over the objection of fellow Council members, occasionally went into the field to carry out operations. Some considered his missions an opprobrium and were concerned with what he might reveal if captured and tortured. Atlas countered that he would never let that happen.

Having been at the Agency for a relatively long time, Atlas was responsible for establishing or maintaining some of the Agency's most elaborate and extensive intelligence operations. Operation Soundpost, for example, made use of spy ships, surveillance planes, satellites, and other sophisticated vehicles to monitor the electronic communications of foreign embassies. Operation Shamrock involved reading copies of international telegrams at a rate of up to 150,000 per month. Skyhawk heavily surveilled civil rights leaders, while closely allied Springboard laid bare the private lives of hundreds of American politicians.

Atlas was under suspicion for his perfidy at the Agency for using methods not entirely acceptable to the Chairman, fellow Council members, and in most cases, to the American public. There was a story that circulated at the Agency about four Russians who were picked up by Lebanese kidnappers during the Lebanese civil war. The KGB, colder and more ruthless than their American counterparts, sent word to the kidnappers that such behavior would not be tolerated and, in doing so, provoked the kidnappers, who killed one hostage. The KGB, through Syrian surrogates, immediately nabbed two younger brothers of the leader of the militia that held the Soviet hostages. Three days later, the militia leader received the genitals of his oldest brother packed neatly in a box, along with a note handwritten in Arabic describing the demasculinization procedure that was allegedly performed while he was fully awake. The next day, the three remaining Russian hostages were released by their Lebanese captors.

Reports had it that Atlas was piqued when he heard this story. A few weeks later, a similar operation was carried out involving a kidnapped American businessman who was being held hostage by

Lebanese Hezbollah militiamen. Subsequently, it was a cell of Atlas's operatives that kidnapped three Lebanese militiamen in return and rendered them to a dark prison in an undisclosed country. Atlas planned the same fate for one of them. The operation severely backfired. Aware of the lack of American resolve and its splintered intelligence units, Hezbollah militiamen did not bend. Instead, they tortured and murdered the businessman they were holding and sent *his* private parts to the American president in a diplomatic pouch through Swiss intermediaries, along with a video of the operation and a message of their own: "Let our brothers go."

The President was sickened and livid and ordered an immediate investigation into where the operation that kidnapped the Lebanese militiamen originated. The head of each and every security agency of government capable of carrying out such a mission denied involvement. Under severe pressure at the Agency and under suspicion, Atlas's cell released its Lebanese hostages.

Another questionable operation linked to Atlas involved the wife of an opposition leader in Central America who was repeatedly raped in front of her husband and children in order to gain critical intelligence information from her husband. There were also similar events that involved groups of nuns in two Salvadoran churches. Atlas had an active mind, a vivid imagination, and a bent for action. He relished combat and advocated for a constant offensive military footing on the part of the United States.

On May 8, Atlas was scheduled to work in the black glass-and-copper-enclosed orthotope at Fort Meade while Harvey Kraft traveled to the NSA's Houston complex for the day before he returned to West Virginia. The sixty-five-year-old Kraft initially came to attention when his espionage novels were popularized. Five of them were made into Hollywood films. Kraft later launched his conservative talk show, which became widely syndicated on AM radio. He was jocular, with a biting sense of humor. It was easier to picture Kraft bumping up and down seated on a drivable lawn mower than riding roughshod on top of a clandestine and sometimes ruthless security agency. With his literary, radio, and film profits, Kraft made extensive investments in properties and broadcast stations in the western and southwestern United States and eventually ranked as one of the country's wealthiest people. He was known to be philanthropic and was a generous backer of conservative causes. In his younger days, Kraft was a social friend and supporter of the current president.

Kraft had dropped out of public sight in recent years. He was rumored to be in seclusion at one of his properties and had taken up with a companion; some would say female, and some would speculate male. In reality, he had been wrapped up in affairs at the NSA and lived comfortably in West Virginia. His thinning gray hair and close-cropped beard, along with his new identity as Reginald Campbell, provided effective cover from the frequent unsuspecting tourists. He was a happy bachelor, with a small terrier being his actual companion. His greatest pleasure outside of work was his biweekly round of golf, usually played with the Greenbrier pros and occasionally a special guest. The Vice President's oldest son, the governor of Arkansas, a former Heisman-winning and NFL running back, as well as an entrepreneur playboy from New York who was toying with the idea of running for president, all occasionally came for a round of golf and a late-night dinner at Kraft's favorite table in the Greenbrier's lobby lounge.

The attitude at the NSA in the early part of May 1987 was smugness. Its huge budget, no-holds-barred philosophy, total autonomy, and close links to other intelligence agencies made the NSA one of the most powerful organizations, if not *the* most powerful organization in the world, the exception being the US military, from whence it had been birthed. The NSA had a strategic vision, and when forced to be operational, it acted deliberatively, with coolness and patience. The amalgamation of geniuses that comprised its leadership, including its Chairman, was confident they could handle any crisis that came their way, and it was unlikely anything could catch them off guard. Within the next twenty-four hours, they would be proven wrong.

DON'T LET ME DOWN

L ate in the afternoon, Hazelton would awaken the napping President with yet another piece of bad news. Hazelton squeezed the President's shoulder firmly and vigorously shook the leader of the free world in order to rouse him. Finally, he tried to communicate with the groggy chief.

"What is it, Steve?" the President asked, still half asleep.

"We have another problem, and I knew you would want to know about it right away," Hazelton told the President. "That son of a bitch at the *Post* is running an exclusive in his column tomorrow detailing your health problems."

"What does he specifically say?" the President inquired, sitting up on the edge of the couch and massaging the left side of his chest with his right hand. He often napped during gaps in his schedule, making up for a sleep deficit due to his heavy workload, health issues, and advancing age. The barbiturate soporific his doctor had prescribed for him at bedtime also had erratic effects, sometimes causing drowsiness in the late afternoon. The barbiturates were in addition to the diuretic and the digitalis he took for an undisclosed heart condition.

"He says you are in heart failure. He has information on your medications and discusses your medical history as well as those of a few senators and congressmen. But you are clearly his target."

"How did he find out this stuff?" the President asked angrily. "Where the hell did he get his information?"

"Who knows? How does he find out anything? The West Wing is leaky. He also must have half of Washington on his payroll. Others have biases and axes to grind. All three network news shows are leading with the story about your health tonight. Betsy has been getting bombarded with phone calls."

Hazelton was now speaking to the back of the President, who was putting a bathrobe on over his boxers and white tank top as he walked toward the white marble fireplace across the room. "I'm not that sick," the President proclaimed, turning toward Hazelton. "Look . . . my feet aren't even swollen anymore," he said with satisfaction, putting his right foot up on a coffee table and pressing the skin over his ankle. "Nothing."

"I know you're not that sick, but it sounds alarming. To the average person, heart failure means your heart is about to stop any second," Hazelton told him.

"The American public loves illness. By tomorrow night, they will all be experts on heart failure, like when Johnson had his gallbladder removed or Eisenhower had his colitis surgery. The public rallied around those guys, and their popularity actually increased. Americans are sympathetic people. They have been sympathetic to me in the past." The President squared off face-to-face with his advisor. "Couldn't we turn this around and make it work in my favor?"

"With the public, that's a possibility, although frankly, sir, you aren't as popular as Ike. I'm not as concerned with the public as I am with the folks you need on Capitol Hill," Hazelton counseled. "Some of them are sticking their necks out for you—not necessarily because they love you," Hazelton said coldly, "but because in the end they expect a favor in return or they fear retaliation. If something were to happen to you—if you were to die, let's say—their IOUs would become unredeemable. They will not be as eager to support you if they think that might happen. They stand to lose more than they stand to gain. They are politicians, not friends. You know what they say about friends in Washington. If you want a friend, buy a dog."

"Hmm," the President said glumly, rubbing his five o'clock shadow. "How do you propose we handle this?"

"To start with, I got hold of Dr. Spencer at Bethesda, and the Secret Service is bringing him straight here. He knows he will go on the polygraph as it says in his nondisclosure agreement. He didn't object. He agreed not to speak to anybody before he talks to us. I also asked him to check his office for a source of the leaks, and he said your records are locked up in his home, as we requested. We are checking for leaks elsewhere. The PR people will get you a lot of exposure over the next few days to show everyone you're still kicking. We'll get a lot of shots in the sunshine. I suggest you get as much sleep as possible. Shave twice a day. We'll use makeup and deep backgrounds. The reporters won't get close to you. Don't take any questions. Betsy will clean it up."

"She's good, isn't she?" the President said.

"Yes, but another thing working against you is your credibility with the public," Hazelton continued. "If you deny the whole story, you may be headed for further trouble down the road. You don't want to be accused of another cover-up. And even if you admit you are sick and say it's minor, people won't believe you. They will ask, 'Why was it a secret? What is he hiding?' They'll start with that forgetting stuff. Whatever you do, don't say you forgot to tell people about it. That will make it worse. Just smile and laugh and let Betsy do your talking. That's her job, and she's good at it. Pretty little liar, that one is."

The President once again sat on the edge of the sofa, dropping his head and staring at the floor. "What a mess. Things are getting worse instead of better," he said, disheartened.

He looked at Hazelton with his head cocked in appeal, fighting back tears. "Steve, don't let me down. You need to find a way out of this mess for me."

EXPLOSIVE CARGO

Screaming sirens and revolving red beacons pierced the cool early May air as an ambulance raced toward a waiting Air Force jet at the military section of the Cincinnati International Airport. The plane stood majestically at the end of a runway, spotlights illuminating its hull against the dark mist. A well-armed Marine stood guard at the bottom of a rolling staircase that led to the plane. Other military women and men, on foot and in jeeps, were stationed and stood stern and silent, forming a circle around the craft. Two limousines parked nearby with their motors running contained a half dozen others, waiting, talking, and plotting. As the ambulance approached a fence, four people rolled open two large chain-link gates. The ambulance sped through.

When the ambulance came to a halt, the siren stopped, but its lights continued to flash. Philip Insbrook and Carly Steiner left the vehicle and greeted three military personnel and a pair of civilians who stepped out of the waiting limousines. Insbrook shook Karl Gruber's hand and introduced the impressive team of experts he had assembled.

The group talked for a few minutes and gestured toward the plane, the ambulance, and the city behind them. They reviewed the details of the plan to transport Katie Shepard to a government installation. No one smiled or laughed or showed any expression at all.

* * *

In the forward section of the plane, Insbrook and Gruber huddled with Carly Steiner and Maxwell Braun, the undersecretary of Health and Human Services (HHS), in conspicuous separation from the military personnel and others aboard the plane. Steiner technically reported to HHS and thought it best to notify her chain of command.

Also with them, in dress uniform, was Air Force physician Major Toliver McDermott, sixty-four, the director of the Atlanta hospital that would house and treat Katie Shepard. Not much was publicly known about the Atlanta facility other than it had a loose affiliation with a sister institution in Bethesda, Maryland. McDermott had completed medical school and training in Atlanta after a tour of duty and had overseen much of the design and construction of the Atlanta complex. McDermott never married and had no known relatives. He would die within days of this flight.

"I'm glad those guys are leaving us alone," Steiner commented, referring to the military personnel.

"I took care of that," Braun told her. "Leave those matters to me."

"What do you think they suspect?" Insbrook asked.

"Suspect?" Braun said. "Everything. But they don't *know* anything. They are just doing their jobs. We're secure here, but don't delude yourself into thinking this matter will be a secret for long. They say there are only two kinds of secrets in Washington: the ones that are too good to keep and the ones that aren't worth keeping."

Insbrook smiled but didn't laugh. He had taken an instant dislike to the ambitious Braun. "I'm not naïve, but I hope we tell as little as possible to as few people as possible for as long as we can until we can figure this out. What does the President know?" Insbrook asked.

"Nothing yet," Braun replied.

"When someone does tell him," Insbrook suggested, "it's probably best to tell him without anyone else present."

"I agree. It's also essential to give him the whole picture slowly, so he can grasp it," Steiner added. "As a geriatrician, I can tell you it looks like he has recently had a significant decline in cognitive abilities. I'm not sure it's even a good time to bring him in."

"That's not your choice," Braun snapped. "I take my orders through my chain of command, not a San Francisco liberal. He must know. If we keep this from him and he and his people find out, I'll be in deep trouble. I would be fired within twenty-four hours. Hazelton doesn't fool around."

"I personally like the President," Gruber opined, "but I can't vote here yet anyway. The FBI guys promised me they would speed up my naturalization process if I moved my labs to Atlanta for a while, so here I am. I hope they keep their word. For what it's worth," he said in his clipped accent, "the President looked pretty good on television yesterday."

"Makeup. He looks like hell in person," Braun told him. "You guys from behind the iron curtain shouldn't believe everything you see and hear. Look, we all stand to gain by dealing with the White House in good faith. Or lose," he added, staring at Gruber. "As for telling the President with no one else present, few people have access to him, and no one can meet with him alone. Everyone must go through Hazelton, who sits in as a babysitter, usually with Betsy. I will get in touch with Hazelton in the morning. The President should know by tomorrow tonight."

"Who else needs to know?" Insbrook asked.

"A lot of people will know right off the bat. Hazelton, Dixon,

State, Justice, and a few others. Turner at the FBI will know for sure," Braun told him. "I would imagine the NSA as well."

"Will the FBI be involved right away?" Insbrook asked with piqued interest.

"They are the only ones who can manage security leaks," Braun told him. "Turner is considered beyond reproach as the one man in government who folks on both sides of the aisle agree can be trusted. The press corps refers to him as the nation's top cop, in a good way. He is honorable and would also stand up to the President if need be."

"I believe that is true, which is why I asked," Insbrook said. "I met him on a few occasions. He seems like a man I could trust."

"I wouldn't worry about this so much. The chances are the President will listen to what we recommend," Braun assured the group.

"The chances are" didn't sound good to Insbrook. He feared what might happen if the President chose not to listen. Insbrook again thought perhaps he should have simply treated Katie for her disease with conventional therapy and allowed her to die. He knew that was her eventual fate, and she would never return to her home in Columbus. But in the few hours he had to make a decision, he felt he had done what was best both for her and his country. He also had fallen in love with Katie. He had read in a novel that men fall in love with women in the first fifteen seconds of meeting them, and he now knew that at least for him in this case it was true.

"What about others, aside from the President?" Steiner asked.

"We have one commander in chief at a time who will decide if we offer to make everyone younger or not," Braun told her.

The thought of making everyone younger continued to gyrate in Insbrook's mind, nauseating him. "How real is that possibility?" he asked.

"Stick yourself with a pin and see if you're alive," Gruber told him. "It's real. A majority of rats I injected with Katie's serum show electron microscopic changes consistent with reverse aging. Subtle changes are already present in the nuclei of their cells. The mitochondrial count is increased in cells and the nuclei display less granularity. Their telomeres have gotten longer. We will have to wait to see if these are coincidental or statistically significant, but there seems to be something there."

"Are you sure about an antibody?" Braun asked Insbrook.

"I am 99 percent sure," Insbrook answered. "I outlined the science behind my theory in the papers I prepared for you."

"Did you take all of your experiments with you? All of the serum?" Braun asked Gruber.

"Yes, I did," Gruber answered. "The biologic materials are all on board with us, and my lab is on the cargo plane that left right after us."

"From now on, the biologic material should be guarded as if it were the specifications for a weapon of mass destruction," Insbrook said. "Did you arrange that, Max?"

"Yes, I did. My end is all taken care of," Braun answered.

"What do we do about the press?" Insbrook asked.

"Maybe you should stay in your own lane, doctor," Braun suggested. "You do your job, and I will do mine. Are you doctors prepared in case we need to meet with the President and his people?" Braun asked. "Are you certain the girl is not merely delusional, and you can explain all this so we don't look like a bunch of fools?"

"I believe we can," Gruber answered. "Professor Insbrook's explanation is sound to me. It all fits with my life's work and theories."

"Everything we need is aboard this plane," Insbrook replied as he gazed into the distance. The jet, with its bombshell load, was headed to Atlanta with no firm plan for dealing with its explosive cargo once it got there. "Personally, I think the world might be better off if this whole damn plane took a nosedive into the field below us," Insbrook muttered.

* * *

In a rear cabin, a middle-aged African American nurse held Katie Shepard's hand and sat close to her, trying to comfort her.

"Where am I right now?" Katie asked the nurse groggily, having been sedated several hours earlier.

"You're on an airplane," the nurse responded.

"Are they going to kill me?" Katie asked.

"No one is going to kill you," the nurse reassured.

"Where am I going?"

"We're flying to Atlanta, baby," the nurse answered. "We are going to one of the finest healthcare facilities in the United States," she said proudly.

Katie fought to keep herself awake. "Is Dr. Insbrook coming with me?"

"I think so," she answered. "Is he good-looking, around forty-five or fifty, with grayish brown hair and blue eyes?" the nurse asked. "There was a doctor here who looked like that."

"Uh-huh. That sounds like him."

"Oh yeah, he's here. He was back here for a little while. He sat over you like a father. He was stroking your hair. I think he was crying a little bit too. He seems to really care about you," she said.

Tears now streamed down the sides of Katie's face as well. "I care about him too," Katie said as she closed her eyes and tried to fall back to sleep. Katie hazily remembered Insbrook explaining to her that she had a medical condition for which she could receive better attention at a research hospital in Atlanta. She remembered him confessing he now believed her story of reverse aging after going to

Milwaukee the day before and gathering evidence to support her claim. Katie, still affected by the large dose of valium she had been given, also remembered Insbrook's request not to speak to anyone else about her growing younger, so she avoided the topic with the nurse and contentedly fell back to sleep.

DAY SEVEN

May 9, 1987

The first forty years of life give us the text.
The next thirty supply the commentary on it.

—SCHOPENHAUER

WELCOME TO GEORGIA

A uniformed guard stood watch at the end of a quiet hallway. Behind one of the doors, Katie Shepard awoke from a long sleep, stretched, and found herself in the comfort of a large suite, with an unconnected cardiac monitor over her bed and medical equipment and carts tucked into the corners. Adjoining her room were a small kitchen, a dining room, a sitting room, and an extra bedroom. Outside the windows was a rolling grassy expanse dotted with carefully pruned trees sporting plush canopies. The lawn in front of her window was crisscrossed with sidewalks surrounded by mature magnolias bearing large white blossoms. In the distance was what appeared to be a tall, slatted fence, allowing light in but intended to keep humans from entering or leaving without passing through a checkpoint.

"Where am I?" Katie asked. "This sure doesn't feel like a hospital. Am I in a mental hospital, or what?"

"No," answered the nurse seated by the door. "This is the National Research Complex. You're in Atlanta, Georgia, baby. Welcome down south. We went over all this last night, but it doesn't sound like you remember it."

Katie paused. She murmured softly, in a dreamlike state.

"Atlanta? Georgia? You know something? I don't even know what's real and what isn't anymore. I don't even know if I'm alive. A few days ago, I was in Columbus. This is a nightmare. What the heck is going on here? Why would I be in Georgia? I feel like Dorothy in the land of Oz."

"You're all right," the nurse said as she walked over to comfort Katie. "The doctors say you're here for some tests. We have some of the finest doctors here, child. Don't worry. They gave you the presidential suite. I hear this is the only time it's been used. They even took out the hospital bed and gave you a king-size bed to make you comfortable. You must be something else. I already asked you if you were a movie star, but you said no."

"More tests? Jesus. What are they going to test now? I have had X-rays and scans. I had a fender bender. Now I'm in Georgia. This is getting stranger all the time. How long will I be here?" Katie asked.

"I don't know. You'll have to ask Dr. Insbrook."

"Is *he* here?"

"Yes. You don't remember him telling you anything, do you?"

"No, they doped me up so much I hardly remember anything. When will I see Dr. Insbrook?" Katie asked.

"I'll call and tell him you are awake," the nurse told her.

"Can I eat?" Katie asked. "I haven't had a good meal in days."

"Yes. They already drew the blood they need and probably then some. There's a kitchen I can call if you tell me what you would like."

"How about eggs and hash browns with toast? And a pot of coffee with cream, please," Katie said, feeling more relaxed. She walked over to a mirror, looked at herself, and fixed her hair.

"There were a lot of folks here looking at you before. They sure thought you were a sight to behold, and they made quite a fuss over you," the nurse told her. "This is the first time I've actually seen you wide awake. You probably don't even remember my name. I'm Lillian White. I am a nurse employed by the Air

Force as a second lieutenant. I've been in the service for almost twenty years."

"The Air Force? What kind of place is this? How come it seems like there isn't anyone here except for you and me?"

"As far as I know, there aren't any other patients here right now. Most of what goes on here is animal and basic science research, but we are outfitted for anything, including a biocontainment unit in case we get an outbreak of some kind of new virus. To tell you the truth, it's a treat for me to have a real live human patient here since there hasn't been one for a while. But don't worry; they let me moonlight at Emory's ER to keep up my skills. It's good money, so I do it quite a bit."

"No family, Lillian?" Katie asked.

"The Air Force is my family. My father left my mother before I was born, so I was raised by my grandparents. They're both gone. So this is it. I'm happy with my life as it is."

"I am, too," Katie answered. "Men are overrated sometimes. You mentioned research before. Do they do experiments on people here? I thought that was somewhere in Alabama."

"No, honey, this is not Tuskegee. No experiments are done on people here. I assume you are pretty special. I don't know why, and I don't want to know why. So let's not discuss it anymore. OK?"

"OK. I think I may know myself," Katie said. "But don't ask me either." Her memory having been jogged, she now vaguely recalled her conversation with Dr. Insbrook and her agreement not to talk about her condition. "Now, how about my breakfast?"

Lillian White informed the doctors the young woman had awakened and called the kitchen to order her breakfast.

TO BE BORN AGAIN

Renee LeSayer was awakened this Saturday by her cocker spaniel, Tripoli, licking her face and mouth. Renee grabbed the puppy from behind its ears and pulled him toward her and cuddled him. She got out of bed and gave him fresh food and water and fed her goldfish with a sprinkle of food. *I need to clean the water,* she thought to herself as she made a note on the small yellow notepad she kept on her kitchen counter, as was her habit.

LeSayer was still wearing the white panties and camisole she had slept in. On her way to shower and get ready for her day, she stopped and looked in the full-length mirror and admired how fit she looked with her rounded, toned shoulders and well-defined biceps and quadriceps. The ninety-minute workouts and six-mile runs she did five days a week kept her in shape, even as her fortieth birthday approached. Renee showered before her workday began behind the green door in the NSA facility sprawled beneath her house.

Renee LeSayer (properly pronounced LE-SAI-YAY) was one of the youngest members of the Council and currently one of only two women. The daughter of both a three-star Army general and a military nurse, born on the Fourth of July, LeSayer was accustomed to moving and was a devoted patriot. She attended Yale for her undergraduate studies, where she majored in French and history, followed by three years at Yale Law School. She never sat for the bar exam, though, because practicing law didn't interest her. Instead, she was recruited by the CIA through a contact of her father. LeSayer had served as an analyst, a field agent, and a Middle East station chief prior to coming to the NSA.

While at the CIA, most Americans she encountered could not speak or pronounce French and called her Renee LeSayer (Le-SAY-er). She was playfully given the sobriquet of "Renee, the man Slayer" as it got around that she could slay a man in more ways than one, including with her bare hands. True to her French heritage, Renee was a petite brunette with piercing blue eyes and fair skin. Most days, she wore a tiny gold crucifix around her long neck and attended Mass on Sundays and holidays when she could. Her clothing on workdays usually consisted of jeans and a blouse or a light sweater and a pair of Nikes. In cooler months, she included a fitted sport jacket.

Renee liked men. And men loved Renee. When it got back to her that some of her male CIA agents in Beirut thought she was drop-dead gorgeous, she joked, "They are right. The minute one of them tells me I am gorgeous, I tell them to drop dead. When I am attracted to one of them, I will let them know."

It was ironic, in light of the Katie Shepard situation, that in French, the name *Renee* means "to be born again."

PEACH TREES, MAGNOLIAS, AND OTHER DELIGHTS

Early in the afternoon, Katie inspected a suitcase that had been packed for her in Cincinnati and found a pair of blue jeans and a V-neck sweater, the same clothes she had worn to the hospital the day she was admitted. She set them on her bed under the watchful gaze of Lillian White, her newfound companion. She stood in front of the large window and stared into the distance.

"It's beautiful out there. Do you think if I get dressed, we can go outside for a while?" Katie asked. "I'm feeling really good today. It looks beautiful out there. I've never seen Georgia or even seen a peach tree. Are there peach trees out there?"

Nurse White chuckled. "Oh, girl, you ask me so many questions. There are plenty of peach trees out there. Peaches and magnolias. If it was up to me, you could do whatever you want, but it's not up to me. Dr. Insbrook is due here any minute, so you can ask him," she said. "It is a shame a pretty young girl like you is locked up in here."

"Yes, it is a shame," Katie agreed. "I better get out of here soon, or I really *will* go berserk."

Just then, there was a polite knock on the door, after which Philip Insbrook entered the room.

"Good morning," Katie said to the physician.

"Good afternoon," Insbrook corrected. In a rare open display of affection toward a patient, he kissed Katie on her cheek. "It's hardly morning anymore, Katie."

"Oh, yeah, I knew that. I was about to get dressed. You guys had me knocked out. Best sleep I've had in a long time. Thank you."

"Don't mention it," Insbrook replied. "Sit down now, why don't you? I would like to talk for a few minutes. Do you think you could leave us alone, Lillian?" he asked the nurse, who dutifully left the room.

"You probably want to know what this is all about," Insbrook began.

"That's an understatement. Why am I in Georgia?" Katie inquired. "I hate the South. I have never been to the South, but I hate it. I know this much: There are a bunch of racists and rednecks down here."

"I don't know about that," Insbrook said. "I don't think your nurse is one. As I told you, and it seems you don't remember, I was in Milwaukee on Wednesday. I met with Dr. Barrett and others who verified your story, and I collected evidence. I now know you are, in fact, sixty-three years old."

Katie sighed. "At least now we both know I'm not delusional."

"I know how you must feel," Insbrook told her. "Like you, I keep telling myself I must be dreaming, and this isn't really happening. But it is happening. So, late yesterday afternoon, I made arrangements to have you transferred here to Atlanta." Insbrook sat on the edge of the bed next to Katie, holding her hand.

"I know I'm not dreaming. I still don't completely understand what is going on," she protested innocently. "Who tried to kill me? Were you involved in that too?"

"No, I was not. Katie, did someone really try to kill you? The people at the hospital thought you had cracked and were about to jump off the roof and kill yourself. Is that not true?"

"No, it's not. Someone really was trying to kill me. I'm not insane. A man came to take me to the psychiatric unit with a wheelchair and tried to strangle me with a rope in the elevator. Somehow, I managed to escape and wound up on the roof near a helicopter pad. It was surreal. Believe me, I wasn't up there to jump," Katie said emphatically. "But I would have!"

"Oh my God, Katie. Now that I know that everything you told me is true, I believe you," Insbrook said. "But I see why it looked that way. I don't know who tried to kill you. I think we might be dealing with sinister people here," he said as he became pale. "That disturbs me."

"It disturbs you? It disturbs me!" Katie exclaimed. "The guy came to kill me, not you!"

"I'll see what I can find out." Insbrook told her. He caressed Katie's hand in a fatherly manner and braced himself for one of the most difficult tasks in clinical medicine: informing a patient they have cancer.

"Katie, I want to discuss your medical condition. It appears you are suffering from a disease, a type of cancer."

Katie looked terrified, and tears welled up in her eyes. Insbrook squeezed her hand and continued. "I believe this illness is responsible for your symptoms, the complaints you told the doctors about in the ER after your accident. I think it is also responsible for what has happened to you—getting younger, that is. I believe what you have experienced is a medical phenomenon as the result of a chance occurrence, not a miracle. It is as a result of chance occurrences that all evolution takes place."

"Cancer? You'll have to go slower," Katie complained. "I'm afraid I don't understand. The only part I heard was that I have cancer. I hardly heard another word after that. Something about revolution? Can you go over this again? Cancer is making me younger? That makes no sense, doctor. Which one of us is delusional? You or me?"

"I'll go through it as many times as you like, but let me give you an overview. Katie, I believe you have within your body the information that could afford medical science the opportunity to change everyone's body in the way your disease has changed yours."

"Make everyone younger? You really *are* nuts."

"I am almost positive that is possible," Insbrook responded.

"So, I am here for you to study? I *knew* there were experiments going on here."

"To study. To protect. Research, not experiments. Hopefully, we can cure you of your disease."

"How long will that take? How long will I be here?" Katie asked.

"I don't know for sure. I will see to it that you are comfortable. It looks like they gave you a pretty nice place," he commented as he looked around. "I feel responsible for you, Katie, and I won't let anything bad happen to you. I promise."

"Happen to me? Like what? What else can happen to me?" Katie asked. "So far, YOU have happened to me. That's bad enough."

"I'm sorry you feel that way, but please trust me."

"You know," Katie began, her young face looking worried, "before, I thought it was some random person who tried to kill me the other night. Now I think there is more to it. What do you think?"

"I'm not sure," Insbrook confessed. "Anything is possible. But you are safe in Atlanta as long as I am here. I'll find out what I can."

Tears began to roll down Katie's cheeks. "How am I supposed to trust you? You drugged me and brought me here. That was a dirty trick."

Insbrook laughed anxiously. "No one seems to trust me these days." He stood and paced, as puzzled and as troubled as his patient. "Who do you think I am?" he asked. "I'm not a bad guy. I don't work for the government. I'm a doctor, as I told you six days ago. I'm trying to work this out in the most optimal way for everyone involved."

"What do you mean, 'everyone involved'?" Katie asked.

"Making everyone younger involves a lot of people," he answered as his brow furrowed.

"I suppose I'll have to trust you because it looks like it's only you and me and Nurse White here, and she is not my type. Lovely woman, though," Katie said. Insbrook finally smiled, and Katie suddenly realized she had fallen in love with him.

"How did you get away from Cincinnati for all this time?" Katie asked. "First, it was Milwaukee, now Atlanta. Who's running your hospital? No wonder the food at your place is awful."

"I have a backup," Insbrook told her. "You met Dr. Shaw, didn't you?"

"Yes. The hematologist; nice man. Do you not have other relationships?"

"If you mean a significant other, no. Not at the moment."

"Too busy for a relationship?" Katie inquired.

"I suppose so," Insbrook answered honestly.

"Too busy to get lonely?" she asked as the physician again sat down on the bed next to her.

"I don't think anyone is too busy for that," Insbrook told her.

"I'm so alone," Katie said angrily. "This was such a cruel trick. First, I became forty years younger, and now I have cancer. First, I became free, and now I'm a prisoner. I have no friends and have cut myself off from my family. Can you understand how lonely I am?" From her sitting position, Katie collapsed sideways onto Insbrook's lap and sobbed.

"I'm sorry, Katie. I really am." Insbrook stood up, and so did Katie. He cradled her in his arms, her head resting on his chest. "I'm lonely, too, believe me. We will find a way out of this," he reassured her.

"You're a kind man," Katie told him. "And handsome. I do trust you." There was silence as they held each other and gazed into each other's eyes.

"I may have trouble sleeping in this place," Katie said. "Do you think you can order a Seconal for me tonight?"

"Seconal? Sure, whatever you want. How do you know about that?"

"I read about it," Katie said. "I'm sorry if I have caused you problems. I know you're trying to help me."

Insbrook held her against his chest as she sobbed and tried to comfort her.

"Philip, can we spend time together?"

"No," he said, rather unconvincingly as he hugged her. "You know I can't do that," he muttered.

Nevertheless, unable to fight an irresistible urge, their lips were drawn together. Katie kissed Insbrook passionately, reaching behind his head and running her fingers through the back of his thick hair.

"Maybe sixty-three is too old for you?" Katie said seductively as she slowly walked backward to the door of the room and locked it. She stood with her back to it and untied her gown from behind her neck and pulled it down gently, revealing pink, prickly, firm nipples. Her sixty-three-year-old breasts hung like plump, ripe fruit. "Doctor, I would like you to meet the fabulous Mrs. Robinson." With that, she let her smock fall to the floor. She was naked from head to toe. Insbrook stood frozen, not knowing which way to look or what to do.

"Make love to me, doctor," she commanded as she rendered her prey helpless while he was in a state of total arousal. Insbrook took her to the bed and obliged her request. They made love passionately and then, lying in their evanescence, they talked about their lives, momentarily escaping all that weighed on them, including the doctor's vaunted medical ethics. Those had apparently left the building with Katie's hospital gown.

"You know I'm falling in love with you," Insbrook whispered into Katie's ear just after they reached climax together.

"I'm falling in love with you, too," Katie replied.

Their intimacy was suddenly interrupted by a jarring series of knocks on the door. The doctor had been in the room for just over an hour, not unusual for a thorough history and physical, which it certainly was. He hurried to put on his shirt, pants, and socks and opened the door a crack. Nurse White informed him that he had an urgent telephone call waiting at the nurse's station. Insbrook's heart raced as he rushed over and pressed a button above a blinking light. "Dr. Insbrook here," he spoke authoritatively into the phone.

"Insbrook, this is Braun," came the voice at the other end. "The President is at Camp David with his closest advisors. He wants us to meet with him tonight. Be prepared to leave the compound by four."

"Got it," Insbrook said as he heard a click ending the call. No matter who one is, no matter what political persuasion, background, occupation, or station in life, there is something awesome and intimidating about a meeting with the president of the United States.

As Insbrook hung up the phone, he trembled. *What an afternoon*, he thought to himself.

THE NSA NETHERWORLD

Stuart Atherton's diligent work and absolute devotion to Alan Atlas resulted in the National Security Agency being among the first to know about the antiaging phenomenon of Katie Shepard and its potential. They knew a day ahead of the executive branch and its apparatchiks. Once the NSA was on to Insbrook, Gruber, and Steiner, not a word murmured by any of them escaped their electronic ears.

The Commission discovered that outside of those who were surveilled with warrants, millions of others had been spied upon as their communications were swept up in the NSA's vast listening farms.

In the late 1970s, the US government attempted to restrict espionage against its citizens. The Foreign Intelligence Surveillance Act (FISA) was introduced by Senator Edward Kennedy and signed into law by President Jimmy Carter in 1978. Its intent was to limit electronic eavesdropping within the United States to listen in on only foreign diplomats, embassies, and agents of foreign powers, the exception being their conversations that included American citizens. Central to FISA was the establishment of a secret federal court located in a windowless room on the sixth floor of the Justice Department building facing Constitution Boulevard. From there, orders could be issued that allowed electronic surveillance of citizens within the United States whose identities were theoretically masked if done in the course of surveilling foreign entities. The FISA court meets in secret, hears no opposing arguments, and issues no public opinions. There are no appeals or other recourses since, in order for it to be successful, surveillance must be done in secret. Up until 1987, each and every request for surveillance under FISA was approved. Once issued, the order is carried out with barely an accounting of its consequences. FISA, like the NSA, is seemingly beyond the control of anyone.

Certain features of the FISA are noteworthy. First, communications leaving the continental United States are exempt from control under the Act. Second, under any circumstances, the NSA is allowed to pull into its vast electronic network every transmission that enters, leaves, or transits the United States. It is a gigantic loophole. Even if not listened to on a real-time basis, these communications could be checked later. The NSA therefore probably broke no laws when it collected many of Insbrook's conversations. Communications involving Americans were scooped up by their government every minute of every day. Such communications were used to inform portions of this report.

* * *

George Christianson flew aboard *Sylph* to the NSA's Houston complex. His Little TEX session that morning had been short but long enough to inform him that he would join Davis, LeSayer, and Kraft for the next three days. He also learned of a new matter with which he was expected to become familiar during his flight. Although it sounded fascinating, involving a woman who had apparently aged backward, he was upset by family matters and unable to concentrate on his work. He would miss his only daughter's performance starring in a high school play the next night. This latest paternal failure was on top of the problems he was having with his son, who was a year younger than his daughter.

If he was a Council member with vast control and power, why did he not have more control over his own life? Why was it necessary for him to be informed of his schedule on such short notice? Why was he scared to even try to change the system at the NSA?

Christianson had been the close associate of a former president, a CIA official, and a high State Department official, at different times. He had declined to be vetted to join the current cabinet as secretary of defense. Prior to 1981, his whole career had been with the United States government, at which point he left to devote more time to his family. By December 1984, however, falling victim to the irresistible magnetism of power that had motivated him since childhood, Christianson was drawn back into government by the clandestine NSA. The Agency's Chairman had appealed to Christianson's patriotism and suggested he was acting at the behest of the recently re-elected president. Christianson accepted the job offer, having forgotten he had left government service in order to achieve peace of mind, something he now felt he might never know. On this morning, he regretted his choice and resolved not to live this way for the rest of his life.

* * *

By half past noon, Christianson was meeting with Renee LeSayer for lunch at Le Bistro, a Council dining room in the NSA netherworld. Le Bistro was informal, decorated with large framed French art posters advertising orange juice and vacations at seaside resorts on the Cote D'Azur. Large rectangular art deco chandeliers were suspended from a tall ceiling. Artificial light sources made the halls outside the windows appear to be outdoors. Outside of the storefront facade hung a large red awning embossed with *Le Bistro* in gold letters. A sidewalk sandwich board displayed the daily specials. George and Renee sat at one of eight tables, simple glass and metal affairs, with paper tablecloths and small vases of fresh flowers placed in the middle. A waiter placed a funnel-shaped container of pommes frites, a basket of bread wrapped in a white linen napkin, a small, round fluted container filled with freshly churned butter, and a bottle of Evian water in front of them. An open bottle of French Chablis was placed in an ice-filled wine bucket at their side as they were handed menus. Christianson and LeSayer were, in fact, six floors below grade in Houston and would be the only customers of the day. They were discussing the topic that was to be covered at the 2:00 p.m. conference, the mysterious phenomenon of a woman who was believed to have become thirty-five years younger. It was all a bit surreal.

"All we can do is wait and see," LeSayer said. "As far as we know, the President doesn't even know of this discovery yet, and we are awaiting word on whether the group in Atlanta will inform him anytime soon. If it doesn't get too far—that is, to him—we may elect to get rid of it early . . . the woman and the whole damn thing. I think the Chairman will lean that way. Don't you?"

"And what if it does get to the President?" Christianson asked.

"Then it'll be big," LeSayer answered.

"Real big," Christianson agreed. "We should act before this gets out of our control. We were lucky we got wind of this early."

"Luck is the residue of skilled scheming. The system works, or at least it has for thirty-five years," the former CIA station chief said. "One thing that appears to be in our favor is that this fellow Insbrook, who put it all together, seems to be a highly intelligent man—levelheaded, and decent. He appears to have called the shots so far. It's unfortunate that it could get messy for him. Collateral damage, as we say in the business."

"A family man?" Christianson asked with interest.

"Separated. Two teenage kids back East. But we're not supposed to ask those sorts of questions," LeSayer reminded him.

"You knew the answer," George volleyed.

"Yes," LeSayer returned. "My job is to know things." Renee was one of the few people on the Council George trusted and the only person with whom he discussed his feelings and emotions. He had lost that in his marriage. Renee disarmed him with her innate feminine guile. Christianson freely broke NSA policy by criticizing the NSA and its Chairman while speaking with her.

"I don't want to get in the position of controlling the lifespan of millions of people," Christianson told her. "Maybe *he* does, but I don't. And I don't personally want to be forty years younger. I couldn't handle this job for forty more years."

"An extra eighty or one hundred, at least," LeSayer corrected.

"On the other hand," Christianson reflected, "if I was twenty-nine again, I could start over with my kids. Maybe I would give them what they deserve, a full-time father."

"So that's it, George. The old weekend-without-the-family blues?"

"That's some of what's bothering me. I think the boss had the right idea when he picked those of you without families. I think it was a flaw in his planning to have picked Chris and me."

"I don't agree. Having a family is only one aspect of a person," Renee countered. "I'm the one whose ovaries are drying up. You have wrestled with these demons before and gotten over them, George. This time won't be different."

Christianson was exasperated as he poured himself a glass of wine from the bottle in the ice bucket. He took a sip and leaned forward as if to tell a secret. "There is not a minute of my life that is truly mine, Renee. That's the thought that haunts me. I would gladly trade my power and money for forty hours a week in a factory, free weekends and holidays, and uninterrupted peace of mind."

"*Pobrecito,*" Renee mocked in Spanish. "Poor little baby. Such is the curse of education and intelligence. You have forgotten what it is like to be poor and hungry and struggle to make ends meet. To sweat your rent. Is that the kind of peace of mind that would make you happy? Do you think your wife and your kids would be happy? Don't kid yourself, George."

Christianson acknowledged LeSayer's argument with a nod but was still troubled. He looked down at his plate and fiddled with the wrapper on a toothpick. "Renee, I need to tell this to someone. Cheryl found drugs in George Jr.'s drawer a few days ago. He's only fifteen. I'm talking serious stuff—straws and a mirror. The boy needs a father, and Cheryl needs a husband. My marriage is a mess. I think I want out of the NSA."

"I'm really sorry to hear all that, George, but frankly, I don't know if there is a way out," Renee answered. "You better think it over. And don't blame yourself for your kid. It's common and almost normal, especially in that private school you have him in for twenty-five grand a year. If that's all that's bothering you, I'm relieved. It will pass. You need to stay with us, George. We need your experience and wisdom."

Christianson sat in silence and still appeared distressed. Renee sought to change the subject. "Did you read the report about what the AG is up to now?" she asked.

"No, I didn't get to it," admitted Christianson.

"That publisher in California plans to use his magazine empire in an attempt to liberalize the drug laws. The US attorney in Los Angeles is planning on putting the heat on him to stop him. From what we picked up, it sounds like he will come down hard on them. There's something about drugs and prostitution at his mansion. He and his pals, including a couple of senators and a governor, have been spending a lot of time there with a lot of young women and a few young men. And white powder. They have photos and informants, and we provided the SIGINT they requested. It will get ugly. Justice is all in. Dillard has given the green light and promised unlimited federal resources," LeSayer told him.

"Oh, God," said Christianson. "What a dirty business we're in. Justice, my ass. What am I doing here?" he asked. His mind drifted to his son's vial of cocaine. "I ought to be home with my boy instead of sitting with you in this bizarre Disneyland version of Paris in a basement in Houston. I will miss you like a sister, Renee, but I'm getting out."

* * *

Later, in a paneled conference room, LeSayer, Davis, Christianson, and Kraft awaited the arrival of the Chairman of the NSA. They each had in front of them a short account of what was known in the Katie Shepard matter, prepared by Stuart Atherton and his team. Medical and scientific information was attached courtesy of their colleague, Preston Knox, who was preparing a more detailed report.

As the clock read 13:59, the Chairman, a man of extraordinary precision, entered the room through a side door. "I am fifteen seconds early," he announced as he looked at his watch with feigned disappointment, his mannerisms slightly effeminate. "We have before us an urgent matter. Let's get on with it."

The meeting opened with Davis summarizing what appeared in the folders of each Council member. "There are two updates," he added. "First, in mice injected by Insbrook earlier in the week, microscopic and clinical changes compatible with the phenomenon of reverse aging have appeared. Under the electron microscope, the rodents' telomeres appear to be lengthening by as much as two nanometers. A nanometer, for those of you who don't know, is 10^{-9} meters in length. An almost infinitesimal amount but significant. As a clinical correlate, the rats are more active on the treadmill. Second, a meeting is scheduled for Camp David at 7:00 p.m. tonight, at which time the President will be advised as to this discovery."

"Thank you, Zvi," the Chairman said. "Are there any questions from the group?"

"Are there any materials available to help explain it to us?" Kraft asked. "I can't quite follow it."

"Those are being prepared," Davis answered. "We should receive a report of what the President is told this evening. That will be a simplified explanation. In summary, all indicators point to the fact that in a short time, we will possess the capability to reverse aging throughout our entire population as has occurred in Mrs. Shepard. Insbrook, his team, and our own experts are pretty sure of that. We in this room must decide if moving forward with such an endeavor is a wise course to take. And if not, what should we do about it?"

"Let us address ourselves to the first question, but phrase it differently," the Chairman said. "Would reverse aging throughout our population be wise, and further, is the mere possession of the capability to do so in our arsenal a threat to national security?"

LeSayer spoke first. "I think the mere possession of this capability *is* a threat to national security. Neither our society nor any society is ready to undergo the massive reorganization that would be necessitated by reversing and stopping aging in the entire population or even the proportion of it who might choose it for themselves. This is a plague that must be quarantined and eliminated like we would a virus. We should act before it spreads out of our control."

"It sounds as if you have some drastic steps in mind, Renee," Kraft said. "Perhaps we shouldn't act too hastily."

"Are you suggesting we don't act now?" Christianson asked. "By not acting, we *are* acting. As Renee said, nipping this in the bud may avoid the need for more drastic measures later. Let's deal with it now."

"And what do you propose we do—cut it off before it gets to the

President?" Kraft asked. "I am not sure we, as part of the intel community, want more heat on us."

"The six people with the greatest knowledge of the situation will be flying to Camp David on the same plane in a few hours. That seems like an opportunity," LeSayer said. "Katie Shepard is isolated in a government installation. It seems to me we could take care of all of these people between now and midnight and be done with it. When I was with the CIA, that's what we would have done. Boom, and be done with it, and the Special Forces would clean up. But I would yield to the Chairman to discuss the feasibility of such an operation in the homeland."

"Feasible? We can arrange to have that plane disappear from the sky without a trace except when it doesn't land. That could be a problem," the Chairman said. "The girl, no problem. We have her where we want her, and the only family she has hasn't seen her in five years. I'm looking for options we can consider other than killing a bunch of people. Not that it is out of the question. Another thing to consider is that the President knows something is up, and if we move too soon, we can't predict how he will react. The White House doctors have started the President on a new medication that sometimes makes this illness worse than when it started. He might become more paranoid. Braun has been in touch with Hazelton," the Chairman continued. "We've picked up their conversations. Hazelton and Dixon would like to keep this top secret and sit on it. State and Defense concur. Hopefully, the President goes along."

"He usually doesn't go against all of them," Kraft said.

"He has at times," LeSayer told the group. "I'm worried he may want to use this information for his benefit. At some point, he may grasp at anything that could save his legacy. What worries me is that his judgment seems so impaired lately. Carly Steiner thinks he has gone senile, especially after the sun goes down. There is talk in Washington of either invoking the Twenty-Fifth Amendment or impeachment. If one of those processes begins, all bets are off. Then he may get reckless. That's why I favor terminating this before it even gets to him."

"Renee, my love," the Chairman said. "With due respect, if people around the President are seriously contemplating invoking the Twenty-Fifth, perhaps we should embrace the opportunity to determine exactly what state of mind he is in. The man has the nuclear codes and the suitcase. He could feel the need to wag the dog.

"If this goes to the President," the Chairman continued, "he has three options. He can crush the matter, and no one will ever know. He can sit on it. Or he can go forth full steam ahead and attempt to reverse and stop aging in the entire population—at least for those who choose it."

"God help us if he does the latter," muttered Christianson as he covered his eyes with his hand.

The session was almost over. The Chairman once again spoke. "All we can do now is develop contingencies based on the three options I outlined. For now, our major challenge is security. We will need to restrict the information for sensitive eyes and ears only. We need to keep tabs on the White House. We should be able to jam and intercept most traffic on the subject, so it's right up our alley. We definitely need to keep it away from the press."

"With the security breaches we've had lately, we'll be lucky if Moscow doesn't know about it already," LeSayer commented. "I'm convinced Camp David is bugged. Other than by us, of course," she joked.

"If the President decides to proceed," the Chairman told the group, "I'm not sure anyone in his inner circle would stand up to him except maybe the Vice President, although we know he has no real influence. Unfortunately, we could face a full-scale showdown with the President. We have never faced this before."

A short time later, a plane and then a helicopter would fly a group from Atlanta to Camp David to brief the President. All ears of the NSA were focused on the President and his close aides to hear how the President would handle the antiaging information once he received it. The Chairman spent the evening contemplating options in the event the President decided to proceed.

THE ETERNAL SEARCH FOR THE FOUNTAIN OF YOUTH

S o now, the elderly President understood more about which of the theories of aging were believed to underlie the reverse aging of Katie Shepard. As he settled into his easy chair and put his feet up on the ottoman, he held up an 8" x 10" photograph of the fascinating woman and felt the desire to see her in person. He was a politician at heart and loved meeting people. Although he was often thought of as being stupid, he was far from it. Strewn on the floor around him were charts, graphs, and reports given to him by the group who had visited him earlier. Their two-hour session had been enlightening and lifted his sagging spirits. The President was engrossed by the material given to him. He sipped cognac from a small Baccarat glass given to him by the French president.

On the table in front of the nation's leader was a copy of the *Report of the Presidential Commission on the Aging and the Aged*, a document he had been reviewing earlier in the day. The report was prepared in 1984 by a blue-ribbon panel of Americans and Western Europeans of varied scientific, academic, political, and social backgrounds.

At the request of the seventy-six-year-old President himself, a significant portion of the report was devoted to research on the process of biological aging, focusing especially on the onset of dementia and the phenomenon of sundowning, something that the President suffered from that often caused him to fatigue in the evenings. Following the publication of the report, the President advocated for more funds to be allocated for research on aging. The report also detailed several of the major contemporary theories of aging. It was these that the beleaguered President had spent his time reviewing to the extent he could stay alert after his earlier briefing.

The Wear-and-Tear Theory of Aging was one of the theories the President found fascinating. It explained how nearly all men who held his office seemed to age ten years in a span of four. This theory suggested there is an irreplaceable life substance that becomes depleted over time, up to the point when it is so depleted that life ceases. The rate at which this substance is depleted was theorized to be related to stress, basal metabolic rate, and total energy expense—in short, to the rate of living. According to this theory, lifespan was inversely proportional to metabolic activity expended over a lifetime.

The Aging Clock Theory was based on observations that on a species basis, the higher the rate of mutation in reproductive cells, the lower the life span. It theorized the existence of an aging clock that counts and monitors mutations in reproductive cells and turns the animals' biological clock on when the damage becomes so high it likely could not produce genetically similar offspring. Factors known to increase such damage include certain drugs, alcohol, poor nutrition, lack of rest, or the like.

According to the Temperature-Dependent Theory, aging occurs as a function of both body temperature and environmental temperature. In humans, it has been observed that long-lived groups such as the Hunzas in the Himalayas or the Abkhazians in the Caucasus live in cooler climates, while those living in extremely warm climates near the equator die at younger ages.

This observation ties into other theories when considering that enzyme-mediated reactions double in rate for each ten-degree Celsius (C) increase in temperature. This thermodynamic principle has been observed in species from insects to mice. Drugs and devices that promote cooling have successfully extended life spans in these species. Physical cooling, although difficult to titrate and regulate, has been tried as a means of resuscitation over the centuries. A group of researchers at Oxford recently published a paper in *Science* positing that cooling could cut the aging process in half and life expectancy in humans could approach one hundred years simply by lowering the body temperature from 37C to 34C by pharmaceutical methods. They also wrote that physical cooling might improve survival rates after sudden cardiac arrest.

The DNA Theory of Aging proposes that aging is a consequence of the accumulation of unrepaired, naturally occurring DNA damage, which happens over time. DNA defects occur in normal cells twenty-five to 115 times per minute, or up to 160,000 times per cell per day. Greater than normal unrepaired DNA damage is associated with premature aging, whereas increased DNA repair facilitates longevity. This theory accounts for processes as mundane as age-related hair loss and skin wrinkles, as well as early onset atherosclerosis.

Related to all of the above was the Aging Protein Theory of Aging. While some researchers believe there is a youth factor that is depleted over time, others theorize that at maturity, there is an aging protein that catalyzes reactions that result in cellular aging. This protein, like all proteins, is under the control of genes and would account for the hereditary nature of both longevity and early death.

The President had difficulty grasping some of the more complicated theories of aging. The Free Radical Theory of Aging (RTA), first proposed by Denham Harman at UC Berkeley in the 1950s, observed that free radicals are unstable chemical structures resulting from unpaired electrons that seek stability by binding with available unbound structures. Vitamin E can slow aging by binding to free radicals.

The Chief Executive was tired and dictated a memo requesting a simplified summary of all these theories to be prepared for him by the next day, and then drifted off to sleep.

* * *

Hazelton and Dixon entered the Executive Parlor in Laurel Lodge and startled the President. The President rubbed his eyes and sat up in his chair. "Is that hour up already?" he asked, disoriented.

"Yes, sir," Dixon replied. "An hour, as you asked for. Have a sip of water, sir. The gentlemen who came to see you are on their way back to Atlanta with a security detail."

"Who? Oh. Very good," the President said. "Have you made all the security arrangements? This is top secret. For our eyes only, right?"

"Yes, sir, of course," Hazelton responded.

"It looks like we have a winner," the President said.

"What do you mean?" Dixon asked.

"I can see this being the big domestic win I need," the President answered. "Imagine what can come of this. The public will love me. Civilization has been looking for the fountain of youth for thousands of years. We won't have a problem finding the money for it. I can sign an executive order and move allocated money around if I have to. We would actually save a lot of money on healthcare costs."

The President suddenly displayed one of his now frequent mood swings. "Are we sure this isn't a hoax?" he asked. "Is somebody trying to trick me? If so, I will have their heads."

"As far as we can tell, it's not a hoax, sir," Hazelton said. "Personally, I wish it were. I think your plan is dangerous. This wouldn't be good for society."

"I actually don't give a fuck what you think," the President shouted, looking angry and tired. "I am the president.

"You really were siding with Insbrook earlier," he scolded. "I didn't think you were serious. You should never have spoken in front of him. He's a total stranger and a university professor on top of it. Those guys are a bunch of useless liberal assholes."

"He's a respected doctor and professor of medicine, sir. He teaches medical students. But I'm sorry," Hazelton conceded.

The President grew serious and sober. "I want you to assemble my strategists during what is billed as the debt conference tomorrow. The Vice President too. I'll need him onboard. I don't want us to drag our feet. The public will hear about this from *me*. It will be the president's decision—mine—to choose if we halt and reverse aging in our population—or at least make the option available to those who want it. Now, you can both leave. I have a lot of reading to do," he said, gesturing toward the briefing books scattered around his bed.

"If you're going to wake up at 5:30 tomorrow morning, you should probably get some sleep. You look tired. You have bags under your eyes and lines on your face. I think you need some rest," Hazelton told him. Then he and Dixon left and huddled in a nearby conference room, making plans for the next morning.

It was 11:45 p.m. on the East Coast, but as frequently happened, the lights at Camp David burned well into the night.

INSOMNIA

Just before midnight, Katie requested another Seconal for sleep. She had been given a 100 mg capsule at ten o'clock but showed no response to it. For Katie Shepard, a woman of light weight and not a drinker, 100 mg should have been an adequate dose, but some individuals metabolize barbiturates rapidly and require a higher dose to achieve effect. All day long, Katie was agitated and restless yet withdrawn, troubled, and uninterested in conversation.

"Why did this happen to me?" she repeatedly asked, making Lillian White wish she was back in the dog lab. Katie had not eaten all day but had requested milk of magnesia to alleviate difficulty in moving her bowels. She refused television, radio, games, and books. The nurse had given up on entertaining Katie and now just wished for her to sleep.

Nurse White telephoned the doctor in charge. "No response. None. She's still repeating herself." She listened, then spoke. "I'm sure she did, but I'll go back and check to be sure." She placed the receiver on the nightstand and went into the bathroom. She checked all corners of the glistening, white-tiled room to be sure Katie had taken her pill. She opened the medicine cabinet, and it was as bare as the national treasury in 1987. Finally, she reached into the pockets of the hanging bathrobe, but those, too, were empty. Lillian finally asked, "Katie, did you take the whole sleeping pill I gave you earlier?"

"Of course I did," Katie replied. "Sleeping pills don't affect me much."

"You were pretty drugged on the plane that took you here. I think another Seconal should knock you out. I will tell the doctor. Maybe then you and I can both get some sleep."

She and the doctor agreed Katie could have another 100 mg of the barbiturate, or even 200 mg, if necessary. It appeared the effects of severe sleep deprivation had set in. Once sedated, Katie would likely crash for twenty-four hours, which would make a lot of people happy.

"I'm merely an experiment now," Katie told the nurse. "I no longer have a life. I know it."

"Maybe tomorrow we can get out for a walk," Lillian said, trying to reassure her. "You will feel better. It's plush and green this time of year. God knows I could stand to get outside myself. We can appreciate nature together."

"I don't want to go out for a walk," Katie said, as she stared blankly. "I think I will be too tired. I'm awfully tired now. I wish I could sleep."

An aide knocked at the door and handed Lillian White a plastic medicine cup, at the bottom of which were two red capsules. The nurse, in turn, handed the pills to Katie and desperately hoped they would sedate her and put her to sleep. "Take one at a time, Katie."

"Thank you," Katie said. "I'll go take this right away." She proceeded into the washroom and closed the door tightly. She stood with her back against the door, unbuttoned the bottom three buttons of her nightgown, squatted slightly, reached between her legs into her vagina, and removed a small aluminum foil packet. As she unrolled the foil, it revealed four other red capsules that were an exact match for the ones just handed to her. Each had the word *Lilly* with the symbol *F40* written in white script below it. She placed the new pills in line with the others, rewrapped them in the foil, and reinserted the stash into her vaginal vault. Katie took a sip of water and walked out of the bathroom, looking satisfied. "Thank you," she said. "I should be able to sleep now."

DAY EIGHT

May 10,1987

*The deep things in science are not found because
they are useful. They are found
because it was possible to find them.*

—J. ROBERT OPPENHEIMER, FATHER OF THE ATOMIC BOMB

JUST SAY NO

Fortuitously, a long-standing conference on world debt had been planned at the White House on the morning of May 10. As a result, when the President arrived from Camp David via helicopter to meet with his top advisors, the press corps was not suspicious. Dixon and Hazelton had circulated the word to five people the President wanted to see in an urgent, top-secret meeting. They included the Vice President, the secretary of state, the attorney general, the secretary of defense, and the treasury secretary.

The Vice President of the United States was a man the President praised in public but did not hold in high regard in private. His public praise was due largely to the President's desire to have his policies carried on for another eight years, which was most likely to occur if his Vice President ran as his heir and succeeded him. Privately, the President was suspicious of the Vice President's close ties to the intelligence community and to big money in the East and in Texas. He generally kept him at a distance. The Vice President was loyal to his boss in public but had grown argumentative during their private luncheon each Friday and lately had tried to distance himself from the President's problems. The nation's number-two man was congenial, intelligent, and well-liked. Polls showed he stood an excellent chance to win the next election.

Clayton "Clay" Van Hall, the secretary of state, probably the second most powerful man in the world, was the scion of an aristocratic shipbuilding family in the Netherlands. He was born in Boston to an American mother, who later divorced while she was visiting family in the United States. Van Hall had been educated in Switzerland, first at the acclaimed Le Rosey boarding school starting at age fourteen, followed by the University of Bern and the Geneva Business School. His summers and school breaks were spent with his mother and younger siblings in Boston and Cape Cod. Clay had a gift for languages and spoke English, Dutch, German, French, Italian, and Romansh. He was methodical, a habit he acquired from his language teachers at his strict European schools. While a businessman, he had run the world's largest oil company, and under his leadership at State, the United States had negotiated several strategic agreements with both friends and foes. His advice to his negotiators was the Dutch proverb *Maak het kleed niet voordat je de beer vang*, meaning "Don't make the rug before you trap the bear." His advice served his charges well. He was straightforward and known to have disputed the President on several major matters. Although not a career diplomat, because of his acumen, people skills, and performance, he was respected at the State Department and around the world. The press treated him favorably.

The attorney general, Stanley Dillard, had formerly been on the masthead of the well-connected Washington law firm of Harriman, Merritt, Lloyd, and Dillard, where he was a partner and high-priced litigator. Dillard's firm had deep connections to both political parties. Through much of his lucrative career, Dillard represented white-collar defendants, including other lawyers, politicians, and lobbyists, many of questionable repute, charged either criminally

or civilly with malfeasance or crimes. One defendant he represented
in a civil case was a well-known member of Congress in a case that
contributed to the evolving body of case law on the tort of sexual
harassment. Dillard lost the case. He was highly political in the
discharge of his duties, accused by his critics of disregard for true
justice, including civil rights.

Roger Whitaker, secretary of defense, was number-one in his
class at West Point and was variously described as stern, hard-
nosed, and brilliant. He had reluctantly accepted his cabinet
position out of a sense of duty to his country and his close friend,
the Vice President, with whom he shared military and New England roots, including their teen years together at Phillips Academy.
Whitaker had fallen out of favor with the Joint Chiefs and the
military-industrial community. Though he envisioned a $280
billion-plus military budget by 1988, Whitaker had publicly criticized defense contractors for not living up to their commitments,
rigging bids, waste, and poor workmanship. After a disastrous
Space Shuttle launch that killed all on board the year before, he
challenged NASA and proposed putting space exploration out to
bid with "better contractors at better prices."

Treasury Secretary Rodney J. Baldwin was a Wharton-trained
economist and finance expert. Baldwin was the only African American member of the cabinet. As governor of South Carolina, he
restored the state to a prosperity it had not enjoyed since the ante-
bellum period. In his current role, he was working to prevent a trade
war with America's trading partners, something being advocated by
an unusual alliance of the President, members of both sides of Congress, and trade unions.

Thus, there would be seven opinions for the President to consider as he decided what to do about the Katie Shepard matter. The
President and his aides had decided that consultation with the so-
called gang of four, the top congressional leaders on Capitol Hill,

was neither necessary nor advisable. The administration had taken its electoral landslide as a mandate to go it alone, a strategy that left them increasingly isolated.

The group assembled in the windowless Roosevelt Room, located across from the Oval Office, and sat around a long rectangular table originally brought to the White House by President Taft. The room was painted buff with portraits of both Presidents Roosevelt—one a Republican on horseback that hung over a white marble fireplace, the other a liberal Democrat, whose seated portrait seemingly kept careful watch on the proceedings from a corner of the room. The current president was seated at the head of the table with his back to the fireplace. The Vice President was seated at the opposite end. In clockwise order, starting at the President's left were Dixon, Van Hall, Dillard, the Vice President, Whitaker, Baldwin, and Hazelton.

Hazelton nodded, whereupon the President began reading from a handwritten script he had prepared, his hands and head trembling ever so slightly, effects of his unacknowledged Parkinson's disease.

"Thank you all for gathering on such short notice for this historic discussion," he began. "Last evening, while I was working at Camp David, five people journeyed to see me bearing news of a discovery I believe will reshape the lives of every person on earth and change the course of human history.

"This discovery, laid out before you with a scientific explanation, is probably the most exciting ever revealed to anyone, anywhere. If this discovery delivers on its promise and the explanation is as it has been explained to me, our roles in managing it will be challenging and complex. The matter will impact every segment of society and every interest represented at this table."

The President looked at the faces of those assembled around the table and continued. "As you are probably aware, the subject of aging has been an interest of mine for some time. Three years ago, I established the Presidential Commission on Aging, and I subsequently ordered stepped-up federal funding for research into the secrets of why we grow old. Little did I know at the time that today we would be on the threshold of fulfilling mankind's age-old dream of immortality. With our new discovery, I propose we proceed with fervor, pausing only long enough to make orderly plans." Those present listened attentively as the President read his prepared remarks as if he were delivering an address to the nation. It felt like a warm-up.

"I propose that in the next few weeks, we begin hinting that we have undertaken a program, hereafter designated the Plasma Cell Project, aimed at arresting and reversing aging. For now, however, I am designating this program top secret, meaning leakers of current information should expect to go to jail for years. In five or six weeks, perhaps on Independence Day, I will address the nation on radio and television and announce that we have had a breakthrough and will be able to halt and even reverse aging. We in this room will need to supervise the societal transitions needed to sustain a population experiencing extreme longevity. I have directed the attorney general to draft the necessary language to assure that each citizen in this country will be offered this gift of life beyond its natural bounds, an idea that, before today, was only the stuff of legends and myths. I will propose an emergency order that will allow us assembled here to remain in charge until a program is fully implemented. In doing so, we will have gone beyond our successes in economics and military affairs," the President said with satisfaction. "This, gentlemen, will be our legacy."

To most in the room, the President appeared delusional, perhaps as a result of the Parkinson's drugs or other medications he had recently started taking.

"Are you ready to begin discussion on this matter, sir?" Dixon asked.

"Yes, I am," the President replied. "Let's go around the room, starting with you, Dan."

"Yes, Mr. President. I will begin by repeating the objections I stated in private last night," the domestic affairs advisor began. "Never before have I gone against your wishes or stood in the way of a politically expedient decision, but I feel compelled to do so now. Sir, with all due respect, this is lunacy. For the record, I am also against any kind of language suggesting we would remain in charge of anything after your current term ends. There is an election next year, you are not eligible, and we should be clear that we will transfer power peacefully when the time comes."

The displeased President scowled and motioned toward Van Hall. "Would the good secretary, whose opinion I value dearly, please tell us where he stands," the President asked.

"Sir, I think you know where I would stand on both issues."

"None of us should stand anywhere until this meeting is over," the President interjected angrily. "I can't believe this bullshit." His face was flushed.

"Let me take issue with Dan's notion of this being politically expedient," Van Hall cautioned. "The other side of the aisle will oppose you. On our side, evangelicals and others of faith will too. People of influence around the world, including the Pope, will oppose you. It's not God's plan. Opponents will see this as evil and fight tooth and nail to stop it. They will impeach you. This will bury you, sir. At the least, I implore you to sit on this whole thing for a while. No announcements."

"So, you favor a wait-and-see approach?" the President said in his gravelly voice.

"I suppose you could put it that way," the nation's top diplomat said, having been trapped by the phrasing of the question.

The President next called on Dillard.

"How can we, as leaders of a society that values life so dearly, turn our backs on this opportunity?" the attorney general asked. "Sure, there will be challenges. In the areas of justice and the law alone, we will need adjustments. Could we still hand out life sentences? Probably not. What would be the legal age of retirement? Could Supreme Court justices still serve lifetime terms? But why not approach this positively? Couldn't we all benefit from TR's common sense today?" he asked, looking over his shoulder at the portrait of Theodore Roosevelt.

"Well said," the President commented. "Teddy could have served longer you know, if he hadn't quit in 1908," he told the group. "I don't quit."

Dillard walked behind his chair and looked around at the group. "Let's get the ball rolling on this thing. I'm in," he said forcefully.

Next, it was the Vice President's turn to speak. He stood to address the group. His slender, tall build was commanding. "I must state my strong objections to this idea. Never have I heard of a more audacious attempt to tamper with nature and the God-given plan for human existence. How can we propose the extension of life beyond all natural bounds for billions of people? How can an administration so strongly opposed to doctors interfering with God's plan be in favor of such a program? This is nonsense."

"I read last night in the Aging Commission's report that the goal of medicine is to prolong life and relieve suffering," the President replied. "Isn't that what this is about?"

"A man-made goal," the Vice President said in an unusually loud voice for him. "No one disagrees with the goal of prolonging the life of a person suffering from pneumonia or removing the cancerous growth in a woman's breast. But the extension of life in this manner is plain wrong. God has a plan, and this isn't it. This program would in no way alleviate suffering. On the contrary, the chaos and crowding it would bring would multiply suffering many times over. Frankly, sir," he said, staring at the President, "I can't support you on a Plasma Cell Project. It would be wrong." It was an unusually firm statement by the Vice President, who was not usually invited to join such high-level deliberations.

"Thank you for your input," the President said without looking directly at his second in command. "You may leave now if you wish," he said as he shuffled the notes in front of him. The Vice President did not wish to be dismissed; instead, he sat back down.

It was Whitaker's turn to speak. "Mr. President, gentlemen, I am not often consulted on nonmilitary matters. I'm not sure whether you want to hear what I think from my cabinet position or from my personal point of view, so I will begin with the former." Whitaker referred to a yellow legal pad placed in front of him and checked off the first item on a list he had compiled. "From the time any mention of a Plasma Cell Project is made, you can be sure of one thing, which is that everyone in the world will try their darnedest to get their hands on our information. Despite our best efforts, we might not be able to maintain control of it. I wouldn't count on it. Second," Whitaker said as he checked off another bullet point on his pad, "sooner or later we will face pressure to share the information with our allies and others. At that point, we will lose control no matter what conditions we attach. That is why we don't transfer our most advanced military systems. Look what happened in Afghanistan with our shoulder-launched missiles. I suppose 'Stinger' was an appropriate name for them.

"Next point," he said as he checked off his final item. "Once the feasibility of reversing aging is disclosed, our adversaries will pursue it as they did with the atomic bomb. The Soviets, for example—those guys are smart. They will see it as a strategic advantage for us if we can halt aging and they can't. I know how they think. They already have entire institutions devoted to solving aging.

Most of them are on the wrong track, and we should be in no hurry to get them on the right track."

"So those are your strategic views?" the President asked.

"Yes."

"And your personal opinion?"

"I think only a madman would want to live forever."

The President winced at the remark but retained his composure. He called on his last secretary to express his views. Baldwin was usually a reliable yes vote.

"We have avoided talking about this in philosophic terms, politically speaking," Baldwin began. "A Plasma Cell Project would lead to government control over every aspect of our lives—the timing of births and even of deaths. It would mean control over jobs and food. It would mean more laws, more agencies, and a larger government. I have spent my career fighting against these things. Still, as a descendant of slaves and a person who believes in personal freedom, I think we need to at least ponder the question of whether every person should be free to make their own choice, whether to live virtually forever or live a natural cycle and let another take their place."

"To have children and grandchildren and watch them grow naturally," the Vice President interrupted. "To follow the path laid down by God," he said sternly with his forehead furrowed.

Just then, Betsy Friar entered the room through a door in the right rear of the room. "Excuse me for being late," she said quietly as she nodded to each of the seated men. "I just broke free," she told them.

Elizabeth (Betsy) Friar was young, clever, and loyal. A petite, spirited, pugilistic redhead, she had worked for the President since his first successful presidential campaign. She had rapidly moved up through the ranks by being sharp, thick-skinned, and tireless. She listened well and committed few errors in her current firing-line job as press secretary. Even as a nonelected, nonconfirmed appointee of the President, she attended all high-level meetings, both at home and abroad. She and her benefactor had a close, practically father-daughter relationship, something Betsy liked to tell people. A rabbi once told her the name *Betsy* derived from a Hebrew name meaning "daughter of God." Many in the White House had grown to resent her and the power she so coolly wielded.

"They're on my back about your health," Friar told her boss. "You need to be out of here in ten minutes, sir, or you will draw more suspicion. There are already a lot of questions about this conference. It was on your published calendar to discuss debt for thirty minutes, and it has been going on for nearly an hour. All the principals, including the secretary of defense, are here. I am shutting this thing down in ten minutes," Friar told the group forcefully.

It was the chief of staff's turn to speak. The ex-Marine was a forceful speaker and traditionally spoke last at such meetings, and his opinion was usually the most highly valued.

"Gentlemen, Betsy," he began in his heavy Boston accent, "Mr. President. I have had a chance to sleep on this. As most of you have appreciated, the legal, political, security, and socioeconomic ramifications of using this antiaging antibody would be protean. I have concluded they would be unmanageable. I agree with those who have stated we cannot allow this scheme to even get into its infancy, or there will be no stopping it. We should abort it early. We can talk about how later. As Betsy said, we have to finish this meeting now."

The President looked at Hazelton with an almost insane stare and addressed the group once again. "I will take all your views into consideration and inform you of my decision in the next few days. If I decide to proceed with it, are there any of you who would oppose me? Or will you stand with me?" he asked.

All remained silent.

"What about you, Mr. Vice President?" he asked as he stared at the man at the opposite end of the table.

"I will not publicly oppose you," the Vice President responded, "but I will not participate either. If it were my presidency, there would be no Plasma Cell Project. This sentence would be remembered. If you do proceed, I will step aside. My resignation letter will be in the center desk drawer in my West Wing office around the corner from here, should you need it. I will prepare it in my own hand." He then abruptly rose and left the room as he had been invited to do earlier.

A FITFUL SLEEP

Back in Atlanta after meeting with the nation's elected leader at Camp David, Insbrook spent a troubled night in bed, sweating, wrestling with his linens and pillows, and trying to cast away the disturbing thoughts that danced in his head. The President had only mentioned a Plasma Cell Project briefly, but Insbrook put stock in his remark based on what he sensed was the President's overall excitement as he heard details about the antiaging protein. Insbrook thought the President was reckless and selfish enough to mount such a program if he thought it would secure his legacy. He knew in his heart the President had not taken heed of his warnings and recommendations. He felt he should never have gone to see him in the first place. In fact, perhaps he should have just left Katie to die of her disease in Cincinnati rather than moving her to Atlanta; he knew she was doomed regardless. But now he was in. He was in love with her.

Over and over, Insbrook asked himself the same questions and arrived at no satisfactory answers. How could he have handled the Katie Shepard matter differently? What could he do now? What would the President choose to do? What if he did something reckless? How could he, Insbrook, be so stupid as to have had sex, as good as it was, with a patient, something that would surely ruin his career if it ever came to light?

In his sleep-deprived state, Insbrook again considered allowing Katie to die but thought it was too late for her death to make much difference unless someone could also get to the guarded laboratories and biorepository on the third and fourth floors of the research building and destroy them. He debated going to the press to convince them to crush a would-be Plasma Cell Project but felt that the revelation would have little chance of stopping the project. Besides, what if the President decided not to proceed with it and Insbrook leaked the information to the press? Hazelton had declared he would designate the program top secret, and divulgence of classified material carried a heavy jail sentence. Another thought that occurred to Insbrook was that he could remain in charge of the undertaking and undermine it from within. He was a confused man. For now, he prayed the President would not make a public disclosure immediately, leaving him time to figure out a way to avert a scientific disaster.

As he brewed a pot of coffee the next morning, Insbrook thought writing might clear his head. In a diary he had begun keeping because he feared he might not live to tell the plasma cell story, Insbrook made an entry.

"With scientific growth compounding, the potential for scientific disaster is increasing at a similar rate. Perhaps the first major disaster has arrived. Soothsayers of doom predict an accidental, uncontrolled thermonuclear reaction will occur in a matter of time, resulting in the loss of hundreds of thousands of lives. We have warned that a change in atmospheric conditions could turn Earth into Mars, yet we defiantly, recklessly damage the climate each day. Some pundits say that in due time, we will inevitably poison, choke, or starve ourselves, while others say that through our ingenuity, we will avoid our man-made devices of doom. Which will come first?

Test tube babies or test tube food? Malignant overpopulation or colonies in space? Pills to make us live longer or pills to make us die sooner? A war is being waged between those who say technology will destroy us and those who contend it will be our salvation. With the choices at hand, does it really matter?"

* * *

Insbrook wanted to pay a visit to Katie, but beforehand he attended to several obligations outside of Atlanta. According to telephone logs available to the Commission, among his calls was one to his medical center, where he was assured all was running smoothly aside from the tragic death of Jim Hartigan, one of the medical residents, who appeared to have been senselessly murdered. Insbrook informed Jack Shaw that he was on special government assignment and would be away indefinitely.

Later he spoke with his two children in New York, assuring them he loved and missed them. He briefly spoke with Doris and avoided uncomfortable matters. He had kind words for his ex-wife, whom he still cared for, and avoided calling her companion "the pool boy" or even mentioning him. Finally, Insbrook called an associate of his, an oncologist at Duke, to discuss the details of Katie Shepard's case, the latest treatments available to her, and her possible enrollment in a clinical trial for multiple myeloma.

Visiting Katie was no longer easy for Insbrook because, as far as he was concerned, her life was probably nearing its end. In the best case, Katie would be allowed to die of her disease. In the worst, the government could either exploit her or expedite her death. In the first instance, they might choose to keep her alive as an example of what the Plasma Cell Project could accomplish. If it came to pass, Katie would become an international spectacle with no real life of her own while at the same time battling to save it. If a decision was made to try to preserve her life and she agreed, it would be no small task. Chemotherapy to palliate the cancer would need to begin immediately, and along with it, the side effects, including vomiting, anorexia, alopecia, loss of libido, and more.

There were no known cures for her disease, so Insbrook exhibited the common behavior of medical personnel who avoided conversations with dying patients, a phenomenon he previously attributed to either a denial of his own mortality or his inability to control his patient's fate. But now, as he struggled to combat *immortality*, or at least using Katie's protein for millions of people, he suspected something else must be at play. Perhaps he was struggling to avoid further intimacy with Katie since the last time he encountered her was in bed, an episode he regretted because it broke a time-honored professional taboo. On top of everything else, Insbrook was ashamed of himself.

On his way across the grounds of the government complex from his living quarters to where Katie was housed, Insbrook stopped into the Eisenhower Building. He passed a security clearance and was escorted by a Marine to the third-floor laboratory where Karl Gruber had set up his temporary shop. Insbrook found Gruber peering through his trusty microscope.

"What does your crystal ball tell you?" Insbrook asked.

"Fantastic," Gruber exclaimed without taking his eye away from the microscope's eyepiece.

"What is?" inquired Insbrook, now looking through a teaching extension lens into Gruber's microscopic world.

"This is a kidney biopsy from a lab rat you injected before you went to Milwaukee," Gruber told him.

"Did you sacrifice it?" Insbrook asked.

"No, not yet; we must keep it alive. I took this biopsy with a needle. The glomeruli, the vessels, and the membranes all look terrific at the cellular level. I couldn't tell this tissue from that of a three-month-old animal. The electron micrographs are even more impressive."

"Yes, you described those previously. The nuclei don't show any evidence of clumping, shrinkage, or fragmentation of chromatin. In other words, it doesn't look old, correct?"

"Yes," an impressed Gruber said. "The mitochondrial structures of the cell have started to reverse age if we assume they had already undergone their expected reduction in numbers and alteration in shape that come with age. This animal was thirty months old, was it not?" Gruber asked as he continued moving the slide as he squinted.

"Yes, it was. I suppose I should have taken some biopsies of the animals before I injected them," Insbrook said. "I didn't think of it."

"You thought of almost everything, professor. I commend you," Gruber said with his clipped Austro-German accent. "I am conducting other experiments of my own. In animals I have injected, the collagen has begun loosening and reverting back to its young form, as if repair is occurring."

"What about your scientists?" Insbrook asked. "How are they doing? Do they think they can reproduce this antibody?"

"As you know, because of the high concentration of the antibodies in the girl's blood, isolation should not be difficult," Gruber replied. "Hopefully, she will stay alive and keep producing her antibodies for us. But just in case she doesn't, we have plenty of her serum in storage right above us on the fourth floor.

"We have a few other ideas," Gruber continued. "We are trying to induce the production of the antibody in lab rats if we can. There is also a new technique for producing something called monoclonal antibodies. If we succeed in isolating the epitope of the antigen, we can expose a mouse to it and then combine its spleen cells with myeloma cancer cells. The resultant hybridoma, as it has been named, should be capable of producing antibodies forever. Another idea is to isolate tissue from the girl's marrow and grow it in tissue culture. We should be able to make it by the truckload one way or the other.

"I will be an American millionaire!" the aspiring capitalist exclaimed. "Give me a few months. One of these approaches will succeed."

"Fantastic," Insbrook said sarcastically, fearing one of Gruber's ideas might actually work.

*   *   *

Insbrook finally entered Katie's suite a few minutes before 10:00 a.m. His hair was tousled, and his necktie was tied unevenly, unusual for him, and there were dark circles under his reddened eyes. With his hands inside the pockets of his lab coat and a stethoscope slung around his neck, Insbrook shuffled into Katie's suite without his usual energy. Not quite the stud he felt like twenty-four hours earlier.

"Will you step outside, Miss White?" Insbrook politely asked the nurse after she let him in the door.

"Yes, sir," she replied.

Katie was propped up in bed, watching her favorite soap opera, *Loving*, on television.

"Doctor," Katie exclaimed as she saw the disheveled physician. "What have you been doing? You look terrible. You're not taking care of yourself," she said in a motherly tone. "You need to get some sleep."

"Thank you for your concern. I have been rather busy."

"I'm sorry I can't say the same," Katie complained. "I am just a poor girl in Georgia. Are there any gentlemen in these parts? You wouldn't be Rhett Butler, would you?"

"That would be me," Insbrook answered. "You're looking better. Do you feel better?"

"Relieved," Katie said with a trace of a smile, trying to watch Ava

Rescott on the soap opera as she was answering the question. "Ava's quite the bitch, but I love her."

"Have those Seconals been helping you sleep?"

"A little, but it seems like I need a pretty high dose," Katie said. "Can I get two tonight? They don't have much of an effect on me."

"I suppose so," Insbrook said, wishing to do anything he could for her. "Let me ask you something. Are you sure you weren't on any pills like this before you came into the ER?"

"Honest," she said, raising her right hand. "But admit I was drinking more in the last few months than I told you before."

"Ah," Insbrook responded. "That will do it."

"Do what?"

"Increase your body's requirement for a barbiturate."

"How can that be?" she inquired.

"It's complicated. It has to do with the fact both drugs are metabolized by the same liver enzymes," Insbrook answered.

"Oh. You are so smart. I love when you talk that way," she kidded as she reached out for his hand and pulled him closer to the bedside.

Insbrook seated himself in a chair next to Katie's bed.

"Can I ask you a favor while we're on the subject?" Katie queried.

"What subject?"

"Wine," Katie replied.

"Sure."

"I would like to have a little with my dinner tonight. Do you think you could arrange a glass or two for me at dinner while I'm stuck in this place?"

Insbrook considered her request. He knew she was destined to die and did not want to deny her anything. "I'll see what I can do," he said. "I hear you haven't been eating well, though. Promise me you will eat and won't drink right before taking the sleeping pills. And only take one at a time."

"I'll eat," Katie reassured. "And maybe you can have a glass of wine along with dinner with me one of these nights."

"Maybe a different night, after I have had the chance to rest. I am glad to hear you would like to share a meal with me. I was told you weren't interested in doing much of anything."

"Oh, that's over, Philip. I feel better. I'm even watching *Loving*, and I finished a crossword puzzle in the *Atlanta Journal-Constitution* earlier.

"I thought you might have stopped by last night," she said. "Did I do something wrong?"

"Believe me, Katie, I would have loved to see you, but I was at an unusual out-of-town meeting last night, and I didn't want to disturb you when I got back."

Just then, Insbrook caught sight on the television of the man with whom he had met only thirteen hours earlier.

"Do you mind if I turn up the TV?" Insbrook asked.

"To hear *him*?" Katie asked disdainfully.

"I assure you, I am only interested in his health problem. Have you heard about that?" Insbrook queried.

"Yes, I have," Katie answered. "It's all over the news." While she had heard about the President's problems, she had no idea he was contemplating actions that would make her a household name.

The mid-morning news update was running a clip of the American president greeting his Salvadoran counterpart on the sunny South Lawn of the White House. It included a close-up of the President's heavily lined, stubbly face, already visibly perspiring under the morning sun. The newscaster continued the thirty-second interlude: "The President emerged today in front of a small group of reporters in order to meet the president of El Salvador on the South Lawn. It is believed to be the first in a series of public appearances designed to dispel widespread rumors of failing health in the seventy-six-year-old chief executive. The nation's leader spent the rest of the morning in a conference with advisors concerning the South American debt crisis. Tonight, he is expected to attend a dinner to honor the visiting Central American president and may answer a few questions on his way inside. There have been rumors of a presidential press conference later in the week, the topic being the Chief Executive's health. We will have more about this on our nightly news tonight, right before *60 Minutes*."

"Is he going to make it?" Katie asked, referring to the ailing President.

"I'm afraid he might," Insbrook replied.

"Am I?" she asked with tears in her eyes.

Insbrook didn't answer.

A RENDEZVOUS AT SEA

When Washington became inhospitable, the President, his wife, and a few advisors accompanied by a Secret Service detail often decamped to the Camp David retreat, nestled in the Catoctin Mountains of Maryland. The Vice President was seldom invited to join them and had his own routine for escaping Washington's rigors, including its summer humidity. For short spells, this usually entailed a sojourn to the charming coastal town of Bar Harbor, Maine, where his family had long maintained a vacation home and where, weather permitting, the nation's second in command would get a chance to captain one of his beloved boats.

On May 10, 1987, after the White House's sham debt meeting, the Vice President made such a trip, leaving his wife behind to entertain foreign dignitaries in the Vice President's residence in northwest Washington. He told his wife he needed to get away in order to contemplate whether to run for the presidency the following year and to write a report for a special White House task force on intelligence he chaired. He expressed to her the need to be alone for a bit, although their eldest adult son and advisor would be joining him, which pleased her. The sun wouldn't set in Bar Harbor that day until almost 8:00 p.m.

The Vice President loved New England. He was born in Massachusetts, raised in Connecticut, and schooled at the finest boarding schools, followed by his time at Yale. Of patrician Yankee stock, he was the eldest son of a US senator. His fine breeding was reflected in his perfect diction and manners. He seemed born to lead, having been, at various times, captain of his college basketball team, class president, congressman, ambassador, and the director of the CIA, followed by an abbreviated stint at the NSA, where he still had informal ties that he refused to acknowledge.

The Vice President was also a war hero of the Second World War. After he refused to be shielded from combat duty by his father's connections in Washington, unbeknownst to his family, he enlisted and became the nation's youngest commissioned pilot. He nearly met an early death in the Pacific when his plane was shot down in flames and his rear man was cut to pieces by a hail of enemy gunfire. Serendipitously, he was rescued by an American submarine that picked up his Mayday call while on its way to the Sea of Japan for a mission and surfaced long enough to pluck him out of the sea. The young pilot spent the next six weeks on board the sub and thoroughly enjoyed watching the torpedoing of enemy ships, physically helping, and cheerleading, as was his nature. He was comfortable at sea; he liked to say he loved being *on* the water rather than *in* it.

On this Sunday afternoon, the same man, now vice president of the United States, would make another critical contact on the ocean's waters, this time in the chilly waters of the Atlantic off the coast of Maine within American territorial waters.

The Vice President boarded the larger of the two vessels dedicated to him during his term with his aide-de-camp General Leland Arthur III, his two most trusted Secret Service agents who also served as crew members on the boat, and his loyal terrier, Derrick. General Arthur, special assistant to the Vice President, was his most faithful advisor. He was well placed, with a seat on the National

Security Council as well as a high-level appointment in the Defense Intelligence Agency. "Have you swept the vessel for bugs?" the General asked one of the agents.

"Yes, sir. Twice," the agent answered. "All clean."

"Would you mind sweeping it again?" the Vice President asked politely. "I want to be sure you haven't missed anything."

The agent nodded. He and his partner walked over to the van parked near the dock and pulled out their equipment. The larger of the two agents donned headphones and held a meter in one hand and a probe in the other as he scoured the craft. The second agent, of slighter build, capable of crawling into tight spaces or climbing poles, proceeded with a manual recheck of the boat, accompanied by his well-trained Belgian Malinois shepherd. There were no traces of explosives or listening devices, the agents reported. The general then turned on a jamming device that rendered the vessel undetectable.

The *Wanna Bee* pushed out to sea, followed at a distance by a support cutter filled with Secret Service agents and a speedboat available for rescues if necessary when the Vice President was at sea on the New England waters. To the west, over the mainland, the skies were gray and ominous. They reflected the mood of the *Wanna Bee*'s skipper, who appeared somber and quiet as he leaned back against a highly varnished wooden wall, his long legs slightly extended in front of him. He looked up at the heavens, to the left and right, looking for guidance, but mostly saw only gulls. As tough as he was, he was frightened by the uncharted territories his office was carrying him into.

As his ship bobbed at sea, the Vice President peered through the lower portion of his bifocals at some intelligence reports he had brought along with him. He was amazed at how the paths of so many presidents and vice presidents had crossed in the past ten or fifteen years. It was President Gerald Ford who, on January 4, 1975, set up a commission headed by Vice President Nelson Rockefeller:

"The Commission on CIA Activities within the United States," otherwise known as the Rockefeller Commission. The final report was generally recognized to have whitewashed the subject of intelligence abuses. Ronald Reagan, as California governor, was a member of the Commission but left before the conclusion of the opening session and missed three of the next four meetings.

The Vice President's briefing papers also turned up the name of Edward M. (Ted) Kennedy, a perennial candidate for the nation's highest office. The senior senator from Massachusetts had made three attempts to introduce legislation meant to regulate wireless eavesdropping prior to finally introducing the Foreign Intelligence Surveillance Act (FISA) in 1976, which was signed into law by President Jimmy Carter in 1978. Ironically, Kennedy's martyred older brothers had used information from such sources, provided by NSA's Operation Shamrock, to try to break the back of organized crime in America.

There were also Senators Church and Biden, either of whom the Vice President himself might face in the next election should he decide to run. Both were members of the Senate intelligence committee. Church was the chairman of a select committee formed to investigate NSA abuses, among other things. During one of these committee hearings, then Senator, later Vice President and presidential candidate Walter Mondale doggedly questioned the legality of Operation Shamrock. He was summarily rebuffed in those hearings by NSA officials.

Fuck Mondale, the Vice President thought as he read the reports. This was exactly what was planned the last time he and his expected visitor rendezvoused at sea.

It was July 14, 1984, less than twenty-four hours after a Minneapolis media event during which the presumed presidential nominee had revealed his female choice for running mate. At a hastily arranged meeting at sea, it was revealed to the current Vice

President that Mondale's campaign would face questions about the tangled finances of his proposed running mate's husband. Damaging information would soon be leaked to the press and the US attorney's office.

"Is there a price for this?" the Vice President asked at the time.

"This one is free," he was told, jokingly. "But who knows? We might want something later. A future draft pick, if you will."

On this afternoon, the Vice President was aboard his own boat, rather than the ship of state, and patiently awaited his rendezvous with the head of one of America's most powerful agencies. He called one of his crew members over, leaned over a table, and unfolded a map. He pointed at nautical coordinates with his left index finger. "Here's where we have to be between 15:30 and 15:45. Tack between these two points. Do you think you can handle that?"

"Yes, sir," the agents replied.

At 15:35, another vessel came into view amidst light Atlantic fog, flashing a secret password in standard naval code. The Vice President read the message himself and uttered his reply to his attaché, who flashed it. "The Eagles have landed and are healthy," he said. This was the pre-agreed-upon message that signaled the all-clear to proceed. There was no press at sea in the area, and transmissions could not be picked out of the air from above. There had been no other sea or air traffic in the vicinity for hours except for a couple of parasailers tethered to a rented speed boat that passed a little earlier, too far out to sea for their own good.

The approaching USS *Reindeer* was a 176-foot, 935-ton World War II coastal freighter later converted into a floating intelligence base. The ship bristled with antennas, microwave dishes, and various electronic equipment, and while it appeared to be unarmed, it was, in fact, loaded with surface-to-air missiles, shoulder-launched Stinger missiles, automatic handheld weapons, and explosives rigged to destroy the vessel.

Once the *Wanna Bee* was aside the freighter, the CIA director sent his agents aboard via a rickety wooden bridge and repeated the task of searching it for listening devices. After they finished, the CIA director came aboard with a single aide, whereupon the trawler backed off to a distance of two hundred yards. From his days at the CIA, the Vice President was quite familiar with the *Reindeer* and its elaborate procedures, along with the man who had come aboard his boat to deliver a vital message. The two men had last seen each other in Washington twelve days earlier but had not talked in private for a while. The President's men generally tried to keep the two apart, fearing a conspiracy or the illusion of one in the eyes of the press and public.

"Things are getting hot for me in Washington. My kids at Harvard and Berkley are being harassed," the CIA man complained to his friend. "They hung an effigy of a baby outside my daughter's dorm in California. Sick people. I don't know how much longer I will be up for this job."

"I'm sorry about that," the Vice President said sincerely.

"It's not your fault. As you know, this is a shitty job," the CIA man told him.

"Thankless. How is your wife holding up?" the Vice President inquired.

"Not well. She wants me to step down, but she can't bear the thought of criminal charges and a trial and the rest, although I don't think it will happen," he said. "I have too much dirt on a lot of them, and they know it."

"That criminal business is a bunch of bull crap," the Vice President consoled his friend. This was about as close as he came to cursing in public, although while at sea, he sometimes relaxed his personal code. "How about a beer?"

"Make mine a dirty martini," the CIA director replied.

The Vice President fixed the drink, opened a can of Coors for himself, and sat down in a chair opposite America's chief spymaster.

He slumped down and let out a sigh. "I've got my problems too. I don't know whether to push for next year or not. I'm tired. One of the reasons I'm considering it is because I have a feeling I may be running as an incumbent by then."

"That's not a bad thought," the CIA chief said.

"So what have you got for me? What's on your mind?" the Vice President queried.

"I think we'd better go outside," the CIA chief replied.

The two men walked out onto the side deck of the boat and made their way to the bow, far away from any of the others on board. They leaned over the edge of a wooden railing facing out to sea. They spoke in low tones as the crushing sound of the sea drowned out their voices. After a signal, a marine helicopter hovered overhead, providing additional audio cover.

"Our contact at the NSA has gone back and reviewed some signal intelligence scooped up from the White House a while back," the CIA director began, "and he said there are conversations directly linking the President to the diversion of arms. He's been lying through his teeth."

"That doesn't surprise me," the Vice President replied. "I suspected that."

"That's not all. There's obstruction of justice, destruction of evidence, and a lot more. I never knew about any of this. And I am not going down for it," the CIA man said.

"Nor me. Does it get worse?" the Vice President asked.

"Unfortunately. The NSA apparently can tap into the Swiss banking systems."

"No shit?" the Vice President said, having completely lost his inhibition against cursing.

"No shit," the crusty CIA man affirmed. "There is money in Dillard's accounts and a few others' as well that came from foreign sources and have not been declared."

"Wow. What else do you know?" the Vice President asked.

"The Chairman has been subpoenaed to testify to the House banking committee behind closed doors in the Capitol skiff next week."

"Does this contact think he has anything on me?" the Vice President asked directly. "I mean, he wouldn't because I'm clean as a whistle, but I am just asking."

"He didn't say. He wouldn't say. You can't read the man. But I know you are clean."

"I see." The story seemed to be deliberately murky and vague. "The fact the Chairman has something on the President's closest friend . . . am I supposed to tell the President?" the Vice President asked.

"It's your call," the CIA head said.

"I see."

"You will have to read him and keep an eye on events over the next couple of weeks," the CIA man advised. "Report back to me, and I can tell the Chairman."

"Right," the Vice President agreed. "What else did you want to meet about? You said it was urgent."

"Have you heard anything about this Plasma Cell Project?" the CIA chief asked as the boat bobbed up and down.

"Yes, I have," the Vice President answered as he winced. "And I don't like it one bit."

"The Chairman doesn't like it one bit either. He wanted you to know."

"The Chairman and the NSA know about this already? Jesus Christ," the Vice President whispered.

"The Chairman wants it stopped," the CIA chief stated matter-of-factly. "Stopped."

"I see. So is this the quid pro quo? I mean, no Plasma Cell Project, then no diversion of funds testimony?" the nation's number-two man queried. "I have nothing to hide, but I don't want to get dragged into either issue if I decide to run for president. I am opposed to a Plasma Cell Project, regardless."

"I'm not sure it's a quid pro quo. No threats here—the Chairman doesn't want the President threatened. Not directly—that's out of the question. He would never take the chance of having any of us testify before a congressional committee or tell some reporter or write in our memoirs that the Chairman of the NSA blackmailed the President of the United States. He's too smart for that. I'm not doing so either." He looked up to the skies. "Do you guys hear me?"

The head of the CIA paused and collected himself. Two more choppers moved into place and began to hover. Their din echoed over the ocean and was practically deafening. "He didn't link the two issues; I am linking them. All he said was that he would do whatever was in his power to stop this Plasma Cell scheme from happening. From what I know of him, I wouldn't doubt him."

THAT DOG WON'T HUNT

"I hope we decide to do something instead of waiting around with our dicks in our hands," Atlas ranted to Bouchikas as the two men rode an elevator to a lower-level conference room in the NSA's Houston headquarters at around the same time the Vice President had arrived for his rendezvous at sea.

"I don't know what the Chairman is waiting for. We should have acted yesterday," the decorated commando continued. "We should have disposed of this quickly and cleanly."

"That might have been a bit premature," Bouchikas told Atlas. "The President is sick. He's busy; he's worried. I don't think he will rush into an initiative as big as a Plasma Cell Project. Better for us to wait, Alan."

"Wait, hell," Atlas growled. "It will be that much more challenging if we wait. The White House will add security and involve its own people. Unlike you, I have been in war. People who wait tend to come home in body bags. Not to doubt your bona fides on the subject, Saint Christopher, but that's not my preferred mode of travel."

"Maybe he'll decide not to proceed. Did you ever think of that?"

Bouchikas asked his counterpart as the elevator doors separated. "Then we don't have to have a confrontation or kill anyone."

The men stepped out of the elevator and walked briskly down the long hallway, undoubtedly monitored by omnipresent cameras and microphones.

"Not proceed?" Atlas asked. "It sounds like he has made up his mind. The man has gone bananas, Chris."

"He's grasping at straws to secure his beloved legacy," Bouchikas replied. "But his advisors all shot it down, except for Dillard. Dillard's a schmuck."

"The President is a schmuck too," Atlas answered. "I don't know about you, but I didn't fly down here to twiddle my thumbs and wait for a disaster to occur. That's not what I signed up for."

"Sometimes the wisest thing to do is wait," Bouchikas counseled. "We can't just go around killing people. That's not our job, either."

Atlas was tense after his hurried journey to Texas. Although NSA bylaws required only five NSA Council members to be present when a Category II was extant, the Chairman had asked the two of them to be in Houston in case the situation worsened; only Abrahamyan and Knox remained at the Fort Meade headquarters.

Bouchikas had left home that day over the strong objections of Diana. He had been home only one night in the previous four and didn't talk to her then because he fell asleep before she arrived home after their son's T-ball game. When Bouchikas informed his wife early the next morning that he had been summoned out of town on urgent government business, she cried and said it was important he stay so she could tell him something important. Their conversation turned tense, and she demanded he not leave town and he give up his "damn" government job. One word led to another until tenderness turned to bitterness, and finally, Diana threatened she would leave Chris—for good—if he left her that morning. He, however, believed his duty to his country to avert a grave threat was his primary duty under God that day and felt he could patch up his personal problems once the threat had ended.

Atlas was agitated and tense for more selfish reasons. He had recently felt pushed aside by the NSA's Chairman, who often seemed to not schedule him for key meetings when Atlas's point of view ran counter to his. Atlas operated as he wished despite not being included in such meetings. The cells of commandos and contractors he ran and paid for out of his slush fund were airtight and practically untraceable. Yet failures attributed to him were beginning to mount, like the Lebanese hostage affair and the murder of the Salvadoran bishop. Or the botched attempt on Katie Shepard's life and Hartigan's messy murder, which were perhaps unnecessary and premature. In those cases, Atlas had taken matters into his own hands after being tipped off by Atherton. Atlas's misfires were beginning to weigh on him; he became concerned and paranoid that he had drawn suspicion at the Agency, where no secrets were safe.

Atlas had begun to openly express doubts about the NSA's Chairman, joining a growing list of Council members considering leaving their jobs. Perhaps the average tenure for them was the limit at which people carrying such burdens collapsed. Bouchikas and Christianson were collapsing because they could no longer satisfy the needs of both the Agency and their families. Abrahamyan had carnal yearnings, while LeSayer had the desire to bear a child. Atlas was at the point of collapse because he had lost perspective on what his role at the NSA, and the role of the NSA itself, was.

"We've done our waiting," Atlas said. "Waiting invites disaster. Doesn't the Chairman realize that?"

"He may be playing a longer game than you are, Alan. If the President really is that reckless, isn't it better to find out now than later?" Bouchikas asked. "We still have time to act."

"We'll see," Atlas responded. "I hope you're right."

* * *

Later in the day, Bouchikas and Atlas huddled with Kraft and LeSayer while waiting for dinner to be served in an authentic pub in the NSA's netherworld. The wooden sign hanging over the door of the establishment read "That Dog Won't Hunt Pub and Grill" and featured a painted image of a Chihuahua puppy. "That dog won't hunt" was a common Texas expression, said bluntly in response to a non-starter of a proposal someone had floated. The Chairman used the expression often.

"Have we heard anything new out of the White House?" Bouchikas asked the group.

"No, it's been quiet," LeSayer said. "Almost too quiet. I'm concerned about the presidential address the White House has scheduled."

"It's on?" Atlas asked.

"Yes. Thursday night at 6:00 p.m. Washington time, prime time on all the networks. Rumors are he will discuss his health," LeSayer told them. "There is also speculation about resignation, but I think that's wishful thinking."

"And you think he may talk about a Plasma Cell Project?" Bouchikas queried.

"I'm afraid he might," the CIA analyst said.

"What have we heard about the President's health?" Bouchikas asked LeSayer. "Have you received anything from Preston?" Preston was Preston Knox, the only physician on the Council.

"Yes. Preston's report is in each of your files. The President is suffering from congestive heart failure, meaning his heart is failing to keep up with the demands on it to pump blood to his organs. In an attempt to keep up, more and more blood is returned to the heart during each beat, causing it to enlarge. This increased volume can't all be expelled by the diseased pump, so the body becomes congested, ergo the name. Fluid backs up into the lungs, liver, and soft tissues where you can see it in the legs and ankles."

"How serious is that?" Bouchikas asked.

"It's treatable," LeSayer answered. "The treatment is twofold: a diuretic to get rid of some of the congested fluid, and digitalis, a drug that improves the contractility of the heart. Together, they compensate pretty well for a while."

"Digitalis," Kraft said. "I've heard of it. Do you know what that is, exactly?"

"It's in a class of drugs called cardiac glycosides," LeSayer answered.

"Ah, yes," the novelist recalled. "I believe it comes from the leaf of a plant. The Borgias employed it in Verona to poison their enemies, right?"

"That's correct," LeSayer said.

"How can it be a poison if it's the President's treatment?" Bouchikas asked.

"It's paradoxical," LeSayer answered. "The therapeutic range of digitalis is narrow, meaning that two to three times the therapeutic level can be lethal. A toxic dose can potentially cause a lethal cardiac rhythm or even stop the heart completely."

"Those Italians were clever," Kraft remarked. "As I recall, the plant is rather pretty, so they grew it right in their own courtyards. Just boil and serve."

"So he's not seriously ill?" Bouchikas said of the President.

"I wouldn't say that. Congestive heart failure carries a poor prognosis. Three-quarters of patients with the condition will be dead in five years. The body can compensate for a while," the former CIA station chief explained, "but eventually the overstretched heart muscle is overburdened and gives up. It will kill him," she opined definitively.

"Not soon enough," Bouchikas said. "How will he explain it to the public?"

"Who knows," LeSayer responded. "They have been tight-lipped. We haven't picked up any reliable chatter. In our cat-and-mouse game, the White House has spots where we can't listen."

* * *

Later, the seven NSA Council members gathered in the Old English dining room in the pub in front of a large hearth. After the meal, once the wait staff was cleared out of the room, the Chairman addressed the group.

"Thank you all for coming down to Houston," he began. "I know some of you prefer we take immediate action against a Plasma Cell Project. I acknowledge waiting carries a risk, but it has its advantages. Let me assure you all that we will act if we need to once we have all the information.

"Preston has put together a presentation on Katie Shepard's disease and the exact mechanism believed to have caused her age reversal," the Chairman continued. "I've asked him to present it to us in person on Tuesday morning, which will give us plenty of time before the President is scheduled to go on TV. Dalia will also be here to discuss the population implications, including what we could expect, and when."

"We will all be here?" Bouchikas asked.

"Yes. I am designating this matter a Category I," the Chairman informed the group. "Once it is resolved, you can each take some much-needed vacation time. I know you have all been working overtime and need to recharge."

"That sounds good to me," Christianson said. "Do you know something new to make this a Cat I?"

"Nothing of any substance," the Chairman answered, "but we have picked up that there is heavy pressure on the President to make some sort of a decision in the next few days. He promised his close advisors he would. I thought it would be prudent if we were all here in case we need to act quickly. One way or another, this will be resolved in the next few days. Does anyone dissent to the Category I classification?"

There were no dissenters. So, with that, the Plasma Cell crisis, the case of the sixty-three-year-old woman from Ohio who had undergone age reversal of some three and a half decades, and whose body potentially held the secrets to provide a similar outcome to billions of people, was designated "a clear and present danger to the national security of the United States." For now, it was in the hands of the President to either worsen or end the crisis. In the meantime, the collective attention of the NSA's leadership focused on the White House.

A LATE NIGHT SNACK

T he President was rummaging around the kitchen as he often did when he couldn't sleep, clad in a pair of well-worn slippers and his monogrammed, burgundy-colored velvet bathrobe with the presidential seal embroidered over its breast pocket. Although there was a small kitchen in the personal living quarters on the second floor of the White House, the President preferred the large commercial kitchen on the ground floor with its walk-in refrigerators, commercial stoves, and hanging pots and pans. This was where the First Family's meals, as well as special event menus, were prepared by the White House chef. A notebook displaying the next day's fare was open on a stand atop the counter; the President reviewed it while he poured himself a glass of milk and ate chocolate chip cookies his wife had baked two nights before. On her rare nights alone in the White House, the First Lady liked to bake for her husband, something often written about by the press corps who despised her. The Chief Executive loved anything his wife made, even when not prepared particularly well. The cookies he was eating tasted salty (something he was supposed to avoid because of his heart failure) and were overbaked, but he happily devoured several of them anyway.

The Chief Executive's location in the White House was constantly monitored on a terminal in the Secret Service control room on the ground floor. Appearing as number one, he was shown to be in room 1639, the kitchen. The First Lady, number two, was in the presidential bedroom, while number three, a daughter, was staying in the Queen's bedroom. Number four was shown to be in New York, while number five was listed to be in Los Angeles. The Secret Service control room was small but efficient. Multiple monitors displayed feeds from the White House grounds, the biggest nuisances usually being fools, often intoxicated, trying to scale the fence bordering Pennsylvania Avenue. Two closets were filled with automatic weapons and man-portable Stinger missile launchers. Another cabinet stored what the White House Secret Service agents dubbed fag bags (technically, fast-action gun bags) with breakaway canvas cases. Also in the control room were two telephone receivers labeled with large red letters. The phone on the left was labeled Residence, while the one to the right was labeled FAA, a line that was also monitored by US Central Command. Flying in unauthorized air space near the White House was sure to trigger a quick, lethal response, along with a trip to the White House bunker by the First Family accompanied by key staffers if in residence.

That the various security services kept close tabs on the President was no surprise. Indeed, they had done a remarkable job of safeguarding first families, frequently with the aid of information supplied by the NSA. What is surprising was how little presidents have kept tabs on the NSA. It was as if it were somebody else's job. The problem was, it wasn't.

From the start, as detailed earlier in this report, the Armed Forces Security Agency (AFSA), which later evolved into the National Security Agency (NSA), was a spinoff of the National Security Council and reported solely to the executive branch. But along came the infamous Directive #9, which created an exemption that placed

AFSA beyond the reach of even the President or his attorney general unless a subsequent executive order changed it. The intention of the directive was to allow the flow of intelligence communications to continue unimpeded by conflicting directives and policy decisions. On October 24, 1952, President Harry Truman issued a memorandum ordering the establishment of the National Security Agency to succeed AFSA; Directive #9 applied to it as well. The actual establishment of the NSA came later that year, in a memo issued by Defense Secretary Robert Lovett on November 4, which curiously was the day of the 1952 presidential election. The agency that was created could carry out work the FBI and the CIA were banned from doing by laws that separated and forbade them from communicating with each other directly or spying on Americans. The NSA became the workaround. It was so shrouded in secrecy that other US intelligence organizations referred to it as "No Such Agency." To evoke a Churchillian phrase, it was a riddle, wrapped in a mystery, inside an enigma. The missing dimension of the missing dimension was another way it had been described. For the NSA, this served its purposes.

Truman left office shortly after he signed his directive. The year 1953 ushered in the Eisenhower years, and as usual, it took nearly a year to fully staff the new administration. In the vacuum that ensued, the NSA was off and running and pulled down huge budget allocations for the construction of facilities and for recruiting some of the most talented people available to help achieve its goals. The push to build huge, powerful, ultra-fast computers began in earnest. Project Lightning, launched in 1957, had as its goal to increase circuitry capability by a thousandfold. It was enthusiastically backed by Eisenhower, who approved $25 million, a large sum for its day, for the effort. Eisenhower, the brilliant tactician of World War II, was all about logistics, infrastructure, strategy, and force superiority, a combination meant to overwhelm the enemy.

Eisenhower's stewardship as president produced mostly quiet years for the US foreign policy establishment, with two notable exceptions. In both cases, the NSA played a key role. The first instance was the Suez Crisis of 1956. Despite public pronouncements to the contrary, the surprise attack by Britain, France, and Israel on the recently seized Suez Canal was well known to the Eisenhower White House, thanks to the NSA. For better or for worse, signals intelligence collected by the NSA was withheld from allies and helped shape developments in the Middle East for years to come. It led to a rift between the United States and its key allies, who suffered politically at home.

The second instance was on September 2, 1958, when an American spy plane on assignment for the NSA along the Soviet-Turkish border was shot down by Russian MIG-17 fighters. The US spy craft, on an intelligence gathering mission, had accidentally veered across the border. Its pilot and eleven crew members were downed and unaccounted for, and Eisenhower, through diplomatic channels, pressed for answers as to their fates. Indignant over the American intrusion into their airspace, the Russians refused to cooperate. Initially, for reasons beneficial to each, both sides agreed to a story that the aircraft had accidentally crashed in the Armenian mountains. But eventually, in order to pressure the Kremlin to release the flyers, Eisenhower went public with transcripts of cockpit conversations between MIG jet fighters that proved the American plane was intentionally downed. The NSA was furious that its eavesdropping capabilities were revealed against its wishes. To this day, the American flyers remain unaccounted for, and the NSA's distrust of the commander in chief endures.

President John Kennedy and his younger brother Robert had a complicated relationship with the intelligence community. The Kennedys were eager consumers of NSA intelligence, sending hundreds of requests for information on racketeers as well as individual

US citizens with ties to Cuba. It was NSA U-2 reconnaissance information that launched the Cuban missile crisis and an NSA contrived plot handed over to the CIA that led to the disastrous Bay of Pigs invasion. To his credit, President Kennedy recognized the future role of satellites in gathering intelligence and, in 1963, established the Communications Satellite Corporation (COMSAT). But Jack Kennedy got in trouble with the intelligence community and the mob because of differences over Cuba and because of the women he shared with Mafia bosses, his brother, and other government officials. His pillow talk with one particular woman was suspected to have compromised him.

It was around that time the NSA is believed to have established its ultra-secret, extralegal operational wing. Unlike the CIA, the NSA was not subject to political winds or congressional oversight. To this day, it has not been publicly revealed what roles, if any, the NSA and CIA might have played in President Kennedy's assassination.

Lyndon Johnson was too preoccupied first with building the Great Society and then by the Vietnam War to issue directives that would rein in the behemoth the NSA was becoming. The turbulent later years of the Johnson administration changed the focus of NSA watch lists from racketeers and Cubans to protestors, civil rights leaders, and drug dealers. As a forerunner to the famous Nixon enemies list, Johnson's watchlist contained such names as pediatrician Benjamin Spock, folk singer Joan Baez, the Reverend Ralph Abernathy of the Southern Christian Leadership Conference, and Dr. Martin Luther King Jr. The FBI, under the direction of J. Edgar Hoover, put increased demands on the NSA for information about US citizens. By 1968, the NSA occupied a five-million-square foot campus of buildings in Fort Meade and two other equally large underground complexes, one in Houston and one in West Virginia. It operated spy ships like the USS *Pueblo* and the USS *Liberty*, farms filled with giant listening dishes, and twenty-five-hundred intercept positions. It employed more than a hundred thousand people, was the largest single employer in the state of Maryland, and was Baltimore Gas & Electric's largest customer. An espionage monster had been created.

Under Nixon, the power of the NSA grew enormously. The demand for domestic intelligence went unchecked during this period, as did the role of secret missions. In the era of shuttle diplomacy that carried the secretary of state between Cairo and Jerusalem, Peking and Moscow, and Hanoi and Geneva, where our adversaries' old-fashioned counterintelligence was arguably a match for our capabilities, the celestial eyes and ears of the NSA became all the more essential. Eventually, however, Nixon's secret international missions gave way to missions inside a psychiatrist's office and the Democratic National Committee's headquarters. Nixon was driven from office in disgrace.

The post-Watergate era of Presidents Ford and Carter brought forth calls for intelligence reforms detailed elsewhere in this Commission's report. But while the operations of the intelligence apparatus, the software, were reduced, the hardware grew enormously. NSA-operated satellites in low earth orbit could read license plate numbers off of cars on Beirut streets and intercept telemetry signals from Soviet ICBMs launched from locations as remote as Tyrotam or Plesetsk. There were setbacks in this era as well. Iran and its listening posts on the Russian border were lost due to the incompetence and dithering of Carter and company. American voters moved to unseat and replace Carter. The NSA became more and more convinced that only its extralegal operations, which needed no one else's approval, could right things in the world.

So it was that in the early 1980s the Agency went into overdrive. Arming death squads in El Salvador, mining Nicaraguan harbors, and supplying *contras* in Honduras were operations aided by the NSA so as to keep the CIA's hands as clean as possible.

No fingerprints; no witnesses at congressional hearings. No Such Agency. It was a convenient arrangement. The President asked no questions and received no answers. As Oliver Goldsmith recommended 250 years earlier, "Ask me no questions, and I will tell you no lies."

As the President snacked on his wife's slightly burnt cookies and sipped warm milk, he had no idea the NSA had taken such a keen interest in his own affairs—namely his failing health and his contemplated Plasma Cell Project.

DAY NINE

May 11, 1987

In a strange game
I saw myself as you knew me
When the change came
And you had the chance to see through me
Though the other side is just the same
You can tell my dream is real.

—NEIL YOUNG, "ON THE WAY HOME," 1968

AN INTIMATE DINNER

Insbrook gazed at Katie's delicate profile as she leaned forward to light the candelabras she found in a cabinet in her presidential suite. At her request, Insbrook had arranged to have groceries delivered so she could finally cook the dinner she had promised him back in Cincinnati. Insbrook had arrived a short time earlier with a chilled bottle of white wine under one arm and a bouquet of freesias in his opposite hand. The low lights, the music playing on the CD player, the toasty smell of home-baked bread, and the simmering garlic pasta sauce created an eerily serene environment amidst the mysterious compound in which they dined. It was surreal and reminded Insbrook of a scene in a French film he had recently watched about life in hiding during World War II as a Jewish family celebrated a peaceful *Shabbat* dinner in a cellar while Nazi soldiers rummaged above them. The human brain has an innate ability to compartmentalize matters, a mechanism that aids in survival.

Insbrook was enraptured by Katie. He admired her face and décolletage as she poured each of them a glass of wine. *Under a different set of circumstances*, he thought, *I could marry a woman of her qualities even if she was in her late twenties. Or sixty-three.*

He couldn't quite figure out which way to think of her. Her outward beauty was in part secondary to her disease-induced age, her artificial youth a fact that did not bother him at all. He liked it. Her wisdom, her charm, her wit, and her vast array of knowledge were due to her true chronological age. Unfortunately, such virtues were often not appreciated in those less beautiful and older in appearance than Katie. *What a shallow man I am*, he thought to himself as he leaned back and continued to admire her and enjoy the wine and the needed break.

"A toast to you," Insbrook said as he lifted his glass, feeling more in love with Katie than he ever had been with Doris.

"No, to you, my dear Philip," Katie responded as she gently touched her glass to his in a kiss of crystal. They each sipped a bit of the wine. Katie was resplendent in the ambiance she had created for their intimate dinner. "How was your day?" she asked, as a wife would ask a husband. "You looked so tired yesterday morning."

"Today was busy again," Insbrook said with a sigh. "But I went to sleep early last night and caught up on my sleep. I have to admit I haven't been sleeping well because I'm not sure what to do anymore."

"You mean with me?" she inquired.

"With the whole thing. You know, this idea of making everyone younger."

"They really want to do that?"

"Some people do."

As she served dinner for the two of them, Katie opened up in a way she never had before. She reflected on her long life, her girlhood, her courtship years, World War II, her husband's death, and the days when she went through the metamorphosis. She reflected on how she so missed seeing her daughter and grandchildren over the past few years and admitted that, all in all, despite the thrills she experienced being a young woman for a second time, she had probably made the wrong choice. Insbrook was quick to point out she really didn't have a choice. Katie saw some truth in the statement but felt she should have been honest with her daughter at the outset. That would have given them five extra years together and maybe given the doctors a better chance to help her. Katie felt guilty for having welcomed the changes so much. Now, fearing death might be near, she expressed hope her daughter would never know what had happened to her.

"Katie, you know there's a chance everyone in the world will know what happened to you, don't you?"

"I've sort of gathered that," his dinner partner replied as she twisted pasta onto her fork.

"Nothing shocks you, does it?" Insbrook remarked.

"Not really. What else could shock me? I became almost forty years younger. Besides, I'm somewhat resigned to the situation. I've had five years to mull it over. The cancer part shocked me, though."

"You are so level-headed," Insbrook told her. "Maybe I can talk to you about *my* problems. I can't talk to anyone else, and you obviously can't tell anyone anything I tell you while you are locked up here."

"Not a word," Katie reassured, raising her left hand and placing her right hand over her heart.

"I'm frightened, Katie," Insbrook told her, focusing on his fork as he loaded it with pasta.

"For yourself?" Katie asked.

"At a lot of levels. But yes, for myself," he admitted. "The irony is that while I'm against making mankind nearly immortal, as I recently told high government officials, I myself don't want to die. No one does."

"And who or what is going to kill you?" Katie asked as she set her glass on the table.

"I'm not sure, but I have encountered some rough types around here—military and FBI types. You know, crewcuts. Goons. There is also a guy I met today they kept referring to as the Chairman. The

Chairman of what, I don't know, Katie. It sounds like mob talk. He was definitely in charge."

"I think your imagination is getting the best of you," Katie said. "Solitary confinement will do that."

"I don't think so. This particular guy came and left in an unmarked black helicopter. He was surrounded by heavyweights. They were tough guys in a five-man bodyguard formation. They took a lot of photos, too, and they weren't sightseers. There was also the attempt on your life. And, of course, someone killed Hartigan."

"Hartigan? You mean the tall male intern?"

"I'm sorry, Katie," Insbrook said quietly. "Yes, he was killed while jogging in a park in Cincinnati the other day."

"Murdered?" Katie asked, now frightened.

Insbrook nodded. "I think it was murder, yes. Maybe a hit. An assassination, the day after you ended up on the roof. You said someone chased you up there. Or maybe my mind is wandering."

"Oh my God, someone *was* trying to kill me," Katie murmured. "Hartigan seemed like such a good kid. He would have been a good doctor."

"Yes, he was a good kid," Insbrook told her. "Aside from fearing for myself, I fear for the nation and the world. This talk of making everyone younger is crazy. And even if this particular program doesn't work out, I have discovered we have a president who has gone half-senile and a bunch of madmen around him running the country. I mean, let's just say I was able to confirm it."

"Your mind *has* gotten away from you. Those are not exactly your personal problems," Katie reminded Insbrook.

"They are, sort of. I started this. And besides, it depresses me. And then there's you, Katie," he said, reaching around the table to take her hand and holding it warmly. "I worry about you; I care about you."

"As I do for you, Philip. I have come to realize, however, no matter how much you worry about me, it probably doesn't matter anyway, does it?"

Insbrook focused on his plate, trying to keep tears out of his eyes.

"Philip," Katie said to break the silence. "I'll serve dessert in a few minutes. Does homemade cappuccino ice cream with a zest of shaved orange peel sound good to you?"

Insbrook looked up at her and shook his head from side to side. "Sounds delicious. That is truly incredible, Katie. You amaze me."

"But before I do," Katie continued, "I want to suggest something. Why don't you ask to leave Atlanta and see if you can stop the madness? If you think making everyone younger is so awful, maybe you can convince others. And you could protect yourself. Weren't you responsible for bringing me here in the first place?"

Insbrook reached for the wine bottle and topped off their glasses with the remainder of its contents. "Yes, I was," he said, "but I have lost control. And to be honest, I'm not sure who to go to for help. The President and his men are a dead end. They will make their own choices. The press? That would probably backfire. It might protect me personally, but it will never stop this antiaging thing from going forward. I might be able to get personal protection from the FBI, but who knows for sure? I know Jack Turner, and I trust him, but I'm not sure who it was who tried killing you and killed Jim Hartigan. I think something bigger is going on here than I know. Something we can't quite see and don't understand, Katie. *The missing dimension of the missing dimension* is a term I've read."

"Maybe the CIA or someone like that?" Katie reasoned.

"I don't know," Insbrook said as he shrugged his shoulders. "There is also a gag order that was served to me this morning, supposedly issued by a judge in the Fourth Circuit. I'm not allowed to talk to anyone, or they will jail me. So please, don't say anything. I probably need to consult with a good constitutional lawyer to find out if this order is even real or legal or what they can do to me. I'm a doctor, not a lawyer," he exclaimed. "I know the governor in Ohio, so maybe I could get some advice from him.

"Maybe I should leave since I don't feel safe here," he concluded, having frightened himself. "I will find myself an attorney."

"You should do that," Katie said as she cleared the table. "You should do that, my love." As she spoke, she stood behind Insbrook, crossing her arms around him while pressing her breasts against the back of his head. "I'll be fine here."

* * *

Philip Insbrook finally broke into tears as he made his way back to his own quarters across the windswept Atlanta grounds amidst the susurrations of mature magnolias and white oaks. After Katie's encouragement, he resolved to ask for leave from the complex for a few days. They both agreed his spending the night in her apartment could only create problems and complications for them. So shortly before midnight, as the doctor went to exit the building, Katie embraced him as she shivered, whimpered, and clutched him in fear. He hugged her back tightly, also afraid, and fought back the tears until he was a safe distance away from the building.

Insbrook's tears streaked his cheeks, and the wind drove them back behind his ears. He walked briskly, his hands in his coat pockets with his head down. He could have been crying for Katie, the world, his nation, his family, or himself. His own life had become as disordered as Katie's. Like her, he had been sidetracked in recent years by unhealthy and unwise pursuits. If only he could get back to a quiet life of relative anonymity with family and friends, Insbrook thought, he would be happy. If he could steer the President away from a course of madness and obsessive preoccupation with his legacy, Insbrook resolved to seek the peaceful life he had once known in Long Island. First, he had to fulfill his wish to halt the Plasma Cell Project.

Back in his suite, Insbrook made an entry in his diary. "The biological laws of nature—of evolution and of natural selection—have brought our species to where it is today, and it will only be through the continued observance of those laws that we will survive as a species and a civilization. We must live within nature's grand plan that has served us so well for countless millennia. Nature makes her plans. We live within them.

"When it comes to aging, the laws of nature operate for the good of the species, not the individual. While the process of natural selection—survival of the fittest—strengthens the species, it is of no value to the individual who is inferior and eliminated from the gene pool. The same is true of aging. Each individual must eventually die so a newer, stronger individual can take their place. Otherwise, we would be left with one of two situations: a world in which there is no reproduction or one that is unbearably overcrowded. Neither would lend itself to the long-term well-being of the species. So, as would be expected, nature has an ideal plan, an orderly succession of the stages of life, the goal of which is to perpetuate the species. The cycle evolved by providing positive reinforcement—physical or psychological pleasure—to the individuals involved in its perpetuation.

"Each stage of human life, be it infancy, childhood, adolescence, adulthood, middle age, or old age, accomplishes a purpose in the perpetuation of the species. The infant and child are lovable, cuddly, and alluring to their elders. As such, they assure care and comfort from those on whom they depend until they can fend for themselves.

"The adolescent is inquisitive, daring, and mischievous, learning the skills and limitations they must be aware of in order to successfully navigate life's curves that lie ahead.

"Young adulthood is the time of courtship and mating. Soft skin and flowing hair, comely faces, and fine physiques. Smooth, round breasts and proud genitalia. Lust, arousal, and sexual pleasure. Mating instincts. All evolved to assure one end: procreation, the essential function members of a species must perform if they are to provide a link in the chain of its perpetuation.

"Up until reproduction occurs, the laws of natural selection apply. Those who are fittest, healthiest, and most desirable are more likely to reproduce themselves in the greatest numbers, while the rest do not. Thus, Darwin postulated, the fittest individuals and their genes survive. Once procreation occurs, there are no longer selective pressures on the individual. Those who become weak and sick or old have already reproduced copies mirroring their genetic selves. Then, nature follows the path of least resistance, conserving biological energy by allowing the organism to age and die. However, society and nature combine forces to create useful roles for humans even when they are beyond their reproductive years as they pass through the remaining stages of life.

"As an adult, individuals occupy themselves with the fulfillment of primary goals by providing essentials for themselves or those dependent upon them. For some, a strong marriage bond and child rearing are sources of satisfaction and stability. The mature adult also seeks secondary goals, including wealth, power, and fame. As physical attributes diminish, social skills, knowledge, experience, and wisdom assume greater importance.

"Middle age gives way to old age as the physical being continues its decline. The human brain often remains intact and further provides wisdom, experience, and advice to future generations. The elderly bask in the glory of their accomplishments and are honored by those who come after them. They give love, and they are loved. As in infancy, they become cuddly, warm, alluring, and helpless, assuring care and comfort as they peacefully pass to a commonly imagined afterlife.

"Such is the formula for happiness, deemed so by nature's design. Indeed, at this point in my highly scientific and technologically oriented life, I have come to believe there is more value in one life lived properly from start to end than in ten lifetimes muddled by science and technology."

DAY TEN

May 12, 1987

To everything there is a season,
and a time to every purpose under heaven:
a time to be born and a time to die;
a time to plant and a time to reap.

—ECCLESIASTES 3:1-2

HARD KNOX

Early Tuesday, the last two Council members flew on *Perseus* to the urgently assembled gathering in Houston. Aboard *Perseus* were Dalia Abrahamyan and Preston Knox, along with their attachés. Abrahamyan slept while Knox prepared for the lecture that would be the most memorable of his career. The aircraft touched down in Houston at 7:15 a.m.

Preston Knox, like several of his counterparts, had been with the Agency for about five years. He had been a diligent Council member, universally respected by his peers. Prior to his arrival at the NSA, Knox was the chief pathologist at the storied Massachusetts General Hospital. Knox's rise through the ranks of the nation's top intelligence agency was not as unlikely as it seemed. In Vietnam, he had served in the Green Berets as a weapons specialist. This Army Special Forces unit was founded in 1952, the same year the NSA was founded. Seeing combat duty at his own request, Knox was the most highly decorated physician in the history of the Army, the only ever to receive the Congressional Medal of Honor for valor on the battlefield twice, having risked his own life to save comrades who were under fire. Knox liked to say he knew as much about

Kalashnikovs as he did about corpses. In either case, he knew a lot about caskets.

After his tour of duty, Knox stayed on in the military as a reservist and was called upon for several sensitive missions where a highly trusted weapons man/physician came in handy. Eventually, he was recruited by the CIA and later by the NSA. Two years later, he was handpicked by the Agency's Chairman for a spot on the Council. He offered diversity in multiple dimensions, which was to the Chairman's liking.

Knox kept a low profile at the NSA but exerted influence through hard work and the common sense he learned as the son of working-class African Americans in Alabama. His churchgoing parents determined he would overcome America's lingering racism and succeed. Knox seemed to churn out twice as much work as his counterparts, largely due to the administrative skills he acquired while running a large pathology department. Other attributes of a good pathologist also served Knox and the Agency well: He was thorough and meticulous, could follow a protocol perfectly, resisted all temptation to deviate from it, paid close attention to fine detail, and was amused and enthused by what might bore the ordinary person.

His assignment was to present as simple an explanation as possible of the medical aspects of the Plasma Cell crisis, while Abrahamyan would discuss population biology implications. The pathologist hoped the others would comprehend their presentations and take heed of their warnings on the Promethean ramifications of a Plasma Cell Project. The 8:00 a.m. meeting brought together one of the greatest brain trusts that could be assembled in 1987 America: Christopher Bouchikas, Zvi Davis, Renee LeSayer, George Christianson, Dalia Abrahamyan, Alan Atlas, and Harvey Kraft.

"Good morning, my friends," Knox began in his baritone voice. "I have been asked to present to you what is believed to be the scientific basis for the phenomenon that has come to be known as the Plasma Cell phenomenon. At your desks, I have distributed background materials." At each station were white folders labeled "Plasma Cell," stamped at the bottom in red with its security designation, "Top Secret/Umbra," and the familiar admonition: "Sensitive: For Your Eyes Only."

Knox continued, "While I am sure you are familiar with the underlying facts in this case, I will review them briefly. This crisis began when an apparently young woman was admitted to a university hospital through their ER after a minor automobile accident, bearing a fantastical tale of having grown some thirty-five years younger in all outward ways. While the physicians assigned to her suspected she was delusional, they nevertheless persisted in trying to establish a basis for her symptoms, including her apparent psychosis. After a few laboratory tests, the astute Dr. Philip Insbrook established the diagnosis of a serious medical illness. Insbrook went on to prove the woman had indeed grown forty years younger and linked the cause to a disease called multiple myeloma."

The words *MULTIPLE MYELOMA* appeared on the screen, and Knox relayed the cause and symptoms of the disease. "Multiple myeloma is a malignant tumor of white blood cells called plasma cells. It is akin to leukemia or Hodgkin's disease but involves a different part of the hematologic system. Its incidence in the population is two to five cases per 100,000 per year—uncommon as diseases go. It occurs in a 2:1 male-to-female ratio, with a peak incidence in the fifth through seventh decades of life. Eighty percent of cases occur after the age of forty and are extremely rare below the age of thirty.

"Multiple myeloma arises from unchecked multiplication of a single clone of plasma cells. Subsequently, all cells produced by this clone—and there are millions—are identical. While these cells are being produced in abundance, the production of other bloodlines is concomitantly diminished, resulting in anemia and susceptibility to infections. Both of these findings were present in Katie Shepard, who was found in the emergency room to be anemic and have a urinary tract infection. The young woman, as I will refer to her hereafter to avoid confusion, also complained of severe, dull bone pain in multiple locations, including the pelvis, hips, ribs, and skull."

The slide changed and projected a series of dots that simulated the outline of a woman. "This bone scan taken of Katie Shepard shows why she complained. The darkened areas, or 'hot spots,' indicate areas of increased cellular activity where the marrow is working overtime to crank out plasma cells. On plain X-rays, these same areas appear as punched-out lesions, areas where the solid bone has been destroyed and replaced with an expansible tumor."

The title of the next slide was *PLASMA CELLS*. "Katie Shepard has a malignancy of plasma cells," Knox continued, "which accounts for her physical complaints. You might ask, how does this account for her reverse aging? The astute Insbrook scratched his head and came up with an answer to the question. To understand it, you must understand the function of plasma cells under normal circumstances. They are part of the immune system that protects the body by the essential function of producing antibodies."

The slide changed to one with the header *ANTIBODIES*. "Antibodies are complex structures, normally produced in response to the invasion of the body by a foreign protein or a bacteria or virus. It is the job of antibodies to attack and destroy such invaders."

The next slide was entitled *ANTIGEN*. "An antigen is any substance capable of inducing an antibody response," Knox lectured. "Antigens are present in bacteria, viruses, and foreign bodies, including transplanted tissues. The body possesses the uncanny ability to recognize its own proteins and will not produce antibodies against itself except rarely in autoimmune diseases. Conversely, elements not recognized as the self stimulate the production of antibodies to attack and reject them, as sometimes happens with transplanted organs.

"What does all of this have to do with Katie Shepard and her reverse aging, you may ask? Insbrook's ability to piece this together astounds me," Knox commented. "This is what he reasoned, which I believe is correct:

"In multiple myeloma, millions of identical plasma cells are produced by malignant foci within the marrow. In turn, these cells churn out billions of uniform antibodies. At the same time, the body decreases the production of other antibodies, which results in susceptibility to infection, as was found in Mrs. Shepard. The high level of protein production from the manufacture of antibodies results in high serum and urine protein levels, also found in Katie's tests. Other markers, including a high serum calcium level, led Insbrook to the rapid diagnosis of multiple myeloma.

"Normally, in multiple myeloma, the antibody produced is what is termed a nonsense antibody. It is not produced in response to a particular stimulus and has no antigenic specificity. In the case of Mrs. Shepard, by pure chance, the lock is believed to be the long-sought-after aging protein. It is postulated that Katie's myeloma antibodies combined with the naturally occurring aging protein present in her body and neutralized it."

"Tell us a little bit more about that," the Chairman encouraged him.

"Sure," Knox responded. "Gruber and others in his field have long hypothesized there is an aging protein, an enzyme that catalyzes the aging process at the cellular and subcellular levels after the cell reaches maturity. This manifests in clinical aging at a prescribed time, with some tissues aging faster than others. The enzyme also appears to act through a feedback loop to block processes that promote DNA repair. Thus, in the absence of this protein, the cell and the organism maintain their mature states and undergo cellular repair when cellular structures are damaged. Nature is highly efficient, so the explanation of a single protein that both turns on aging and blocks cellular repair makes teleological sense. The production of this protein is likely turned on by a clock embedded in our genes, triggering aging and senescence.

"We believe the chance production of Katie Shepard's particular antibody resulted in the absence of the aging protein from her body. The halting of cell aging appears to have occurred first, as has been demonstrated in a rat model and cellular repair, and changes in her physical appearance occurred afterward. Katie's clinical changes appear to have taken approximately six months, which is not surprising for an organism as complex as a human.

"I've been speaking for a long time," Knox said. "Why don't I stop and entertain questions you may have."

Bouchikas spoke from his second-row seat. "Excellent talk, Preston. Can you tell us how your explanation relates to other theories of aging?"

"Yes, I can," Knox answered. "It fits well. The demonstration of an aging enzyme is consistent with the observation that a decrease in the body's temperature slows the aging process since enzyme-mediated reactions are cut in half for every ten-degree (C) drop in temperature. Another theory states the increased rate of living hastens the aging process by increasing cellular metabolism, which would increase the rate of aging protein synthesis. In summary, an aging protein is consistent with most current theories. Probably the final common pathway."

Davis pressed the button on his microphone, illuminating a red light.

"Zvi," Knox said.

"Thank you, Preston. You mentioned the disease progeria before, the phenomena whereby children age prematurely, take on features and afflictions of early adults, and usually die by age thirteen. This has always struck me, a computer scientist, as a programming error. How does the aging protein theory relate to this?"

"Your observations are spot-on, Zvi. In progeria syndromes, the aging program appears to get switched on at around age one. Thereafter, as the child struggles to mature, it physically ages while cellular repair mechanisms are blocked. Multiple papers on the progeria enzyme and a substance labeled Lamin-A demonstrate this."

Kraft raised his hand next.

"Harvey," Knox said.

"Thank you for a brilliant lecture," Kraft said. "If Katie's case arose as a chance occurrence, it likely has before or will again. Can you comment?"

"Gladly," Knox said. "It's always helpful to have a shill in the audience. I had the same question, so I had my staff research it, and they found some fascinating accounts from the past. The earliest mention of a similar occurrence is found in the Babylonian literature of about thirty-five hundred years ago. The book of *Adata-rubis*, originally written in ancient Akkadian, describes a man named Fakim who lived, and I quote to the best of my Akkadian, 'a clean and holy life, of meritorious deed, vigorous labor, and daily prayer. In his seventieth year, when he had unto him three sons, two daughters, and children unto them numbering seventeen, this man, to the wonderment of all who lived in his village of Zara, underwent the most spectacular change in appearance until when the moon had come and gone six times, Fakim could not be told from his grandson.'

"He lived this way for four years but, in the meantime, 'changed the ways of his life, committed sins of the flesh, and brought shame on himself and his family by replacing the worship of the gods with worship of wine and harlots.' Fakim, who had never known sickness in his life, became severely ill in the last year of it and complained of excruciating pains, quote: 'deep within his marrow,' unquote. This, of course, was interpreted as a punishment by the Babylonian gods for his sins, described as forces of nature, for having turned to an unclean existence. Fakim's story was set forth as an example of what happens when one transgresses against the gods. It seems possible Fakim underwent the same phenomenon as Katie Shepard and died of his disease, multiple myeloma, which is progressively painful and fatal. Historiographers believe this episode might have inspired the Sumerian King Gilgamesh in his own storied search for immortality as described in epic poems discovered from the era.

"Plutarch, the Greek historian of the first and second centuries, described in *Parallel Lives* a member of the Greek senate who 'underwent a metamorphosis over a five-month span from the aged, withered habitus of a septuagenarian senator to the youthful, finely muscled physique of an athlete.' Had other senators not seen the physical changes with their own eyes, they would have thought that those making the claim were mad. No physician of the time could offer an explanation for this physiological quirk, which destroyed the mind of its victim. Unable to deal with it, the senator poisoned himself with *Conium maculatum*, commonly known as hemlock, the agent of choice for suicide at the time.

"The next apparent victim of the Plasma Cell phenomenon met a similarly poor fate. Proceedings of the Court of Salem, Massachusetts: *The People vs. Priscilla Wentworth*, from the year 1692, describes the trial of an alleged sorceress brought by her neighbors from her home in Connecticut to Cotton Mather's court in Salem. The woman, Priscilla Wentworth, was said to have been born in 1627, married, and raised three children. She had lived a good Christian life—devout, in fact—and took to living alone after her husband died. It was during that time neighbors noticed Priscilla to be growing younger, eventually achieving the facial appearance and habitus of a twenty-year-old girl. No one talked to Pricilla, fearing her to be a witch, resulting in her becoming a recluse. Over a short period of time, she became sick and complained of terrible pains, worse than those of the arthritis she had suffered as an old woman. The doctor of the town refused to see her, so Priscilla confined herself to her bed from which, as the months passed, blood-curdling shrieks could be heard at a greater and greater frequency. Finally, although she was paralyzed below the waist and incontinent, most likely from spinal cord involvement by a malignancy-related vertebral collapse, the woman was taken to Salem by frightened neighbors and put on trial for sorcery. She was convicted of witchcraft and put to death by hanging before a mocking, jeering crowd in the public square of Salem Town. Eighteen others met the same fate."

Knox paused and sipped from a glass of ice water. "The final report my team found was by an Englishman, Sir William Harper, an eighteenth-century physician who first observed and described numerous disease processes that went on to further elucidation as science advanced. In 1793, in a second-floor parlor at 1 Wimpole Street in Mayfair, London, Harper delivered this fascinating oral account to a meeting of the Royal Society. It was probably the first attempt to medically define the Plasma Cell phenomenon. Allow me to read this, as recorded by the Society's secretary:

"'In my entire career as a physician, I have never witnessed anything as thoroughly curious as what I observed a fortnight ago. My paternal cousin Sir Henry Harper of Gloucestershire, also a surgeon, summoned me to his town so that I might offer an explanation for a bizarre occurrence: A man who resided in a small town just a few miles away seemed to have aged backward over a six-month period from a man of sixty-one to one in his mid-twenties. The man, despite his youthful appearance, was said to have been in extraordinary, gripping pain throughout the depths of his body, but especially in his skull. Whilst the parsons of Gloucestershire insisted that Satan and the Lord Jesus Christ were waging a battle within the man's body, Cousin Henry suspected something else might be occurring.

"'To my dismay, by the time I arrived in Gloucestershire, the man had expired—two days before—after his third bout with pneumonia in as many months. While his age was difficult to determine due to the state in which I found him, he appeared to be a young man, although wasted and cachectic. A cluster of townsmen, including elders, testified that six months before, he was as heavily muscled as an apprentice laborer, but two years before that, he had been an aging, flabby widower. Cousin Henry informed me that before the man's death, he had been weak and pale, with dropsy and occasional mottling of the skin. At autopsy, we found quite abnormal lungs due to the previously described pneumonia, markedly distorted kidneys, a swollen liver, and a spleen enlarged threefold. Most mysteriously, there were unexplained fractures of the third, fourth, fifth, and sixth ribs on the right, the ischium on the left, and several vertebrae. In addition, there were extreme irregularities and thickening of other bones, including the skull and sternum. It appears that a cancer of sorts was present in this man, but I cannot explain why he should first have become younger in preparation for his demise. We await further reports of this affliction,' Harper reported to the Society's meeting near the end of the eighteenth century."

Knox finished his remarks and acknowledged the raised hand of Dalia Abrahamyan.

"It sounds like William Harper was more accepting of the possibility of such a medical phenomenon than we are. Perhaps he realized that if a person, as a biological organism, can grow older, they can also grow younger. It makes sense to me. I also want to point out that each of these individuals went on, or would have gone on, to eventual death from their underlying disease. The exceptions are the senator, who poisoned himself, and Priscilla, who was mercifully hanged. It is only now that science can manipulate the disease, alter its course, and offer its seductive fruits to millions of people; it is a danger to the world's well-being. In the past, it didn't matter."

"Let me get back to my original question," Kraft said. "Now that you have detailed previous occurrences, what about the future? When is this likely to happen again?"

"I will preface this by saying, as an experienced pathologist, I can't be certain that all four of these people had multiple myeloma, but their syndromes are remarkably similar to Mrs. Shepard's," Knox answered. "Mathematically, the probability of a chance antibody being active against the aging protein is quite small. However, as people live longer and as the world's population increases, the odds go up. The probability of when this phenomenon occurs again in our world of five billion people is maybe fifty to one hundred years. But it could happen tomorrow. It's all chance."

"How do we know Mrs. Shepard's antibodies will be effective in reversing aging in other humans?" LeSayer asked. "What about the specificity you mentioned?"

"Good question, Renee," Knox answered. "Remember, specificity refers to the fact that antibodies attack specific antigens. Once produced, the antibody will attack the epitope, the target site on its trigger antigen, anywhere, even *in vitro* in the laboratory. In some instances, serum containing antibodies, antiserum, produced in animals or harvested from humans, is injected into others to fight disease. This transference of preformed antibodies into another person to neutralize or destroy an antigen is termed passive immunization. Thus, as long as the antigen, the aging protein, is the same in all humans, Mrs. Shepard's antibody will be effective against it. In the laboratory, samples of her blood mixed with random human serum have shown agglutination to occur in all cases—strong evidence an antigen-antibody complex has formed."

"What about supplying enough?" Davis asked. "Is Katie Shepard's antibody reproducible?"

"It will be," Knox said. "As long as she is alive, she is a biochemical factory for it. Gruber has stored her serum. Work will soon begin on determining the exact sequence of amino acids comprising it. From there, chemists should be able to synthesize the antibody in abundance. This could take a year or two to complete.

"Gruber is clever," he continued, "and is trying a couple of other techniques in order to complete the process sooner. Gruber believes he can elute the protein from the antibody that binds it, manipulate it, inject the new molecule into an animal, and induce antibody production. This would result in an inexhaustible supply of antiaging protein antiserum. There is another new approach he will try, too, something called monoclonal antibodies made in a lab. It's all in your packets."

The morning discussion continued with further questions and answers. All present were convinced Katie Shepard possessed an antiaging protein antibody capable of halting and reversing aging. Just allocation of the antibody, how it would be paid for, means of its distribution, and geopolitical implications of doing so were discussed.

"I want to thank Dr. Knox for an excellent presentation," the Chairman said. "We will have to decide if we should attempt to harness this phenomenon or if it is too dangerous to do so.

"Perhaps the Babylonians had it right about Fakim," he said as an aside. "It's probably better not to battle 'the forces' and travel down the path of an unclean existence.

"Speaking of natural forces," he said as he looked at his watch, "it's about time for lunch. Before we break, let me bring you up to date on a couple of developments. As of an hour ago, the President's address to the nation is still on for Thursday evening. We believe he will talk about his health, but not even his staff members are sure. Our intercepts don't shed any light on it.

"A problem has also cropped up in Atlanta. Insbrook and Steiner have requested to leave for a while, but there are no provisions in place to do so. If the White House sends its own team to monitor events, that could limit our options. We will have to decide at what point it becomes more dangerous to wait than act."

At exactly noon, the Chairman adjourned the meeting. "The Italian place is open today," he said. "*Mangia!* But please work through lunch and be back in your seats by two. Dalia will present to us then."

"This is one fine hot mess," Kraft muttered in his folksy vernacular as the group departed for their break.

"One fine hot mess," LeSayer repeated, dressed in her signature jeans, sports jacket, and running shoes, arms folded in front of her chest with a look of consternation on her face as she ascended the pitched steps of the Friedman Auditorium with Kraft.

* * *

"How the hell did she get ahold of that stuff?" George Christianson, who was covering events in Atlanta, yelled into the telephone. "She drank wine and took *what* else?" he asked excitedly.

"Seconal," the man at the other end answered. "Apparently, she's been hoarding it in her vagina for a few days."

"*Where?* Her what?"

"Yes. There. Tango, Whiskey, Alpha, Tango. There. She wrapped the pills in a piece of tin foil and hid the bundle of joy in her bundle of joy, if you know what I mean," the salty military man replied.

"Roger, copy that. Do you think Insbrook was involved?" Christianson asked.

"Collusion? No. No way."

"It's quite an oversight for a person as smart as Insbrook," Christianson observed.

"Yes, but he has been quite upset, and he's been with her ever since. If he wanted to kill her, he has had plenty of chances. Besides, we think he's been giving her the high-hard one. They found some fresh gism in there where she was hiding the pills. He's the only man who has been in and out of her room."

"I'm jealous," Christianson said glibly. "I guess he's not so righteous after all. Are you sure she's out of danger?"

"Reasonably sure. She's groggy but awake. They have her on I.V. fluids in order to flush the crap out of her system, and she's being monitored. They pumped her stomach too. She has tubes going in and coming out of every place you can imagine. Poor thing. She should never have had that fender bender in Cincinnati."

"God knows we would be better off if she had succeeded in this little episode, but it wouldn't solve all of our problems," Christianson commented. "As long as Gruber's experiments are intact and they have her serum, the Plasma Cell Project remains a possibility. By the way," he asked the NSA's Atlanta man, "have you had a chance to get up to see what Gruber is up to?"

"We've seen it all. We collected and photographed whatever we could without being detected, and the courier is on his way to you now. It's a two-hour flight. I sent you copies of Gruber's notes and everything else we found."

"Good," Christianson said. "This suicide attempt worries me. The President will strengthen security, which will make it more difficult for us to operate. This may also be all it takes to push him to go through with his project while he thinks he still can. He's quite paranoid these days."

"The President's mental state may actually be working in our favor for now," the Atlanta man said. "At least in my estimation."

"How's that?"

"Two cliques have formed here. One composed of those who favor a Plasma Cell Project and one made up of those who oppose it. Insbrook and Steiner are leading the group that is opposed. They are physicians and have been caring for Katie, so no one outside of their clique is aware of her attempted suicide. I suspect the doctors have chosen to keep it a secret out of fear of reprisal in one form or another or an irrational reaction on the part of the President."

"That's a good assessment. You're doing well," Christianson told his charge.

"Thank you," the trusted agent said. "It's all in my report."

"What's the mood there?" Christianson asked.

"Insbrook is on pins and needles," the field man told him. "He's in a daze. He doesn't know what to do. He wants to go home for a day or two, allegedly to think the situation over and take care of personal business. He definitely complicated things for himself by getting into bed with that girl."

"For sure," Christianson agreed. "If nothing else, we can black-mail him if need be. He's ours. Another man is thinking of the wrong organ. See what you can save from the video feeds. Mark and copy them. Get me some stills too. Those sell newspapers."

"Roger. It's done. We have DNA, too," the Atlanta deputy said. "God forbid it was someone else. My perception is Insbrook is gen-uinely in love with her. They had some kind of romantic dinner last night, but he didn't stay over with her. How are things in Houston?"

"Tense. We're in Category I, as you know. This suicide attempt points to the fact that the longer we wait, the more complications we risk. We'll have to make some decisions soon."

"Don't you think maybe we've already waited too long?" the offi-cer asked.

Christianson knew better than to second guess the Chairman. "I don't think I'll comment on that," he answered, knowing he was likely being monitored or recorded.

LOCKED AND LOADED

Even through the midday break, all thoughts and conversations in Houston revolved around the Plasma Cell crisis. A confrontation with the President seemed unavoidable. The calm that existed within the Agency a few days before had evaporated.

"The Chairman seems to be coming around to my point of view," Atlas told LeSayer and Kraft as the three met in a conference space.

"Alan, I wish you would keep something in mind," Kraft said. He leaned forward as if to tell a secret, which was both unnecessary and impossible within these confines. "No matter what justification we have for it, the course of action you prefer is *illegal*," he said, whispering the last word for emphasis. "We could be prosecuted and strung up by our balls or spend the rest of our lives in solitary for what you suggest. An assassination in Tunis or Santiago is one thing; Washington is another."

"No one will know it was us," Atlas replied.

"Don't be ridiculous. Things are changing out there," Kraft countered. "People are asking questions—the Senate, the House, the media. The only protection we can still count on, ironically enough, is from the White House itself and Directive #9. That's only because the President thinks he knows everything going on, and Dillard is, in fact, a dildo."

"He's right, Alan," Renee said. "They're investigating everybody— the FBI, the IRS, the CIA, everyone. It's the zeitgeist in Washington at the moment. Soon, I fear, it will be our turn on the barrel. At least three oversight committees that have unlimited subpoena powers can get involved. A girlfriend once told me that everything that ends, ends badly. Well, almost everything," she added, blushing with a naughty smile on her face.

"The only one with real information about the NSA is the Agency itself," Atlas confidently told the others. "No Such Agency, remember. Unless one of us talks, we are safe."

"Don't be naïve," Kraft told him. "What if someone on the outside begins to put the pieces together? They could intimidate one of us and offer immunity from prosecution. They could use this RICO thing like Giuliani is doing in the southern district. The mob guys in lower Manhattan are singing to the feds like canaries. Someone here might do the same."

"That's not going to happen. We were psychologically screened, not like those goombahs. We're supposed to be committed to die for this damn agency and country," Atlas said.

"We are human," Kraft replied. "Those mob guys squealed to save their own hides even though they're marked for the rest of their lives. And don't tell me you haven't laid awake at night a few times worrying about the possibility. This is a dangerous game, Alan. They say there is no honor among thieves or spies."

"It's shitty about the possibility of prosecution, but it's a fact," LeSayer agreed. "As Harvey said, they would probably string us up by whatever we have if they knew what we are doing. And for the record, guys, I have bigger balls than the two of you put together. The shame is we are not doing any of this for ourselves. I am not deriving any pleasure from this work anymore. Personally, I'm ready for a baby or two."

"The Army can kill thousands of people or a few people, spend $250 billion a year, and wear medals on their chests," Atlas lamented, "yet if people found out what we accomplish for a couple billion a year and a few deaths, they would send us to prison. How does that make sense?"

"Most of our operations are nonlethal," Kraft responded. "Overhead surveillance, opening people's mail, and looking at telegrams are our strong suits. Not killing our own citizens or the President."

"Yes. But if we need to kill a few people to keep this country safe, so be it," Atlas said. "According to NSA lore, when Ralph Canine became impatient, he used to say, 'When are we going to stop rolling cheek-to-cheek'—by that, he meant jerking off—'and get moving on this?' That's all I'm saying."

"Alan," Kraft responded, "one of the problems with being locked and loaded all the time is the tendency to want to pull the trigger. No disrespect for Ralph intended, but it's not always the wisest thing to do. You do know Ralph died suddenly and unexpectedly, don't you?"

There was momentary silence at the table. People often felt tense around Atlas. Just then, Kraft leaned back in his chair and spotted Bouchikas making his way through the hallway with a broad smile on his face. "There's Chris," he said. "I wonder why he looks so happy. Maybe the crisis is over." The three waved their arms over their heads and attracted Bouchikas's attention.

"Guess what?" Bouchikas announced to them. "There's going to be four in my house soon."

"Is your mother-in-law moving in?" LeSayer joked.

"Ha-ha, Renee. No. Diana's pregnant."

"That's wonderful. You're the man," Atlas told him. "I hope."

"Don't listen to him. That's terrific," Kraft said to Bouchikas in a fatherly manner, standing up to shake his hand and put his arm around him. "When is she due?"

"February first. She's wanted to tell me in person for days, but I never gave her the opportunity. I have been too busy or too stupid to sit down and listen. I'll make it up to her."

"Something will happen by tomorrow night," Atlas assured his colleague. "As soon as we are out of Category I, I'm sure some of us can go home and you can see her."

"I hope you're right," Bouchikas said. "Have you guys heard the news about the Shepard woman? She took an overdose but is still alive. Apparently, she has been hoarding pills. George has the whole story. He will fill us in later," Chris told them. "Things are getting stickier all the time."

"Are you referring to the gism?" Kraft joked, having heard the salacious details of the story already. LeSayer covered her eyes and tried to hold back a laugh. She, too, had heard it.

"Hey," Bouchikas interrupted, "it's almost two o'clock. Let's go."

A MOMENTOUS DECISION

Betsy Friar trotted up the west portico's driveway and rushed past familiar Secret Service agents on her way to the Oval Office. She entered the White House through an unlocked door and almost ran over the chief of staff as he stepped out of his office. Hazelton, the former Marine, was startled by the diminutive Friar and reacted with fright.

"What's going on?" Friar asked Hazelton, having broken a sweat in the Washington humidity.

"I don't know. He called me and said I should come over because he has something urgent to tell us," Hazelton answered. "We only have a few minutes. He's scheduled for a private meeting with his legal counsel. It's on his official calendar. And he has a scheduled dinner afterward."

"I know his schedule," Friar said with annoyance, feeling devalued as a woman on the team.

"Of course you do. Sorry," Hazelton told her. "He asked me to get Buck over here too."

"Buck? Oh, shit!" Friar exclaimed. Buck Donohue was the President's favorite speechwriter, used when he wanted soaring rhetoric for a big occasion.

"Yes," Hazelton answered. "I've been trying to reach him, but I think he's out for a run at Rock Creek. We have a page out for him."

As the two reached the door of the Oval Office, Dixon approached from the opposite direction.

"Dan," Friar said. "Do you know what's going on?"

"I'm not sure. I think he's going to go through with it—the Plasma Cell Project," Dixon speculated.

"So do I," Hazelton agreed. Hazelton knocked on the door, immediately opened it, and the trio continued inside. The President looked relaxed, his brown suit jacket laid across a chair and his shirt sleeves rolled back to his elbows. His tie was loosened, and his stocking feet were resting on his treasured *Resolute* desk, a gift of Queen Victoria to President Hayes. The President was wearing his horn-rimmed spectacles and reading from a report that rested in his lap.

"Come in, come in," the President said. "I'm looking at this garbage from that congressional committee. Some of those guys will be sorry when this is all over. They ought to get off my back. Haven't they heard of the separation of powers? I should impeach *their* asses. Where is Buck, Steve?"

"We're still trying to get hold of him. I paged him and left a message with his service."

"OK. You three can fill him in. Sit down, will you," he said. The President was in a better mood than he had been in for weeks. "I've come to a decision with regard to this Plasma Cell Project," he said in a relaxed tone.

"And?" Hazelton inquired.

"I have decided to go ahead with it," he said. "It's the domestic issue I need. I can't pass it up. I cannot choose for millions of people whether or not they want to participate in such a plan. Each person can decide for themselves. I will take the helm and lead this effort, and I hope you will all be on board. We will bring in the most talented experts and advisors we can find. Maybe even this fellow

Insbrook can help us. He seems like a smart guy. What do you say? Can I count on you?"

"I'm not thrilled about it," Dixon responded. "But of course I will stick with you."

"And you?" the President asked Hazelton as he coldly looked him in the eye.

Hazelton turned away. "You know, it's crazy how elected officials are called upon to make decisions about areas in which they have no real knowledge."

"What are you saying?" the President queried.

"Nothing, really," Hazelton said, looking back at his boss. "You are the commander in chief. It's your decision. I'm not a firm no, but I will need to think it over. I might want to spend more time with my grandchildren. I will give you fair warning if I decide to leave."

"What about you, my dear?" the President asked Betsy in a patronizing tone.

"Whatever you say," the press secretary, who secretly hoped she someday would replace Hazelton and become the first female chief of staff to the President, answered.

Face-to-face with the President in the confines of the Oval Office, each person's resistance largely crumbled. The President had operated this way for years, with creepy charm, psychological manipulation, and arm-twisting when necessary.

"I will be going on the air Thursday to inform the nation. Not a word is to be leaked as to content to anyone beforehand. I will need Buck to help me craft something. Afterward, the only information that will go out will originate from this office. This is still classified," the President said firmly. "I don't want any leaks—do you understand?"

"Yes, sir," Hazelton said. "We will start making arrangements."

"The press corps is already asking questions about that address," Friar informed her boss. "They want to know what it's all about. What would you like me to tell them?"

"Tell them they will have to wait," the President replied. "You are good at handling that bunch."

A DYSTOPIAN FUTURE

The Chairman and his fellow Council members assembled in the Friedman Auditorium. The room was named for and dedicated to William F. Friedman, the founder of the US Signal Intelligence Service and generally considered to be the father of cryptology in America. In fact, Friedman coined the very word, a term that encompasses both the sciences of code-making and code-breaking. A Romanian-born Jew (born Wolf Friedman in 1891), Friedman developed an interest in the subject of secret codes after reading Edgar Allen Poe's short story "The Gold Bug." By 1920, he had written eight monographs on the subject. Along with a team that included his wife, Elizabeth, also a cryptologist, Friedman is credited with cracking the Japanese Purple code, akin to British mathematician Alan Turing and his Ultra team at Bentley Park cracking the German Enigma code during World War II. Friedman spent the remainder of his career at the NSA after its founding in 1952.

Prior to his death, at the request of the NSA, Friedman prepared a series of six lectures titled *On Cryptology and Cryptanalysis*. The source materials for these lectures were considered so sensitive that the Agency forcefully confiscated them from Friedman's home after his death for storage at its Fort Meade facility, where they remain classified today. Though the Agency traced its roots back to him, Friedman himself, a man of unquestionable intellect and honesty, could never have imagined what the NSA would morph into or what it was about to take up in the auditorium that bore his name.

Dalia Abrahamyan was at the lectern. Her comments referred to the slide projected on the screen behind her.

LEADING CAUSES OF DEATH, 1986

ETIOLOGY	PERCENT
DISEASES OF THE HEART	30.9
CANCER	16.8
STROKE	10.9
ACCIDENTS	6.1
CHRONIC OBSTRUCTIVE PULMONARY DX	3.3
PNEUMONIA and INFLUENZA	3.0
DIABETES MELLITUS	2.8
SUICIDE	2.6
PERIPHERAL VASCULAR DISEASE	2.0
CHRONIC LIVER DISEASE	1.9
OTHER	19.7
TOTAL DEATHS	2,105,361

Source: CDC/NCHS, National Vital
Statistics System. Mortality

"As you can see in this chart, most of the leading causes of death in the United States in 1986 arose out of the aging process. Fifty years ago, the list of leading causes of death was vastly different, with people dying earlier and much more often of infectious diseases and childbirth. Conditions such as cardiovascular disease, diabetes, kidney ailments, and others were treated less effectively than today. If we were to remove aging as a factor, the list would undergo an even more drastic change and in a few years might resemble the next slide."

LEADING CAUSES OF DEATH, EX-AGING, 2001 (THEORETICAL*)

ETIOLOGY	PERCENT
TRAUMA	22.1
HOMICIDE	17.6
SUICIDE	11.1
WAR	9.9
INFECTIOUS DISEASES/PESTILENCE	9.1
STARVATION	3.3
CANCER	2.2
PNEUMONIA	1.8
DIABETES	1.5
OTHER	20.4
TERMINATION OF LIFE	?
TOTAL DEATHS	451,291

The Nobel-winning population expert continued to expound. "Just a few days ago, we discussed the concept of carrying capacity in reference to sending food to starving regions of the world, and I emphasized that unless birth rates and death rates are closely matched, the planet's already swollen population will not be sustainable. If we eliminate the common factor that underlies the leading causes of death in most parts of the world—aging—we would be faced with the choice of placing draconian controls on birth or enacting a government program of termination of life. Neither is universally acceptable, certainly not in our country.

"By keeping the population young, we would be maintaining them in their most reproductive state," Abrahamyan continued. "Let me quickly dismiss birth control. There are few successful birth control programs in the world, and successful ones uniformly depend on abortion as a backup, something a large proportion of Americans, including the President, oppose. In a piece I recently wrote for *Population*, I suggested that countries might one day need to control their populations by putting a potent contraceptive in the drinking water and making an antidote available to selected individuals. Such programs would be difficult to administer and be heavily fraught with privileges, prejudices, value judgments, and other evils not acceptable in democratic societies. It would amount to modern eugenics, a discussion of 'lives not worth living.' A Plasma Cell Project would put greater pressure on our scarce resources and only hasten the day for such dystopian options."

Chris Bouchikas, the newly informed father-to-be, spoke next. "I, for one, am not ready to trade my right to have children and grandchildren for increased longevity for myself," he said. "I am against this scheme."

"Most people will not want an either/or choice," Abrahamyan said. "People will want both. We will have no control over other countries' choices. Past attempts to export American values and norms have failed miserably. In crowded streets around the world, food exports from the West are wildly received while contraception goes unfetched. Similarly, I suspect we would see a clamor for the aging antidote but not for concomitant birth control."

"A critical point," the Chairman commented. "We will have no control over the proliferation of the Plasma Cell Project were it to begin. Each country will go its own way as to how to develop and use it, like the bomb. Our country is affected not only by our own decisions but by those of other countries. The demands for sharing our resources are already at a fevered pitch in parts of the world, driven largely by their teeming populations, envy, and desperate circumstances. Underdeveloped countries would wage war against us, and migration pressures would increase. This is what we will face if we unleash a Plasma Cell Project. Dalia, can you tell us what kind of numbers we are talking about and how soon can we expect them?"

"The population in this country could double in around eighteen years," Abrahamyan answered. "For countries with high birth rates, the doubling time would be shorter."

"What would be the consequences in this country?" he prompted.

"Housing two hundred million more people would mean the construction of thousands of urban high-rise projects with their attendant social problems," Dalia answered. "Demand for raw and processed goods will double and quickly wipe out our surpluses. Prices of everything will rise. Beef will become scarce and only be available to the affluent. Reserves of energy sources and other commodities will be used up twice as fast every eighteen years. Water will become scarce for some. Because of further industrialization and efficiency, including through robots that don't eat, as the population increases, jobs will not keep up. Education will be a challenge. A larger percentage of the population will be unemployed and in poverty. Crime will skyrocket, and policing will be a challenge. Sewage systems will be strained. In short, we will have an increasingly hazardous society with widespread ignorance, poverty, crime, infectious diseases, and violence. As an earlier slide indicated, suicides, homicides, and accidents will skyrocket in our Soylent Green America."

It was 2:52 p.m. Time had run out for Abrahamyan's doomsday peroration. "Why don't I open this up to a discussion," she suggested.

"A Plasma Cell Project is obviously intolerable," Davis said. "I think any action we may take in conflict with the President's is legitimate," he said, looking at his boss.

"I think it is clear any action we take would have the nation's best interests at heart," the Chairman responded. "Whatever we do would be a patriotic act. It is arguable that the President is impaired and could be removed from office under the Twenty-Fifth Amendment if there were time. I would prefer to see it play out that way."

"I would like to bring up a related issue," Christianson said. "The goal of most medical research is the prolongation of life. The Plasma Cell discovery is consonant with that goal and yet undesirable. Should we also be addressing other research?" he asked.

"What you say about the goal of medical research is true," Abrahamyan answered. "If we examine the cost-benefit analysis of what we spend on such research, we might conclude that the money could be better spent on sustaining the present population with a better quality of life. Better education, housing, and all that. Of course, this is my own prejudice as a population biologist and an avowed liberal," she mused. "But to your point, there is research in this country and elsewhere directly focused on the goal of eventually 'curing' aging, if you will. If someone were to discover something similar to what was stumbled upon, we might be faced with this same situation again."

Suddenly, a red light flashed on the phone in front of the Chairman. He picked it up and turned visibly pale as his conversation progressed. The rest of the conversations in the room trailed off. The Chairman was trembling as he informed the others. "The President has made up his mind. He plans to announce the Plasma Cell Project to the world Thursday evening."

Bouchikas stopped thinking about his pregnant wife. Renee forgot about getting pregnant. Atlas was no longer interested in battling with his fellow Council members. Abrahamyan's disquisition was finished. There was much work to be done.

DAY ELEVEN

May 13, 1987

After life's fitful fever, he sleeps well
Treason has done his worst: not steel nor poison,
Malice domestic, (nor) foreign levy.
Nothing can touch him further.

—WILLIAM SHAKESPEARE, *MACBETH*, 1623

OPERATION FREEDOM

Atlas looked at himself in the mirror in his Houston living quarters. Clad in a camouflage T-shirt, fatigue pants, and high-laced leather boots, with a muscular chest and biceps and a stare so focused it previously drove chess opponents to the breaking point, he was a fearsome man.

"Hee-yah!" he yelled as he kicked high and spun around, practicing his Tae Kwon Do and Krav Maga. He was scheduled to leave in fifteen minutes, and the excitement was overwhelming him.

Were it for any other reason, Atlas would have hated to leave on this night, but the major issues had been settled, and it was left to the Chairman to complete the execution of the plan. This was the moment Atlas had been waiting for. As he kicked and twisted and cut the air violently with his hands and feet, Atlas could almost taste blood. He could smell the jungles. He could feel a revolution.

The orders had come across only two hours earlier in an envelope marked *Top Secret/Umbra*, hand-delivered to him by a uniformed Marine officer accompanied by a security flank. The details were sketchy, but more would be provided at a classified staging facility near Miami. The orders came from the very top. If the National

Security Council and the Joint Chiefs were involved, obviously so was the President.

Atlas wondered whether this was what the crafty President really planned to announce during his press conference the following night. He speculated on this possibility to Christianson when he called to say goodbye and gave his friend a vague idea of his assignment. He also expressed disappointment the NSA was totally frozen out of the planning. How did the final planning for this operation, the seeds of which Atlas himself had sown four years earlier, escape NSA ears? Perhaps the Chairman was losing his grip.

The NSA and its Chairman were not Atlas's greatest concerns. His thoughts were focused on something far more exciting, intoxicating, and appealing to his alpha male instincts. Soon a helicopter would arrive to carry him from a small private airfield on the outskirts of Houston to the Florida Everglades, where the Yankee Transport Company (YTC), secretly run by the CIA, based its operations. Inside a hangar at YTC, he would hook up with other members of the command for Operation Freedom. By dawn, Operation Freedom would embark on its historic mission to overthrow the government of Nicaragua's charismatic strongman, Daniel Ortega.

As he waited for the call to leave his apartment, Atlas stopped in front of a framed 24" x 48" poster from the 1972 film *Last Tango in Paris*. Marlon Brando was seated, crying, across from his dead wife, Rosa, who had committed suicide and was surrounded by a bed of flowers. At the bottom of the poster was a quote from his emotional soliloquy.

Even if a husband lives two hundred fucking years
He'll never discover his wife's true nature.
I may be able to understand the secrets of the universe
But I'll never understand the truth about you. Never.

It was decidedly Alan Atlas. Machismo, vulgarity, cynicism, unrequited love, obsession with secrecy, and bitterness. All there for him to absorb each time he entered or left his Texas dwelling.

PAPA SETTLES THE SCORE

The fearsome Chinook 47D helicopter with its tandem rotors was an awkward beast but got the job done. Atlas loaded his two oversized duffle bags onto the craft. One was filled with clothing, books, and a sleeping bag. The other contained papers, radio-communications equipment, a chess board, an ArmaLite-15, and a cache of fuses and explosives. His last time in the field was off New Zealand during the not-too-challenging task of sinking an antinuclear group's peace ship. His role during the Grenada campaign, to his extreme displeasure, was limited to observing and reporting from a destroyer. This time, he was assured, he would hit the beach with the leathernecks on the western side of Nicaragua.

Such were the visions that danced in Alan Atlas's head as the Chinook began the horizontal portion of its flight, lumbering over the Florida Panhandle when, from behind a curtain, stepped the familiar silhouette of the Chairman.

"Alan, you son of a bitch," the Chairman said quietly. "You can't work for yourself in this business." He pointed an automatic pistol at Atlas, the martial arts specialist, as he kept a safe distance from him. "You either work for me, or you work for no one."

Having not yet understood, Atlas looked at his superior in defiant disbelief. "You can't take this mission away from me, too," he protested as beads of perspiration appeared on his forehead. "I'm going in this time."

"There is no mission, Rambo," the Chairman said in a steely tone. "Your treachery is over. Echo Tango Sierra. Expiration, Term of Service, motherfucker." With that, he plugged the troublesome councilor between his eyes with a single round fired from his M9 service weapon.

"Take care of him," he told his lieutenant. "Put a Band-Aid on his head and wrap him up, will you?" he said as he dispassionately reached for an overhead bin, grabbed his briefcase, and stored his Beretta inside for another day.

THE BURDEN OF RESPONSIBILITY

L ate at night, the NSA Chairman sat at his desk, alone in his apartment at the Houston complex, and made a notation on the outside of a manila file, anticipating that he would be the one to eventually pen the final Plasma Cell Report. The Chairman was only the third person to hold the post in the NSA's thirty-five-year history. During that time, the position, like the Agency, grew and evolved from its roots. By 1987, the NSA Chairman was one of the most powerful people in the world, having at his disposal the most heavily financed, technologically advanced, and far-reaching espionage web ever spun in the free world and probably anywhere—its chief rival for the mantle being the USSR's KGB.

The Chairman was a master at finessing related agencies into carrying out the NSA's plans. The NSA employed thousands of people who were also on FBI and CIA payrolls and often didn't know exactly for whom they worked. All government employees received the same colorful treasury checks Americans are used to getting for their tax refunds. Some NSA employees assumed they were working for a super-secret branch of the CIA and dared not ask questions. They had signed nondisclosure agreements punishable by years in prison.

The Agency's chief took advantage of presidents, using them to request other domestic and foreign intelligence agencies to do the NSA's bidding. The Chairman knew he could give the President misleading or false information as justification for an NSA operation, and once he approved it, it would be carried out without question by the FBI, CIA, the military, or a law enforcement agency.

Like his predecessors, the Chairman persuaded the President to adopt an attitude of benign neglect toward the NSA and by precedent to look the other way. As a result, the Agency operated beyond the reach of the President. One reason the NSA was able to stay so anonymous was that its internal organization, including its leadership, was stable and not subject to elections while eight administrations had come and gone.

The NSA carefully controlled the information about itself that was released to the executive branch. The NSA chairmen convinced each president that their agency's work was essential to national security and that asking too many questions might upset the NSA's delicate operations. If asked about a matter directly, the chairmen often quoted Director Canine, who famously told an inquiring congressman during an intelligence committee hearing, "I don't think you would want to be burdened with the responsibility of that information."

Besides, there was Directive #9, which was never challenged, repealed, or replaced. It wasn't intended to be this way when Truman initially authorized the NSA, thinking he was merely creating a placeholder, but left unchecked, it evolved into a well-financed, powerful, and entrenched deep-state actor, not accountable to anyone.

The only information Council members themselves knew about the Agency came from the Chairman, who kept them as ignorant or well-informed as he thought advantageous. He sought to humble these geniuses to the point where they could work for someone without questioning their authority. In corporate parlance, he was the CEO, and the rest of the Cs all rolled into one. There was no board of directors, no CFO, and no audit committee. If an Agency employee had an objection to an action of the Chairman, they had no recourse; they had no one else to turn to except one another, an action that carried risks.

Each Council member had a personal relationship with the Chairman, the nature of which was unbeknownst to the others. The Chairman insisted that while he treated his Council members firmly, it was always fairly, and he believed he meted out punishments and rewards like an old-fashioned father: fairly, with good reason, clear explanation, and a strong hand.

Perhaps that's why he did the dirty work with Atlas himself, face-to-face.

Some on the Council had begun to feel that the Chairman forced his preferences past them and used them as a rubber stamp when it came to critical decisions. Council members were, in fact, integral parts of the Agency's operating machinery. Each was a capable administrator who oversaw critical matters in their areas of expertise and supervised dozens of employees and contractors. The Chairman preached there were four elements necessary for success: vision, planning, execution, and follow-through, and he demanded adherence to his mantra.

In difficult matters, it was the Chairman who had ultimate responsibility for executing the NSA's plans. While this made the job of the Council members easier, it reciprocally made the Chairman's job more burdensome. From where did the Chairman's authority come? Who made his word absolute? Why should he control the fate of millions of people? The Chairman knew these would be the questions prosecutors would ask if the Agency's operations ever came to light, and these were the questions he asked himself on nights like this. Those who knew the head of the NSA might have assumed he did not lie awake at night thinking about such matters, but he did.

The Chairman's job was thankless and lonely. He was believed to be without family or friends. The son of a four-star general and a high school principal, he was a deeply religious man who prayed to his God in private and kept his secrets between the Lord and himself, having given up sacramental confession after his altar-boy days. Even when he confided in an associate at the Agency, his confidence was calculated. While he maintained a residence in a Washington suburb to avoid suspicion, the Chairman was mostly domiciled within his NSA confines in Houston and rarely ventured outside. He had no real time off, a modest salary, and little need for money. For entertainment, on weekends he sometimes picked up videotapes and microwave popcorn at the local Blockbuster store, where he was anonymous. He had little contact with the outside world. No women and no known friends. He received no praise, no thanks, and no recognition for the work he did, nor did he ever expect it. In his own way, he was a patriot who had devoted his life to his country in the belief he was safeguarding it from harm.

The aging Chairman, now out of shape and not at all the trim man he had been as a Notre Dame track star decades before, rubbed his eyes and ran his hands through his shock of white hair. He drank from the rare glass of wine he poured himself, cinched up his silky bathrobe, and continued work on his journal. Perhaps trying to ease his conscience and justify the actions his covert organization had authorized, as well as the assassination he carried out earlier in the evening, the Chairman made a tabulation, presumably in part as supplication for success in the days to come.

"America is dependent for its survival on its three branches of government, as well as its agencies, corporations, mainstream institutions, and a free press. Let us examine the accomplishments of all these on their most recent workdays.

"**The President:** Attended a private prayer service and received

Eucharist at St. John's Episcopal Church on the advice of his political team. He later met with two influential advisors, both nonelected, one a lawyer and the other an ex-senator, during which he planned his legal defense against charges that he supplied arms and cash to freedom fighters in violation of the will of Congress. In the evening, the President entertained the leader of a country who had seized power in a military coup seven years earlier.

"**The Senate:** The finance committee voted to reduce next year's budget by 2 percent. A bipartisan group pushed through an anti-busing amendment to an appropriations bill as it moved through committee. The majority also voted not to authorize federal funds for mass transit projects in major cities.

"**The House:** A subcommittee killed a bill that would have increased GI benefits and VA funding. The full body voted to post-humously award the Congressional Medal of Honor to a Marine of Guatemalan origin who saved the life of a general by throwing his body over a live hand grenade during the last days of American involvement in the Vietnam War. A retired Army colonel appeared before the armed services committee testifying as to his role in illegal weapons sales.

"**The Two-Party System:** A leading candidate for the presidency threw in the towel because of charges of sexual misconduct including adultery. In a poll, the majority of Americans believe spying on politicians' personal lives is acceptable.

"**The Supreme Court:** In a dinner speech, a justice criticized the Constitution as a flawed document because its original text discounted the rights of Blacks and women. Separately, the Court, with one woman and one Black justice, refused to hear arguments in a case that alleged discrimination in the way the death penalty was applied in Texas.

"**The Military:** Five Marines were charged with spying in

exchange for sexual favors from prostitutes at American embassies in Moscow and two other Eastern bloc countries. Dozens of others are under investigation.

"**The FBI:** A committee of Congress ordered the FBI to remove listening devices in Washington embassies meant to monitor the conversations of foreign ambassadors. It was revealed the FBI was investigating alleged bribes paid by government agencies and public corporations to Gulf State sheiks. Jack Turner, the FBI director, declined to comment.

"**The CIA:** Illegal activities on American soil and the death of an African head of state killed in a plane crash several months ago have been linked to the CIA. The current director of the CIA was vacationing with his wife and college-age children at an undisclosed location.

"**The NSA:** The Agency intercepted five thousand letters and telegrams, uncovering a plot by terrorists to explode two backpacks filled with shrapnel in proximity to the wife and children of a former US president in New York in an effort to change US foreign policy in the Middle East. It also handed over to the Justice Department tapes of conversations gathered under FISA warrants of foreign citizens meeting with Americans in the Hay-Adams Hotel across from the White House who intended to commit crimes. It delivered evidence to federal authorities meant to lead to the destruction, dissolution, and prosecution of a $3-billion-a-year international cocaine ring.

"The NSA Council also convened a Category I meeting and debated what to do about the President's intention to deploy on a massive scale an antiaging antibody being produced naturally by a terminally ill woman named Katie Shepard, in what he called the 'Plasma Cell Project.' The Council unanimously adopted three resolutions:

" 1. Katie Shepard, her antiaging antibody, and any knowledge thereof shall be destroyed. Efforts underway related to building a Plasma Cell Project shall be destroyed.

"2. Worldwide experimentation aimed at extreme test-tube extension of lifespan through halting or reversing aging will be thwarted if possible.

"3. The NSA will accomplish these objectives, without limitation, as soon as possible."

After the Chairman penned this, he closed his journal, finished his drink, and headed off to bed in his modest apartment. The next few days were expected to be hectic.

A RIDE WITH MR. COOPER

Shortly before midnight, Philip Insbrook flew to Cincinnati at his request in order to attend to affairs at home. He was told a little earlier that security clearances were complete, and his "pass" from the Atlanta complex had been approved by the President. He was instructed to prepare to leave as soon as possible because his private flight would need to be "wheels-up" within thirty minutes to avoid detection. He was further instructed not to speak with anyone about what he had seen or heard regarding the Shepard matter.

Katie Shepard's condition had stabilized. The most serious residual effect of her suicide attempt was a small upper lobe pneumonia, probably due to aspiration of secretions while she was comatose, an event that could have been catastrophic because of Katie's decreased ability to battle infection. Although he was concerned, by the time Insbrook left, the ill-fated woman was not systemically ill, with stable vital signs and normal oxygenation of her blood. Insbrook judged leaving her in the hands of a competent military pulmonologist was not perilous. In any event, he could not back out of leaving since it would risk exposing the suicide attempt, which he mistakenly believed he had successfully covered up until this point.

Insbrook was confused as he left Atlanta. He did not under-stand exactly who was in charge. Somewhere along the way, the Plasma Cell affair had gotten too big for him to control, and he found himself taking orders from unknown commanders. He also found himself behaving extremely defensively out of fear, which was unusual for him.

He needed to keep trying, though, to prevent the Plasma Cell discovery from destroying the world. So, he would go home for a day or two and try to clear his head. He sought to separate from Katie as well since he realized he had crossed professional boundar-ies and knew nothing good could come of their relationship. In the meantime, he planned to further extricate himself from his univer-sity responsibilities, signing himself completely off of his hospital cases and having Shaw tend to his administrative responsibilities. Insbrook wanted to arrange an official leave of absence from his job but wasn't sure where he could go for approval. He had been handed a court order not to discuss the Plasma Cell Project with public offi-cials or anyone else. Some of the people he encountered in Atlanta weren't what he was used to in medicine and seemed like they would play rough. Insbrook had begun to fear for his life.

The physician was met at the door outside of his Atlanta quar-ters by a running limousine with three occupants inside.

"My name is Cooper," the man in the rear seat told him. "I'm with the State Department. We're going to take you to the airport," he said, motioning to the open rear door for Insbrook to get inside.

Insbrook bent over, looked suspiciously at the man in the car, and reluctantly obeyed. In the front seat were a driver and a female partner in the other seat, who each turned to greet and shake hands with their special passenger. Both sported faintly tinted sunglasses, despite the hour. Cooper got out to close Insbrook's door, scurried back around, got in, and slammed the door. "Let's go," he said.

The limousine sped away from the Atlanta complex, clearing a guardhouse without stopping at the gates that flung open as they approached. The doctor looked back nervously. It occurred to him he might not survive this trip to the airport. Cooper pressed a button on a console, and a thick panel separating the front and rear cabins rolled up and sealed shut. Insbrook's heartbeat accelerated as fear gripped his entire body. The State Department man placed his black briefcase on a small table he folded down in front of him.

"Do you mind if I turn on a light?" Cooper asked.

"No. Go ahead," Insbrook replied nervously.

Cooper opened the briefcase and took out an envelope from atop a stack of papers. "For you, sir," he said to the startled Insbrook, hand-delivering a linen envelope bearing a gold-embossed presidential seal on the rear top center. Flicking on a reading lamp, Insbrook opened the envelope and read the letter inside.

Dear Dr. Insbrook,

Thank you for your help in uncovering the Plasma Cell situation and bringing it to the early attention of the government of the United States. It has been most valuable. Your dedication, foresight, and unselfish patriotism have averted the improper application of this information and the ramifications thereof. On behalf of the American people, I would like to thank you for your actions.

According to your suggestion, the Plasma Cell information will be destroyed. Mrs. Shepard will be adequately looked after until the time of her natural death. It is the intent of the government that no report of this whole affair will ever see the light of day.

As the above matters are of vital interest to the national security of the United States and will be attended to by the proper agencies of government, you are hereby relieved of your duties in this matter. You are advised not to mention any of the events of the past week and a half to anyone. To avoid suspicion, it would be best if you returned to work and assumed your professional responsibilities as soon as possible.

My representative will remain in touch with you and will supply details regarding the final disposition of this matter. For obvious reasons, you are asked to kindly return this letter to Mr. Cooper after you have read it.

It has been my honor to work with you. Thank you for your service.

Sincerely yours,

The letter bore the familiar signature of the President of the United States.

Insbrook's hands trembled as he passed the letter back to Cooper, leaned back, and let out an audible sigh. He was both shocked and relieved the President had made such a turnaround and accepted his advice. But then, he was suspicious too. Why was he, Insbrook, informed in such an unusual manner? Why was he given the letter only after the limousine cleared the health complex? Who was this Mr. Cooper, and why had Insbrook previously neither seen nor heard of him?

The one thing Insbrook knew for sure was that he was out of the picture, and whatever the White House had really decided was beyond his control. If, in fact, the President decided what was stated in the letter, all would be well—except for Katie, of course, who was doomed either way. But if the White House decided differently, Insbrook was left without recourse.

So, the prominent physician flew home late Wednesday night, intent on resuming his former duties as advised, while hoping and praying that for the good of mankind he was being told the truth.

DAY TWELVE
{PRIVATE}

May 14, 1987

Do not try to live forever. You will not succeed.

—GEORGE BERNARD SHAW

AN EARLY MORNING CALL

At 5:30 a.m., the familiar persistent ring of a phone filled Insbrook's spacious, mostly empty residence. The doctor, who had only slept for a few hours, stumbled toward the phone as he had done hundreds of times before in the middle of hundreds of other nights. Francisco Gomez, Insbrook's houseman and sometimes driver, got to the phone first and picked it up on the seventh ring. He handed the receiver to his employer and awaited instructions.

"This is Dr. Insbrook," Insbrook croaked into the receiver.

"Dr. Insbrook," a female with a Belizean accent whom he didn't recognize said. "This is the hospital calling. I'm sorry to call so early. A patient you saw is comatose, and we can't reach his attending physician. Mr. O'Neil suffered a respiratory arrest and is being moved to the ICU right now. He was intubated by the code blue team. His blood sugar is normal. Could you come to the hospital to see him?"

"Is the resident not there?" the exhausted Insbrook queried.

"She is, but she is exceptionally busy," the nurse informed him. "She got called to another code and asked me to call you."

"I'll be right there," Insbrook responded.

Philip Insbrook hurriedly dressed and raced out the wide front doors of his colonial-style home, intent on saving the life of a patient. His dark silhouette appeared in the night in a black suit, still tying a thin black necktie as he rushed out into the early dawn, past a cluster of bushes, toward his car.

It is safe to assume the victim never saw the barrel of the shotgun that fired twice on target, exploding his skull and splattering brains across the white bricks of Insbrook's stately home. The ski-masked man who fired the shots reached over the lifeless body, retrieved a wristwatch, and rushed to a waiting van that sped away. Ironically, as he had tried to get to sleep earlier in the morning, Insbrook had thought that unless the Plasma Cell Project could be destroyed during his lifetime, he might only achieve peace of mind through his own death.

Buried in the afternoon edition of the *Plain Dealer* was an account of Professor Insbrook's brutal murder. His wristwatch was taken in a senseless robbery. An anonymous caller told Cincinnati police he saw three African American youths commit the horrendous crime and flee the scene on foot.

THE DEATH OF A PRESIDENT

T he headlines on May 14, 1987, did not only concern Philip Insbrook. They were *PRESIDENT DEAD*, below which, in a smaller font, was *Vice President Sworn in in Private Ceremony*.

The President had gone to bed a little before 1:00 a.m., at which time the White House physician administered a short-acting sedative, evening doses of his Parkinson's medications, and digitalis per the usual routine. A few hours later, the same physician who slept close to the private residence was summoned to attempt to revive the President, who was found pulseless and apneic by his wife. An hourlong attempt at resuscitation failed, and the nation's leader was pronounced dead at 5:00 a.m.

The world was informed of the peaceful demise of the American president three hours later. He died of a badly diseased heart on the morning before he had been scheduled to address the nation, reportedly to discuss his health problems. Thus, on May 14, 1987, the moral and righteous Vice President who vehemently opposed the Plasma Cell Project ascended to the nation's highest office, having been sworn in by the Chief Justice during an early morning ceremony at his residence.

The President's family refused an autopsy, and an elaborate state funeral was arranged after the President spent twenty-four hours lying in state in the Rotunda. Thousands streamed by to view his flag-draped casket. As Insbrook had feared about himself, the President would achieve peace through his death that he could never have known during life. Supporters of the President claimed he left a legacy of economic rebirth, strengthened national defense, made America proud, and stood up to the evil forces in the world. They also cited diplomatic advances, opening up whole regions of the world to better lives for their people and better relations with the United States. Detractors pointed to a morally weakened America, a national debt that had doubled in seven years, a battered dollar, and a world armed to the teeth. Only time would tell which epitaph would survive.

* * *

Meanwhile, the blighted Plasma Cell Project suffered disasters of its own.

As he did every morning, Karl Gruber arrived at his laboratory at half past six and lit one of the Prima cigarettes he still had imported from Ukraine. He turned a key, opened the door to his lab, and was met by a thunderous explosion that rocked the Eisenhower lab building and blew the body of the gerontologic researcher to pieces. A flash fire occurred instantaneously and consumed the entire third and fourth floors of the research building. According to an examination of records from Southern Company Gas, the cause of the explosion was believed to have been the ignition of natural gas leaking from a feedline to a row of Meker-Fisher burners that accumulated after a recent repair. The intact body of Major Toliver McDermott, who apparently had fallen asleep near the lab the night of the explosion, was thrown clear of the fire and recovered nearly sixty feet from the building. According to the Fulton County coroner, autopsy findings confirmed primary methane poisoning along with blunt force injuries as the causes of his death, deemed accidental on his death certificate.

Carly Steiner of the NIH was killed in a fiery auto mishap as she headed home early on the morning of May 14. The brakes on her older model Volvo, devoid of brake fluid, had locked up. On call in Washington, HHS Undersecretary Braun was struck by a hit-and-run driver as he stepped from a taxi into oncoming traffic while inebriated. Lillian White became seriously ill that day, was placed on a ventilator at Grady Memorial Hospital, and died ten days later of a rare meningoencephalitis. Dr. Jack Shaw, who had recently been depressed, was found dead in his bed in Cincinnati, a glass of whiskey on his nightstand and an empty bottle of painkillers beside him. Stuart Atherton was sent on a classified assignment in Marrakesh, never to be heard from again. Coincidentally on May 14, a grand jury returned indictments against Secretary Stanley Dillard and several of his associates on charges of conspiracy, bribery, money laundering, and mail fraud. By dusk, a distraught Betsy Friar fatally shot herself through her chest in Fort Marcy Park after filling her station wagon with mementos from her years of service in the White House as keepsakes for her children. The Vice President's press secretary had replaced her earlier in the day.

Thousands of people die in America each day, often from accidental and violent causes. Unsolved crimes were a staple in American society in 1987. There would be no reason for anyone to suspect any connection between the various events of May 14. Consider that over the forty-seven-hour span that began with the assassination of President John F. Kennedy at 12:30 p.m. CST on November 22, 1963, and ended with the killing of Lee Harvey Oswald at 11:21 a.m. CST on November 24, six policemen were killed, a famous American author died, a prominent journalist took fatally ill, an influential Chicago banker was killed by a hit-and-run driver, and a high-ranking military official died of cardiac arrest at Walter Reed Hospital in Bethesda, Maryland. These facts are only included in this report to support the notion that even when a president dies, life and death in America go on.

A GRISLY TRIP TO THE MORGUE

An NSA operative had one last task to oversee before he left the National Research Hospital complex Wednesday morning. His heart raced with fear and anxiety as he would momentarily complete the last phase of his sordid mission and then head back to Houston to join his NSA compatriots. The highly trained saboteur was pleased with what he and his assistants had accomplished in Georgia and was elated thinking of the accolades he would receive from his superiors at the NSA. For now, he concentrated on disposing of his last problem: completing his assignment.

Most of the commotion at the Atlanta complex had died down as city firefighters doused the smoldering Eisenhower laboratories from which multiple dead and injured people had been removed. News crews assembled outside the perimeter fence while competing helicopters flew overhead under FAA control. Noxious smoke produced by a combination of chemicals and burning flesh permeated the air, including that of the isolated underground corridors that the senior agent and his assistant traversed. The fumes sickened the junior officer who complained about it and vomited, while the hardened senior agent held a wet hand cloth over his mouth and ignored the smell.

The two NSA field agents moved briskly alongside a gurney they wheeled between them. After a series of right-hand turns in the basement hallway, they arrived at a short corridor that ended abruptly. They stopped in front of a door starkly marked *Morgue*. The stretcher they were transporting bore the corpse of a slender young woman, covered with a double layer of white linens. The aide turned a key and opened the door to the animal crematorium located in the vivarium while the senior agent pulled back the shroud slightly and took a final photograph of the peaceful, lifeless face of Katie Shepard. Inhaling another breath of foul air, the aide resisted an urge to vomit as he entered the furnace room to complete his gruesome task. He forcefully shoved the woman's petite body into an oven built for dead mongrels, ignited it, and firmly closed the door behind him.

Minutes later, once they had concluded their assignment, a helicopter arrived to ferry the men back to base. Once the chopper was in the air, the junior officer fell to his death in the marshlands below.

DIFFICULTY SLEEPING

George Christianson was reading *Red Storm Rising* when he heard a knock at his door and saw Renee LeSayer through the peephole. He opened the door a slight bit. "Renee, what's wrong?" he asked.

"I can't sleep," she said. "Can I come in?" Dressed in a white terry cloth bathrobe, she was holding a bottle of white wine in her left hand.

"Sure," George told her. "I couldn't sleep either. I was reading the latest Tom Clancy book before bed, the follow-up to *Red October*. But I would rather have company. Come in."

She poured each of them a glass of wine. "I hate these nights," Renee told him in a gentle voice. "It reminds me of my nights in Beirut or Erbil when I heard shelling and explosions and knew an operation was going to go down. Tomorrow, there will be children without a parent and parents without a child. There will be funerals. Widows and widowers. Lives ruined. Whole families destroyed." She looked out the window with tears streaming down her cheeks.

"Yes. And there will be lives saved. This is a tough business we are in," Christianson said, trying to comfort her. "We have to focus on the big picture."

"I know you're right, but we are responsible. I'm sorry to seem needy. What about you, George? Better?" LeSayer asked, trying not to focus only on herself.

"Not so great. That's why I was trying to read myself to sleep. I spoke with my wife earlier, and I'm afraid we're pretty much done. We don't see eye-to-eye, nor do we understand each other anymore. We agreed to stick it out until the kids are out of high school," he confided to her. "We are both pretty much resolved to it all. I have no emotional connection to her whatsoever anymore."

"I'm sorry," LeSayer told him. "George, I don't want to sleep alone tonight. Do you think I can stay here with you?" she asked as she opened the tie on her bathrobe and let her silky nightgown peek through.

"Of course, Renee," he said as took her by the hand and led her to the bedroom. Their long, difficult day was almost over, even as their erotic tension was piqued. They would finally spend the night together as they both had desired to do for years.

DAY THIRTEEN

May 15, 1987

Every man's life ends the same way. It is only the details of how he lived and how he died that distinguishes one from the other.

—ERNEST HEMINGWAY

DEAD MEN DON'T TALK

"I tend to agree with the Chairman," Davis told Christianson. "There is only one way to be sure a man won't talk. No exceptions," he preached to Christianson and the other two Council members as the limousine whizzed them away from the Houston headquarters. "Dead men don't talk."

"I don't disagree," Christianson responded. "All I said was that if we had acted sooner, we might not have had to kill as many people. Insbrook, Gruber, and the Steiner woman, for instance. I liked them all. They didn't do anything wrong."

"It was a matter of weighing risks versus benefits," LeSayer said. "If the President had shown better judgment, no one would have had to be killed. The few additional lives were the price we paid for our gamble on his judgment. It turns out it was a bad bet."

"His judgment has cost more lives than this in the past," Davis said. "We took the gamble in order to assess his state of mind. What we discovered was invaluable. His judgment was clearly impaired beyond what we knew. To me, the question is how to prevent this from happening in the future. How do we keep a person like him out of the White House?"

"People like him gravitate to the White House," LeSayer said. "He was probably a decent man at some point in his life. Harvey, you knew him at one time, right?"

"Yes, I did. He got old rather quickly," Kraft told them. "An irony under the circumstances. He also got caught up in his own interests and lost sight of what was best for the country. A common fault in politicians, taken to an extreme by a man in his mental condition."

The quartet was on their way to the airfield, where *Sylph* waited to shuttle them back to Washington. They discussed the same subject over and over again during their twenty-minute ride, trying to convince one another they had taken the best course available to them in order to prevent the Plasma Cell Project from causing ruin. As they had sworn to do, they had acted swiftly and coolly to protect national security.

"The man's health situation gave us an easy way out," Christianson said of the President. "We nailed him right in his own bed. His own physician gave him a toxic dose of digitalis along with his sedative, and that was it. No one will suspect it."

"I have to admit it was brilliant," Kraft chimed in. "Papa," as they sometimes referred to the Chairman, "initially considered a nerve agent until he realized an overdose of digitalis, which is notoriously difficult to regulate, might be better. Even if they were to do toxicology tests on his blood, they won't suspect anything. The switched vial of concentrated digitalis is probably in a New Jersey dump or at the bottom of the ocean by now. The form we used is nearly immeasurable," Kraft added. "He probably never knew what hit him, and for sure, it was painless. Not the worst way to go out considering what he was facing with the banking records and a likely impeachment trial."

Davis, LeSayer, and Christianson mustered smug smiles. "Chris will finally get to see his pretty wife," Kraft said. "I'm glad for both of them. He's a good kid, and she's quite lovely. They are both over the moon about the new baby."

"He's going back too?" Davis queried.

"Yes, I saw him leaving for the airport a few minutes before we did," Kraft informed him. "We would have been tight in here, so he got his own car."

"I saw Dalia and Preston leaving too," LeSayer remarked. "That would make all of us, except for Alan. I don't know about you, but I won't miss him on our flight."

"Maybe the chief is planning the first of those vacations he promised us," Kraft commented.

"As a matter of fact," Davis, who informally acted as the Chairman's deputy, said, "he wants us to lie low for a while. For the next few weeks, he wants us operating only behind the green doors under our homes. All scheduled meetings have been postponed indefinitely. It's in tonight's briefing memo."

"Did he say why?" Christianson asked.

"He suspects the press and the FBI will be snooping around," Davis told him. "The FBI guys are good, and Turner doesn't leave a stone unturned.

"We don't want the new president to investigate too heavily either. After all, he knows the business. So, we will tread lightly for a while. The government changeover should be minimal and orderly. Our task, for now, will be keeping track of the changes and, as always, watching what our adversaries are doing."

"That sounds like a wise course to me," Kraft said as he loosened his tie and ran his fingers between his tight shirt collar and his sweaty neck. "I don't know about you guys, but I could use the break. A round or two of golf would be great. The boss said he might even meet me for a round and stay for dinner. The crab cakes at the Greenbrier are excellent this time of year, if any of you have time to join us."

The NSA's stretch Lincoln arrived within the confines of Hobby Field and approached the private runway on which *Sylph* was perched. As it did, the car's headlights illuminated the movable stairway leading from the tarmac to the door of the unmarked aircraft, highlighting the silhouette of the Chairman as he deplaned and made his way down the steps. When he reached the bottom, the Chairman exchanged a few words with a small group of high-ranking NSA officials waiting to board the plane. Among those waiting was the NSA cleanup man who had returned from Atlanta without his partner a little while earlier. The rest of the group shook hands, briefly chatted, and then made their way on board the plane. The Chairman waited for the limo to come to a halt. When it did, its occupants stepped out into the warm, humid Texas wind, which slapped their weary faces.

"Your baggage arrived earlier and is already aboard," the Chairman told his associates, speaking loudly over the roar of other jets as they took off and landed. "I told you I would have you home by Friday night. The four of you are holding up the show. Time to go."

"Thanks, Chief," Kraft said. "What are you doing all the way out here?"

"It was an impulse. I wanted to thank you for all of your loyalty and devotion. I left each of you a goodie bag by your seats and put a cheese tray and some sandwiches on board. I won't see you for a while. We have made difficult decisions over the past few days, but they were for the good of the country. Keep that in mind."

"We all agree with you," Christianson told him. "We were saying the same thing on the way here."

"Great. Now, go ease your minds for a while. I'm covering things myself tonight. You should log in for your assignments tomorrow, but I can assure you none of you will be coming right back to Houston."

"That's good to hear," LeSayer told her boss. "I really need to hit the gym."

Each of the councilors, standing in a circle, their hair blowing in the Texas wind, had a look of satisfaction on their tired faces, loving the attention from "Papa."

"Chris, call your wife before you take off," the Chairman advised. "It's getting late there. She needs to hear your voice. There's a satellite phone in the cockpit."

"They're waiting for us," Davis interrupted, referring to the crew. He reached for a firm handshake from the boss, then turned and trotted up the stairs to the idling plane. Before going inside, Davis looked back and saluted his friend. LeSayer and Christianson made their way up the stairs behind him, leaving only Kraft on the tarmac. The aging author followed, but not before embracing the Chairman cheek-to-cheek with a glimmer of wetness in his eyes and muttering, "God help us, my friend."

By 9:00 p.m., the rolling stairs were wheeled away from *Sylph* and the craft's hatch closed and locked, securing its eighteen passengers and two crew members inside. Thunderously revving its engines, the jet ascended into the dark, starry skies and flew southeast toward the Gulf of Mexico, where it made its gradual counterclockwise turn to the northeast. A few minutes later, the cabin lights were dimmed, and the "fasten seat belt" sign was turned off. The seven NSA Council members and eleven other personnel settled back to relax. In the forward cabin of the specially outfitted 727-23, the passengers sat in plush leather chairs arranged in groupings of four, two on each side facing each other.

Kraft dealt a game of solitaire on a burl wood table while LeSayer got up to fix the two of them cocktails and grab some snacks. Christianson read a book. Knox opened his briefcase and pulled out a journal manuscript waiting for his review. Abrahamyan, tired from the long week, tilted her seat back, flipped off her overhead light, and fell asleep. Bouchikas, the expectant father, wanted to do the same, hoping to be rested when he got home to Diana that night. He reached up to an overhead rack in search of a pillow but came up empty-handed. They seemed not to have been loaded aboard.

"Do you know where any pillows might be?" he asked Zvi Davis, who was seated across from him.

"I don't see any. Why don't you try the rear compartment past where the rest of the folks are sitting," Davis suggested, gesturing toward the back of the plane. "The chief has a bedroom back there too. I'm sure you can find pillows there."

Bouchikas made his way past the plane's conference room, and quietly passed through the second cabin, craning his neck in search of a pillow as he walked, but with no luck. The cleaning crew had apparently forgotten to load any aboard. Eventually, he arrived at the rear compartment, where a number of packages, baggage, and boxes were secured behind curtains that were pulled together, intended to protect the forward cabins from noise and odors. The chamber doubled as a vestibule to make sure crew members did not enter the forward cabins while loading the plane and could not identify any of its passengers. A sign on the wall read, "Crew Area: No Passengers Beyond This Point."

By this time of night, after the long week, Bouchikas was more exhausted than obedient and proceeded in search of something soft on which he could finally rest his head. He was relieved as he spotted the edges of two pillows extending over the top of a pair of rear-facing seats, generally meant for extra crew members. As he stretched to grab the cushions, the olive skin Bouchikas became pale as a ghost. He reeled back in horror as he discovered the cold and livid body of Alan Atlas with a Band-Aid plastered on the middle of his forehead, slouched down in the seat, drained of color. Atlas was covered nearly head-to-toe with a blanket. Bouchikas ripped it away along with the Band-Aid, discovering an entry wound caused by a bullet.

"It's a setup," Bouchikas yelled in terror as he barreled toward the front of the plane. "We've been set up!" He rushed toward the cockpit and pounded on its door, pulling at the handle. "Land the plane. Land this goddamned plane," he yelled to the pilot and copilot. The crew in the cockpit had their headsets on and did not respond, although they reported a possible commotion to the control tower.

Bouchikas backed up and then desperately rushed forward, pushing a service cart and trying to force the cockpit door open, but to no avail as the reinforced door didn't budge, and he recoiled to the floor. He righted himself and, with a flushed face, screamed to the startled group staring at him. "Atlas is back there. He's dead with a bullet through his head."

"Goddamn it!" Christianson reacted, pounding his fist angrily against the padded wall of the jetliner. "I suspected something was up when that son of a bitch was at the airport, and we were all on the same plane. Atlas wouldn't have been the one left behind. We all know the Chairman hated him and didn't trust him."

"We're going to die," Kraft mumbled to himself in a trancelike state as he made the sign of the cross. The NSA rules strictly forbade all eight Council members from traveling in the same vehicle at the same time.

Davis stared blankly at the darkness that enveloped the plane. *There is only one way to be sure a man won't talk*, he thought to himself; *dead men don't talk*. Abrahamyan buried her face in her hands, thinking about her parents, and tried in vain not to cry. Kraft fell helplessly to his knees in prayer in the center aisle while Knox, in full combat mode, pulled out the loaded revolver he always carried and instinctively guarded the entry from the rear compartments while glancing at his teammates in front of him. Bouchikas and LeSayer rushed to the front of the plane, screaming to the pilot and copilot to land the plane, and tried again to use the service cart as a battering ram to open the cockpit door. Renee grabbed Christianson by the arm. "Give us a hand, George."

At least some on board must have understood why the Chairman took this action. They had committed what they thought was a perfect crime and assassinated an American president. The knowledge of this and the vast conspiracy by so many people with knowledge of it was itself a risk to both the Agency and national security, and this was unacceptable to the Chairman.

Their screams went unanswered. Within seconds, a detonator in the plane's fuel tank ignited the jet fuel and consumed *Sylph* and its payload in a hellish ball of flames, the wreckage falling miles deep to the floor of the Gulf of Mexico. The Chairman watched on a radar screen from an air traffic control tower along with an experienced pair of controllers, former Special Forces personnel who now worked for the NSA. He told them it was part of a CIA training mission, the passengers were safe, and they shouldn't speak of it.

DAY FIFTEEN

May 17, 1987

There is no death! The stars go down
To rise upon some fairer shore.

—J.L. MCCREERY, 1863

AN EXCEEDINGLY PRIVATE MAN

The Chairman awoke early Sunday morning and kissed his longtime lover on the back of his head. "I need to leave soon, Paul. I'll see you next weekend."

"I hope so," Paul answered in a groggy tone. "You were barely here, but I understand. You must be closing the deal at the bank tomorrow."

"Yes, hopefully. It will be a busy week for me, so don't be upset if I don't call. Take care of our babies," he said, speaking of the tiny dogs lying by their feet.

"I wish you would come out," Paul said. "I would love to meet some of the people in your world. I'm a schoolteacher with kids all day. It's not fair to me."

"You know that will never happen. I told you when we met twenty years ago that I am an exceedingly private man by necessity," the Chairman said as he sat on the edge of the bed, gently stroking Paul's hair. "But I will see you soon. You know I love you."

A TIME TO LIVE AND A TIME TO DIE

Beth Shalom is a cemetery nestled in the rolling green hills of Virginia, thirty-five miles southwest of Washington, DC. It has a calm, parklike atmosphere, with religious monuments, including a large candelabra menorah at the entrance, fountains, streams, and a chapel. Like most modern Jewish cemeteries in America, there is a memorial to the memory of the six million martyrs who perished in the Holocaust, marked by an eternal flame. The plaza it sits on is usually covered with pebbles customarily left around it and occasionally bunches of flowers. Unlike most Virginia public spaces, statues of human likenesses are absent since they are strictly forbidden by Jewish law. There are no vertical headstones—only simple, flush-mounted plaques marking the graves of the deceased.

The cemetery itself is divided into twelve sections, each named for one of the tribes of Israel. A large map posted near the entrance depicts the winding roads leading to the various sections of the cemetery. The hills rise and fall along narrow roads and serve to divide the cemetery into its biblically apportioned parcels. Near the northwest corner of the cemetery at the ten o'clock position is B'nai Reuven, a section almost completely ringed with hills. The only break in this ring is a narrow pass, still a few feet above ground level, where mourners could follow a hearse as it enters on a single-lane private road.

Late Sunday morning on May 17, a small crowd gathered in the valley of B'nai Reuven under clear blue Virginia skies. A canopy was set up, covering a row of white folding chairs overlooking an open grave. Next to the grave was a lift with pulleys and chains that would mechanically lower the coffin into its resting place, and across from the grave were twelve additional white chairs set up for attendees who were not part of the family. Six well-built men serving as pallbearers, in dark suits, with dark sunglasses and dark *yarmulkes* on their heads, delivered the casket from the hearse to the graveside.

"We are gathered here today to remember the soul of Dr. Philip Insbrook," the rabbi began. "The soul of Dr. Insbrook has gone to its eternal home. In his will, he asked to be buried here in a private service, in this Jewish cemetery not far from where he grew up near Washington, DC, the capital of the country he loved so deeply. May he rest in dignity and peace alongside his beloved parents. We mourn with his children and other family members who have joined us here today.

"Will you now please read responsively from the prayer books on your chairs?

"The days of man are as grass," the rabbi recited. "He flourishes as a flower in the field."

"The wind passes over it, and it is gone, and no one can recognize where it has gone," the mourners responded.

"But the Lord's compassion for His worshippers, His righteousness to children's children, remain, age after age, unchanging," the rabbi continued.

"Three scores and ten our years may number, four score years if granted the vigor," the assembled responded. "Laden with trouble and travail, life quickly passes; it flies away."

"Teach us to use all of our days, O Lord, that we may attain a heart of wisdom."

The Chairman of the National Security Agency stood pensively behind the mourners at this spring funeral, reflecting on the words of the rabbi, making sure the disposal of Insbrook was completed.

"The Lord is my shepherd; I shall not want," the assembled congregants chanted. "He gives me repose in green meadows. He leads me beside the still waters to revive my spirit. He guides me on the right path, for that is his nature. Though I walk in the valley of the shadow of death, I fear no harm, for you are with me."

A nod signaled that the casket could be lowered into the grave. As the unpleasant whir of the motors filled the air, the two men who had respectfully paused for the rabbi made their way toward the graveside with intensity, their legs moving in unison, their hearts pounding as they approached.

The familiar Twenty-Third Psalm was concluding. "Surely goodness and mercy shall follow me all the days of my life. And I will dwell in the house of the Lord forever."

The NSA Chairman instinctively felt something was wrong. Sensing he might be the prey of an approaching stalker, he looked up and saw two men on the top of the hill looking down at the ceremony through small binoculars. One was tall and earnest, with straight, conservatively cut hair. He looked like a banker but moved like a cop, with the trace of a magnum tucked away in a holster beneath his off-the-rack suit. The other moved more gracefully, a self-assured, graying gentleman of admirable build in a fashionable suit and tie. The two men were silhouetted by the sun in the sky behind them as they started down the hill and paused for a moment with their heads bowed as the rabbi spoke. One of the men appeared to be speaking softly to himself, perhaps in prayer.

The Chairman recognized them instantly. One he knew well; the second he had encountered for the first time in Atlanta a few days earlier. The familiar man, the one with the banker's looks and the cheap suit, was Jack Turner, head of the FBI, who led the charge. To his right and a half step behind, in a finely tailored lightweight Armani suit, was Philip Insbrook, alive and in the flesh.

Was the man whose skull was blown away in the wee hours of the morning the day before not really Philip Insbrook? the Chairman asked himself. Could the actual Insbrook have rigged the autopsy and arranged for his own death to be reported while he sorted out the events of the previous week? Had he gambled, despite warnings, and sought out Turner, the one member of the intelligence community he thought the Chairman could not control? Were these mourners, in reality, armed agents?

Insbrook and Turner paused on the embankment and gazed at the Chairman. Insbrook glared hard yet sympathetically at the man who would have had him murdered but who inadvertently settled for Francisco Gomez as he went outside to pick up the morning newspaper for his boss. Turner also stared at the NSA Chairman, a man with whom he'd had dealings before, and shook his head from side to side.

The Chairman glanced in the direction of his two bodyguards wearing their earpieces standing at the edge of the mourners. "Call for help. We're in trouble," he mumbled into the microphone embedded into a lapel pin. This was followed by a nod to the body-guards. The aide nearest to him reached for his transmitter as the guards reached for their shoulder holsters.

"There is a time for everything; there is a time for all things under the sun," the rabbi continued. "A time to be born and a time to die. A time to laugh and a time to cry."

The six pallbearers reached for their shoulder-holstered weapons as well.

"A time to dance and a time to mourn," the rabbi chanted.

Then, all at once, on top of the hills forming a ring around B'nai

Reuven, twenty-four special agents took up their positions. Wearing flak jackets and black baseball caps with *FBI* emblazoned on them, every second agent knelt down, pointed a rifle, and took aim at a target below. Four other heavily armed agents moved into place and blocked the narrow pass between the hills leading to the roadway. Yet more agents in noiseless electric vans secured the perimeter of the section of the cemetery, while others worked to round up suspects in the deep state of coup d'état. FBI helicopters circled overhead.

"It's over," Turner said over the chants of mourners for a man who wasn't actually dead.

"A time to seek and a time to lose. A time to forget and a time to remember," the rabbi continued, not knowing what to think or do.

The Chairman looked around in disbelief. Had he been outdone by this medical doctor? He had admired Insbrook from the start, and ironically, they both had the same goal: to stop the Plasma Cell Project from becoming a reality. The Chairman, however, was the only one with the ability to stop the latest nightmare mankind would have unleashed on itself. He had no regrets.

The Chairman had drawn his revolver, and it hung heavily in his hand at his side as he weighed his options. He looked earnestly at Turner and peered into the cold blue eyes of Philip Insbrook.

"Please," he begged of them, "make the nation understand." With that, he lifted the pistol to his own right temple and sent a bullet through his brain.

EPILOGUE

The presses of the government printing office and two contracted private publishers ran twenty-four hours a day for five days, producing an initial run of six hundred thousand copies of what has become referred to in shorthand as *The Plasma Cell Report*. The books were carefully boxed and shipped with an embargo date, and each employee was checked before leaving their plant to avoid leaks. The initial run sold out in a day. The report is now in its seventh printing, with millions of copies in circulation.

Philip Insbrook left academia and is in private practice as an endocrinologist on Long Island.

AUTHOR'S NOTE

Remember that "whatever can go forward can go backward." The science of this book is solid. When Jules Verne wrote *From the Earth to the Moon*, it was science fiction, and no one believed it would ever happen. It did. We are much closer with aging. Undoubtedly genetics plays an underlying role, and we are making great strides in "fixing" genes. We are not prepared for this today as we similarly are not prepared for artificial intelligence.

This book is a novel. Although the chronology of the story may suggest that Ronald Reagan was the President, he was not meant to be depicted as such. The President was mostly modeled after an earlier president but is actually a compilation of several. Some people and places such as William Friedman, Ralph Canine, and the Fort Meade NSA headquarters are historical. Others were fictionalized, including the Houston facility and the NSA portion of the Greenbrier, although the Greenbrier remnant of the government-planned bomb shelter in the event of a nuclear attack is, sadly, real. The operational wing of the NSA is also fictional. I attempted to be apolitical. I tried to be sympathetic to the President, the Chairman, and the other figures, except Atlas, the anti-hero of the story. I respect all of our intelligence agencies in this country, which keep us safe, including the NSA. My knowledge of the NSA came from open sources, although I enhanced it with fictionalized places I mentioned above.

Respectfully,
Joel Geiderman, MD, 2024

ACKNOWLEDGMENTS

"It takes a village" to publish a novel of this breadth and magnitude. I wish to thank many people beginning with my original editors at Kevin Anderson and Associates in New York, Mark Weinstein and Kendra Harpster, who helped me get my original manuscript down from 104,000 words to 87,000 words, now at 79,000. At Greenleaf Book Group I wish to thank my lead editor, Tess Newton; Adrianna Hernandez, project manager; Kristin Noland, developmental editor; Claudia Volkman, copy editor; Neil Gonzales, my brilliant designer of the cover and page layout; Sally Garland, who efficiently obtained copyright permissions; and my trusty consultants, Danny Sandoval and HaJ.

I wish to thank my many friends who read earlier versions of my book and provided feedback including my late dear friend Larry; Matt; Neil R.; Tollie; Shlomo M.; Dalia; Rabbi David Wolpe; Natasha S.; Michael L.; Sharon; Tom B.; my brother, Ralph; and my son, Bram. I also want to acknowledge the time and advice of my friends Jamie G., Sandy Wernick, and Tom Bernstein, who know the publishing business and advised me. I especially want to thank my longtime friend and supporter Suzan Bymel and my longtime assistant Ivette Chacon. I also wish to thank all four of my children, who spent years looking at the back of my head as I typed my manuscript on my word processor.

I wish to thank all of those in our country who keep us safe on a daily basis. Finally, I wish to thank President George W. Bush for appointing me to the US Holocaust Memorial Museum Board, allowing me to better understand the geography, politics, and culture of Washington.

Hopefully, this book will be received well, and we will be seeing Dr. Insbrook again.

ABOUT THE AUTHOR

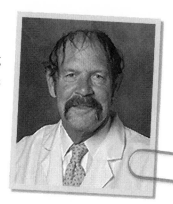

JOEL GEIDERMAN has been practicing medicine for more than forty years. He has been the co-chair of Emergency Medicine at Cedars-Sinai Medical Center in Los Angeles for thirty years. He is a professor at both Cedars-Sinai and the David Geffen School of Medicine at UCLA. Dr. Geiderman was also formerly the vice chair of the United States Holocaust Memorial Museum in Washington, DC, appointed by President George W. Bush. He has authored more than one hundred peer-reviewed papers and book chapters. This is his first novel. Dr. Geiderman lives in Beverly Hills with two of his four children and his dog, affectionately named Reagan.

Made in the USA
Las Vegas, NV
29 August 2024

94581487R00199